FALLING FOR HIM
A Male/Male Military Love Story

~THE COMPLETE SERIES~

IIIII II IIIIIII IIIIII IIIII III
I0624986

KELLY WASHINGTON

KELLY WASHINGTON BOOKS
WASHINGTON DC USA

Kelly Washington
P.O. Box 650092
Sterling, Virginia 20165-0092
www.kellywashington.com
kellywashwrites@gmail.com

Publisher's Note: This is a work of fiction. Names, characters, places, and incidents are a product of the author's imagination. Locales and public names are sometimes used for atmospheric purposes. Any resemblance to actual people, living or dead, or to businesses, companies, events, institutions, or locales is completely coincidental.

Cover Design © 2015 Anita Carroll (race-point.com)
Print ISBN-13: 978-0615832418 (Kelly Washington Books)
Print ISBN-10: 061583415
Falling For Him (The Complete Series), Kelly Washington. – 2nd ed.
An e-book version is available

For those of you who stuck with me to the end: Thank you. Each of you inspire me. Whoever it is that is lucky enough to earn your love, don't let another day pass without expressing it to them. Be without regrets. Be bold. Be loved. Be YOU.

This book is comprised of three novellas that were originally published in serial format. What you are holding in your hands is the *complete series*.

FALLING FOR YOU
A Male/Male Military Romance

-VOLUME ONE-

KELLY WASHINGTON

Chapter One

THE HANDWRITTEN LETTER was folded up in his Kevlar pocket. The day was hot, windy, and Staff Sergeant Justin Hauten—a machine gunner, career Army sergeant, built like the Terminator but still a small-town-Texas boy—had a few minutes to kill.

Justin never put things in his pockets, least of all letters, and he figured it was some sort of mistake, or a joke one of the other Sergeants was trying to pull. For the record, Justin had never once fallen for one of their stupid jokes.

He jumped back into the idling Humvee (the driver, Specialist Walker, was taking a piss), pushed his M4 and a camera to his side, and opened up the carefully folded piece of paper. It quickly became apparent what it was.

Justin, it began, *you make me weak. Every time you walk near me, my heart beats double-time. Can you hear it or feel its pulse? My body radiates heat for you and my body, voice, refuse to obey when we talk. Everything about you turns me on. From your muscular body, your green eyes, to how strong and long your fingers are. Are your lips as soft as I imagine them to be? Will your heat match my own should we ever touch? I long to reach out to you, to skim my fingers along your arm, or back, or leg. And more. I want so much more that my hand is shaking as I write this. I've watched you from afar, desired you at a distance, for all these longs months, and I'm taking a chance now. I have to let you know how I feel. I will burst otherwise. I'll stay hidden for now. But soon, very soon, I will confide in you. I hope you will not be disappointed. All Yours, T.*

He read the letter three times and with each reading, his opinion changed. First, he was pretty sure it was a joke. All of his buddies, even his company commander, called him Hotten, based on his physique and his last name. But this letter, the deep confiding, with its secret longing written in each word, told him that it probably wasn't a joke and that one of his buddies had the hots for him.

He looked at the top of the letter. It was dated four months ago.

Justin refolded the letter and placed it back in his pocket. He wasn't sure how to feel.

He looked out over the Afghanistan landscape, pondering. The red dirt, the mud-hut homes, the deep craters left by some roadside bombs, the Afghani peoples' mixed expressions as they passed by, the eager faces of the children wanting chocolate bars or to practice their broken English. And those were the good days. He didn't like thinking about the bad days around here.

"You ready, Hotten?" Specialist Sean "Nebraska" Walker adjusted his sunglasses and inspected himself in the mirror as he got back into the driver's seat. Nebraska was as tall as a lumberjack and built like one, too. Throw on a plaid shirt and he'd be a dead ringer for the old Brawny Paper Towels man, minus the creepy mustache.

"Yeah, Nebraska, let's go."

As the desolate, yet hopeful, scenery went past, Justin wondered who T was and if there were other letters. Did T place the letter in his pocket four months ago, or did he write the letter then but just now put it in his pocket? Nebraska spoke into the two-way radio, informing the command that they were done for the day and en route. A static reply came back.

"You heard that, Hotten?"

"What?"

"The camera. Captain Phillips wants it first thing."

"Right, yeah, I heard." Justin shook his head.

"You alright, man? You look, I dunno, confused about something. You're not getting cold feet, are you?"

His mind went straight to the letter, but Nebraska wouldn't be talking about that, would he?

"What?"

"Seriously, man," the driver whistled. "Something's stuck in your head, but that's your business. I'm talking about the camera. The mission."

"Oh, right. No cold feet. I'm still game." Justin patted the camera sitting in his lap. *As long as it doesn't get us killed.*

Chapter Two

THE SHOWERS WERE deserted, thank God. Justin stripped down quickly and let the hot water cascade over him. He checked his wrist for the hundredth time, but the white outline of a missing watch made him laugh. He figured it was about midnight.

He had spent the entire day with Nebraska, as usual, taking pictures of the landscape and other landmarks for the commander. So far, the commander was happy with their progress, but he hadn't gotten exactly what was needed just yet. Their mission had begun a month ago. One month left, he thought to himself as he soaped up.

He rubbed the back of his neck, and the muscles screamed at him. Justin turned the water knob all the way to the left and let the scalding water hit the aching muscles and then cascade down his back.

Earlier in the day, another letter had turned up in a notebook he used day in and day out... a letter that hadn't been there yesterday. Same handwriting, but dated two months ago. He could remember some of the words.

This is more than a crush. I want to taste you, feel you, kiss you. I love it when you smile.

Justin was beyond flattered. Unlike how civilians thought the military thought about gay men and women, he had never encountered hatred or the lesser treatment of those living under the Don't Ask Don't Tell rules before that rule was recently abolished. One of his former commanders was gay, and everyone knew it. *And he was one of the coolest guys I've ever known,* Justin thought.

He just didn't know how he was supposed to feel toward the person writing these words to him. He reread the letters as many times as he could get away with—privacy was difficult to come by around here—just to make sure the notes were indeed for him and not for someone else. Justin was pretty easy going and not the type to play things out to the hilt in his mind, but something about the situation combined with this mission set him on edge. He didn't see the scenario ending favorably if he found out who the letter writer was. Did he want to find out?

The shower water was a little less hot now, and it was only a matter of time before his skin pruned up. Plus, any minute now, someone else would come in and steal his solitude.

He wondered more about T. T didn't have to be from his company, though it was more than likely he was. T could be from Kabul at ISAF headquarters, but it was doubtful. His admirer had to have access to his equipment that those at Kabul wouldn't have.

Sergeant Terry Ingram, maybe? God, he hoped not. The man was a sexist jerk and his personality was, well, beyond offensive at all times. What about Lieutenant Tom Ackers, the executive officer? No, he was married with a couple of kids.

Perhaps T was the last name...

Then his mind went in another direction. *Be honest with yourself!* The idea sort of turned him on. It was taboo, new, and intriguing...

A surge went through him.

What would it feel like? To kiss a man, to have his skin covered completely by T? He'd never once thought of this. In his thirty-one years, twelve of which he'd been in the military, he never let the thoughts of another man, let alone a mystery man, enter his thoughts sexually. But had it been there, under the surface?

He tried to think about the girl back home, Julia. His cock swelled a little more, but if he were honest with himself, he would have to admit that he was already slightly hard. He lathered some bar soap and lowered a hand, sliding his palm over himself, then wrapped the hand around his hardness.

He pleasured himself and climaxed rather quickly and intensely, just as the water turned ice cold.

Justin wasn't sure which of the two images—Julia, or T —heightened the experience.

Chapter Three

IT WAS NEAR dusk when he had what he needed. Red and pink streaks ribboned the sky as the sun sunk lower. It was a gorgeous image and one that he would have loved to capture on the camera, but he needed the last bit of sunlight as he dug out his notebook. He motioned for Nebraska to take the camera back to the vehicle as he made a few notes.

Three weeks had gone by, and the commander was beginning to lose patience with him. Three weeks, and three letters—which were getting to him. Justin was both annoyed and aroused by them. The last letter was dated one week ago.

In my dreams, when I touch you, you shiver and beg for more. I'm rubbing your back, hard, digging into your sore neck muscles, when you turn around, push me down, and kiss me like you've never tasted anything so sweet.

But he couldn't discern any odd behavior by any of his friends. The only person showing any behavior beyond the normal was his commander, and Captain Phillips was showing the "I'm pissed at you" kind. At times, the Captain would have an "I'm going to kill you after all of this is over if you don't get what we need" mentality, too.

Suddenly, someone was yelling.

Nebraska.

Justin hauled up to the top of the hill behind him and spotted two M4's and one handgun pointed at Nebraska. Shit!

"Give us the camera," one was shouting at Nebraska.

Justin couldn't tell who they were, but they weren't military men. He sprinted down the steep hill, tripped, and fell down the rest. Everything that could have possibly hit him or poke him did. Rocks. His M4. The holstered M9 firearm at his side. Even the pens in his side arm pocket. He counted himself lucky that none of his weapons discharged.

He did his best to stand up, but his right knee wouldn't cooperate and he quickly collapsed. He pulled out his M9 just as one of the three pointed an M4 at him.

"Hello, Hotten," the man said sarcastically. Captain Phillips? "I understand you got what I need?"

Justin's mind whirled. What was the point of this? He was going to give the camera to Captain Phillips tonight. Why go to all these lengths?

"You okay, Nebraska?" Justin asked.

"Think I just crapped in my pants, but, yeah, doing pretty good. You?"

"Not too excited about the turn of events," he said to his friend, then addressed the commander. "You're a son of a bitch, you know that?"

"Insubordination, Staff Sergeant?"

"Figure that's the least of my worries at the moment."

"Instruct your little friend here to hand over the camera and no one gets hurt."

"First, there's nothing little about Nebraska, and second, you're not in a position to make any demands. The way I see it, we have the camera and I have a gun pointed at your head. I'm pretty sure I know which of us is the better shot, Captain."

"Yeah, but what about Nebraska here? He's not exactly a sniper. He's more like a lumbering oaf, tucked into Kevlar like a stuffed sausage."

"Cute," Nebraska muttered. "But he does have a point,

Justin. Not the sausage part, but the shooting part. And really, the other two fellas here, let's not forget about them. I know I haven't. The good captain failed to make introductions."

Justin desperately wanted to look at the two men focused on Nebraska, but he didn't trust that Captain Phillips wouldn't shoot the second he did. The two other men were not in his company, of that he was certain, but other than that, he was at a loss as to who they were.

"Who are your friends, sir?"

His knee was beginning to throb and, if he wasn't mistaken, a small amount of blood was trickling down his temple. His whole mouth had a metallic taste. A tooth was loose.

Great, just great.

"I like to call them Mr. A and Mr. B."

Clever. These two were either from the State Department or the CIA. Did they really have to be wearing sunglasses? So cliché. It was practically dark now.

"Back down, Captain Phillips," one of them said as he pointed his weapon down to the ground. "You too, Sergeant Hauten. No one is getting shot today." The other man, probably Mr. B, followed suit and lowered his M4. "Do we have an understanding, gentlemen?"

Justin laughed out loud. "The only reason I have my weapon pointed at Captain Phillips is because he has his pointed at me. Perhaps the reason is obvious to everyone else, but why is Captain Phillips pointing his weapon at me?"

"Captain Phillips, I am ordering you to lower your weapon."

"I want the camera first," the captain said, slightly stuttering. Justin could barely make out the sweat pouring down the man's face.

Justin knew what he had recorded over the last two months on the camera currently hanging around Nebraska's neck, and none of it warranted this type of behavior from the company commander.

"Listen, guys," Justin began. "I don't know what's going on, but this son of a bitch doesn't look like he's going to back down, so perhaps you can do someth—"

A shot rang out and Justin's ears began to buzz. It took a couple of seconds before he realized the captain had just shot him. He actually shot him.

"What the fuck?" Justin screamed at the man. Mr. A, or B, quickly wrestled Captain Phillips to the ground and even handcuffed him. Nebraska was at Justin's side, inspecting him.

His shoulder seared and while he knew he wasn't going to die from a gunshot wound to his shoulder, he was so pissed off that he might black out from a sudden stroke. Justin noticed strange things that he probably wouldn't have noticed otherwise.

Nebraska had thick eyebrows, which were now tightly knit in concentration as he tried to stop the bloodflow. Nebraska also had a lot of freckles.

"Jesus Christ, Nebraska. You should wear sunscreen."

"Sure, whatever you say, buddy."

Something banged against his other shoulder: the camera. It was still around Nebraska's neck. A bird screeched in the background. Footsteps, and then he was being carried.

The drive back to the base was the longest and the roughest possible. And not because his shoulder hurt. It hurt like a bitch. It was because Captain Phillips was sitting right beside him, handcuffed, cursing up a storm at the injustice of it all.

What an asshole.

Chapter Four

IT WAS HELL being shot, but the nurses were cute and the drugs felt nice. Justin found out later, after his surgery, that Mr. B confiscated the camera from Nebraska. But not before Nebraska punched him soundly on the jaw.

"My knuckles feel like crap, but that dude deserved it," Nebraska said. He had parked himself in the chair beside Justin's bed two nights ago, after the incident, and refused to leave.

Justin chuckled. "Did Mr. B punch you back?" His friend was sporting a fresh black eye.

"Nope," he smiled, his crooked teeth showing. "It was Mr. A once he realized Mr. B wasn't going to be able to get up on his own."

"Did you find out who they were?"

"I haven't left your side, man, except to take a piss. But I asked around…"

"And…"

"Word is that they are CIA, investigating Captain Phillips on corruption charges or something or another."

"Doesn't sound like a CIA type of operation. We both know what's on that camera. Did it seem like something to shoot one of us over?"

Nebraska laughed and then cupped his face, muttering an ouch. "I dunno, man. Perhaps the man is deranged, or maybe he just hates your guts and needed a small reason to shoot you. Not everyone loves you, man."

"Yeah, yeah." Secretly, Justin hoped that wasn't true.

"Speaking of," Nebraska said and reached into his

pocket. "This was dropped off for you." He handed over an envelope, sealed, with Justin's name scrawled on the outside.

Justin recognized the handwriting immediately.

"Whoa," Nebraska whistled. "What's that look for?"

"What look?"

"That look, when you saw the envelope. It was a combination of dread and eagerness. Odd."

Justin shook his head. "It's been an odd few days."

"True that, my friend. So, are you going to read it?"

"Right now?"

"Yes, right now."

"No."

"No?"

"No."

"Holy shit on toast! You know who it's from. You're holding out on me. For months, all I hear about is Julia from back home and now you get this letter and you aren't going to read it in front of me."

Nebraska snatched the letter away from Justin and ripped it open.

"Hey! You gave me a paper cut, you dork." He tried to reach up, but his bandaged shoulder and sore body prevented him from doing so.

"Let me read it for you, my goodly injured friend." Nebraska cleared his throat and began to read. "It's dated yesterday, by the way," he casually mentioned.

"Shhhhh. Keep it down," Justin begged.

"Ohhh. Maybe it is a love letter. One of the nurses, perhaps. There are a few pretty ones around here." He paused and then focused on the letter. "*'Justin, my love, my wounded soul mate.'* Okay, it has to be said," Nebraska said roughly. "This chick has horrible handwriting, and that opening is just corny. But, anyway, back to the letter.

18 Kelly Washington

'I desperately long to see you, to ensure that you are safe and in the care of skilled doctors. If I could be at your side, at this moment, as your friend Nebraska is.' Wait a minute," Nebraska looked closely at Justin. "This is just creepy. It's like you have a stalker."

"I suppose you do, too. You are mentioned, after all," Justin pointed out as he tried to steal the paper back. Anything to keep him from reading the rest of the letter. Nebraska dodged it smoothly. "Just give me the letter. It's, ah, private."

"You, private? My ass is more private than you are."

"I'd prefer it if you didn't read the letter," Justin said through clenched teeth.

"This is too funny. Your face is turning a deep shade of red. It isn't becoming. Calm down or the nurse is going to inject you with insulin or something."

"Fuck!" he muttered under his breath. What he needed was morphine. "Fine. Go ahead."

Nebraska cleared his throat again. "'Soon I will tell you who I am. I will look into your green eyes and hope to see acceptance, perhaps—if I am lucky—the same feelings in return. Until then, Justin, be well. Yours, T.'"

Nebraska refolded the letter, his eyes narrowing, and stuffed it back into the envelope. Justin could tell he was thinking, trying to figure out who the letter was from.

"The letter makes it sound like you've received others."

"Yeah. I think this one is number four or five. I've been getting them for about two months now."

"So... not a nurse?"

"I don't think so."

"Someone in the unit?"

Justin nodded.

Nebraska jumped up, clearly excited. "This is completely awesome!"

Justin was stunned that Nebraska wasn't ribbing him about the whole thing.

"Why?"

"Crazy Julia has competition."

"What does that have to do with anything? And don't call her crazy."

"I can't wait to see how this whole thing unfolds. And I plan to be there when it does."

"Interested in taking my spot for me?"

Nebraska just laughed and turned to leave.

"Wait, where you going?"

" 'My dearest Justin,' " Nebraska mimicked, laughing, but then turned somewhat serious. "I'm hungry as shit, man. See you later."

Everyone deserved a great friend like Nebraska. Before his friend closed the door, he could hear him talking to himself about guys whose name began with T.

Chapter Five

TWO WEEKS FLEW by before Justin was released from the medical center, and it was two weeks before the Transfer of Authority ceremony was to take place. Two weeks before he and the rest of the Brigade would return to the States. Two weeks of debriefings, interviews, and official statements, ad nauseam.

However, there weren't any new letters.

So, naturally, Justin reread every letter from before. Just to be sure, he told himself. But he found himself thinking more about T and less about Julia. Nebraska, trying to appear helpful but really just being nosy, would ask questions like: Do you prefer blondes or brunettes? Brown eyes or blue eyes? Smooth or hairy chest? Girth or length?

Justin threw his helmet at Nebraska after the last question, but he had to admit that he appreciated how well his friend was taking the situation. If Justin were suddenly transformed into a troll, Nebraska would still call him a best friend.

Nebraska was awesome-weird like that.

A new company commander assumed command almost immediately, just as soon as the Department of the Army could reallocate a captain; and, by then, the rumors about the incident were already well-oiled and oft-repeated machines.

Who was the man of the hour? Justin? Nope. Specialist Sean Walker was. The tall Nebraska native was credited with everything from saving Justin's life to personally taking down Captain Phillips. All at the same time. He also apparently interrogated the CIA operatives. Made them cry and had them begging for their own attorneys after fifteen minutes of his company.

Allegedly, of course.

Nothing about what was on the camera was ever mentioned, not really. Only five people knew what Justin had photographed. One had been shot and hospitalized, one arrested, one credited as the hero, and two were CIA spooks, presumably.

Justin walked slowly into the chow hall just as Nebraska began embellishing another story in between huge bites of his hamburger. "The way I heard it," he was saying, "is that Captain Phillips was trying to smuggle diamonds out of the country, which he hid in the camera, unbeknownst to Hotten and me."

A small group sat huddled around Nebraska, hanging on every word. Most were already done eating, so they stayed for whatever entertainment Nebraska would dazzle them with tonight.

"Yeah, but wouldn't you hear the diamonds rattling around in the camera?" One of his chow-mates asked, clearly not believing him.

"Now that you mention it, yeah. Hotten and I thought that a part was broken inside and that was what the noise was. But it was more a 'thud-thud-thud,' as if they were wrapped up in some sort of cloth strips. It's what I'd do."

A couple of the others nodded.

Justin entered the line before realizing he probably wouldn't be able to carry the tray to the table. He was such a spaz for relying on Nebraska too much.

"I'll help you out," he heard behind him. The voice was very close.

It was Lieutenant Aaron Parris, aka "Texas," one of the

company platoon leaders. A man that was always around... but quiet and observant though very well thought of and respected.

Texas...

T...

Suddenly, Justin couldn't breathe properly. Could Lt. Parris be T? Maybe. God, listen to him. Wasn't the lieutenant married? Or had some sort of serious girlfriend? He turned fully and studied the man. Tall—about his height, maybe a little taller—black hair, brown eyes, tan skin, and, well, attractive, too. Very attractive.

"Thanks, Lieutenant," Justin nodded but offered nothing more.

"Fun couple of weeks you've had," he chuckled. "Seems to me that you took the beating and Nebraska took the fame."

"Nebraska's the good sort and I'm glad he was in my corner. A guy can't ask for a better friend."

"I can imagine," Texas said without much warmth, though his gaze was direct, like he was dissecting Justin or questioning his choices in friends. He didn't seem too interested in hearing about the incident. On second thought, Justin decided maybe the lieutenant wasn't his letter writer.

Justin made his food choices and then followed the lieutenant as he carried the tray to Nebraska's table.

"—then I snatched the letter from his hands and gave him a paper cut in the process," Nebraska was saying as the table burst into laughter.

Justin's eyes grew large and he couldn't believe his ears. He was talking about the letter?

"What?" Nebraska asked. "Your mom's bitter letter to the command. Priceless. Do you still have it? I want to read it to the guys." Nebraska gave him a knowing look.

Lieutenant Parris placed Justin's food down, raised an eyebrow and a slight grin at Justin, and walked away.

"Huh? Oh, no," Justin lied, still watching the lieutenant. "It's in the new commander's office. Apparently they don't want it to get out to the press."

Justin sat. As it so happened, the lieutenant sat two tables up, facing him. There was something about his expression, a knowing look, like Texas knew—just knew—that Justin was lying about the letter.

That pretty much meant one thing.

Lieutenant Aaron "Texas" Parris was T.

Justin wasn't sure how he felt about that.

Nebraska leaned over and whispered in his ear, "At least T isn't ugly. Julia's competition just got real."

Not much escaped Nebraska.

Chapter Six

JUSTIN WAS PACKING, with Nebraska's assistance—which wasn't much help, if he were being honest—for the trip home when he found another letter in his rucksack, dated eight months ago. While he wasn't exactly sure, he felt that this was the first letter and that it had been deposited in his rucksack at the time of the letter's date.

Rather than let Nebraska learn of its existence, he excused himself and promptly sat on the toilet and read the letter.

Justin, I know you. The smell of you. Your movements. I dream about you intertwined with me in our bed, and we make love. Softly, lovingly, before passion overtakes us and we are pawing, clamoring, desperately seeking each other out, pleasuring each other with our hands and mouths, and dare I say it, our cocks. You explore me tenderly, like a novice learning a delicate craft. Your hungry mouth crashes into mine over and over. You cannot get enough; you cannot get close enough to satisfy your craving to touch every inch of me. Your strong, gorgeous body fits mine perfectly. My fingers thread through your short brown hair as you go lower on my body. Your eyebrows are knitted together in deep concentration. Your green eyes seek mine, asking, begging permission to go further still. Yes. Yes a thousand times. But I always stop here. I do not let myself go beyond this part. I stop my mind and will myself to wake up from such a wonderful dream. You are a dream to me. I want you more than I want air or oxygen. Silly words? Yes. But true. I've watched you for two months now, but you do not see me. You know me. You speak to me almost daily. But you haven't a clue. And this is okay. For now, I will reveal myself to you in letters, secreted away in your belongings. I do not know when you'll find them. Maybe you never will. If so, the loss is mine because you'll never know how much you mean to me. Maybe in time I'll tell you. Maybe not. I do not know how far I am willing to let this go. I do not know how you will react to this letter. I know that you will not be repulsed. You will not be disgusted. But you may not be interested, and while this will sadden me, I will respect your wishes completely. But maybe, just maybe, one day you will return these feelings to me. You will ask yourself: who is this person writing to me? And I will say that I am "T" for now. My fingers shake as I write this. I yearn to write more, to describe more. This is more than lust, but not quite love, either. That would have to develop. I desire you, want you, want to be with you in every sense possible. The question is: will you allow yourself to think of the possibilities? I hope you will. Until next time... Yours, T.

The words moved him. They felt sincere. As he read the prose, he imagined Lieutenant Parris, or Texas, in its context. He saw himself lying next to the man, naked, and exploring him. And it... aroused him. His cock was hard, ready to be stroked.

Jesus, he'd never been more confused. He tried to remember all of his interactions with the man. Not many came to mind. Just normal everyday interactions in formations, inspections, and salutations as needed.

I don't think I've ever been alone with the man. Why single me out?

Then another thought occurred to him. Maybe this was all a joke. One big joke. But at whose expense? Justin wasn't sure and as he repacked the envelope and left the bathroom stall and returned to the packing, he wasn't sure if he'd be disappointed if it was a joke or not.

So what did that tell him?

A lot and not much at the same time.

Chapter Seven

TWO WOMEN FLEW into his arms, killing his shoulder. His mother and Julia. He curbed a curse word as tears sprang into his eyes, which the women mistook for tears of happiness, not tears of pain and misery.

The gymnasium was packed with the family members of his brigade. A good thousand or more were in various stages of hugging, kissing, and crying. And that was just the service members. Children ran. Mothers and fathers hugged. Husbands and wives tearily greeted each other.

Nebraska had his entire clan there. His mother, a rather large woman; his father, a tall and balding skinny man; two brothers; and five sisters. While Nebraska didn't have the most family members present, they certainly were the loudest. Screeches and screams, and even loud, very loud moaning from the mother, who thought she was close to fainting in all the excitement.

Justin watched in amusement as his mother refused to let him go, and when she did, Julia stepped in and slapped him. It probably wouldn't have been that big of a deal if there wasn't a sudden quietness in the gym at the same time. So they had an audience, to which he quickly enveloped the woman and kissed her soundly.

"What was that for?" Justin asked.

Julia had a dreamy look in her eyes and he knew instantly that kissing her was probably not the best idea now or, in fact, ever.

"You didn't write," she pouted. Her long blonde hair was tied at the back of her neck and cascaded down in pretty curly locks. She wore a short dress—he saw his mother's disapproving looks out of the corner of his eye— that barely covered the parts that were already barely covered. Her pretty blue eyes sought his before leaning in for another kiss.

Justin pulled away. He forgot that she kissed with her eyes open. That totally freaked him out.

"We aren't dating, Julia. That's why I didn't write."

She humphed. "Well, you aren't dating your mother either, but you wrote to her." She smiled at what she thought was a very brilliant statement.

"She gave birth to me and raised me singlehandedly after my dad died. Not to mention that she'd find a sly and very painful way to kill me if I didn't write to her. That's why I wrote to her."

His mother nodded in agreement. She also had great hearing.

"But, we, you know... got together... at that party that one time," she hinted.

Good God. She remembered? "That was, what, three years ago?"

Julia pouted some more. She latched herself to his good arm.

"Justin, dear," his mother said. "Why don't you introduce us to some of your friends."

"Great idea!" He agreed with the same amount of enthusiasm as if she had said, "Let's all get drunk."

"I can't wait to see Nebricka," Julia chimed in.

"It's Nebraska."

She still looked confused.

"Like the state," he explained. But her mind had already moved on.

Nebraska was still making the hug rounds. The Walker family was huge in numbers and in body size.

"Hotten!" he exclaimed suddenly. "Meet the fam. They all want to meet the man whose life I saved."

"Oh, you poor dear," Mrs. Walker exclaimed in large delights. She hugged him with all her might. His shoulder was throbbing so much that he knew sleep would never bless him that night, but he didn't complain as the Walker brothers did the bro hug on him and slapped his shoulders. The brothers even hugged Julia, who complained that she couldn't breathe.

Nebraska's sisters hugged him affectionately. Apparently, as one whispered, they found him handsome, while another invited him home for dinner and dessert. The subsequent remaining three Walker sisters echoed pretty much the same sentiments, but in ruder and more direct ways.

"Ah," he stuttered. "My momma's cooking chicken pot pie and fried catfish tonight. Can't miss that," he said in various ways to each sister.

Nebraska pulled him aside. "Just go along with whatever I say. There's a girl I'm trying to impress back at Fort Hood. Also, we're lined up for an exclusive with Good Morning Dallas next week."

Justin caught only bits and pieces of the extravagant baggage Nebraska said about the incident and Justin's difficult recovery of three bullet wounds in the shoulder. Justin was even stabbed by one of the CIA operatives in this particular version. Nebraska fought every last one of them and came off without so much as a single scratch or paper cut.

Nebraska grinned at him.

Justin focused on the words paper cut and began to look for the man who was haunting his dreams. Texas was on the opposite side of the gym and surrounded by a small group.

Nebraska's family had just finished greeting Justin's mom and Julia, when the object of Justin's attention caught Nebraska's notice.

"Mrs. Hauten, Miss Julia, why don't we meet another person from the unit? A Lieutenant Parris, also known as Texas." Nebraska offered his arm to Justin's mother as Julia latched onto Justin's bad arm this time.

He winced as they crossed the gym. Justin could feel Texas' eyes on him just as Julia's fingers tried to fix his hair, saying something to the effect that his hair was parted on the wrong side. Justin tried to dissuade her by moving his head as far away from her hands as his neck would allow. But Julia's attentions immediately ceased when she spotted Lieutenant Parris. Justin watched Texas closely as he made several glances between Justin and Julia, smiled in a sort of bemused way, and then introduced his family.

Julia made goo-goo eyes at Texas. This made Nebraska bark with laughter, but he rescued Justin by taking Julia off of his hands and began to launch into a more bedazzling embellishment about the incident.

The Mafia? Did he just hear something about the Mafia making an entrance in this particular version? It was only a matter of time before Samuel L. Jackson made an appearance in a made-up theatrical version.

Justin found himself partnerless, a predicament he didn't necessarily think was a bad thing. His mother spoke animatedly with Major General and Mrs. Parris, Texas' parents.

Suddenly Texas was beside him. Was it him, or did the air conditioner just break?

"I didn't know your father was a Major General." Justin looked straight ahead, as did Texas. Anyone happening to look at them would think they were rigid spies trading secrets but trying not to be obvious about it.

"Retired now."

"Oh," Justin replied lamely. Did it just get stuffy? The air was so thick.

"Since you made it a point to see me and my family, should I assume you know the letters are from me?" Texas turned and looked at him. His gaze was so direct, so heated, so... meaningful.

"I..."

"Can I come by to see you this weekend?"

"I..."

"Justin?" his mother called. "I think we're ready." Julia stood beside her. Her top was even lower and her bottom was even higher. Seriously, what went through her mind when she got dressed this morning? Her outfit was almost no bigger than a wide scarf wrapped around her.

Nebraska, ever the astute specialist he was, quickly started another series of questions directed at Justin's mother.

"Lunchtime, on Saturday?" Texas asked. His gaze never wavered.

Justin breathed in deeply. Just say yes, dammit!

"Y...y...yes," he finally answered.

Texas smiled. His teeth were perfect. His smile gorgeous.

Justin smiled just as big and didn't stop for quite some time.

Chapter Eight

JUSTIN THREW OPEN his apartment door, kicked his duffle bag inside, and crashed on the couch.

Just one minute of rest...

His shoulder felt about twice the normal size from all of the hugging he suffered through and, he chuckled, also due to Julia clutching on to him for dear life, like a child pulling down on a parent's arm.

His injured arm. For some reason, Julia never quite understood that her tugging on him actually hurt.

"But you're such a strong soldier, Justin," Julia had innocently responded to his near-crying pleas. Leave it to Julia to confuse shoulder with soldier... Then Julia had spotted Lieutenant Parris and promptly forgot all about Justin. It was a lovely feeling, and he sort of felt sorry for her.

Now, as his eyelids felt way too heavy, what Justin wanted was a beer and a half bottle of painkillers.

And sleep. Lots and lots of sleep.

But his momma would skin him alive if he didn't show up for the chicken potpie slash fish fry dinner tonight. Everyone would be there. Uncles. Aunts. Cousins.

If he could only fast forward to Saturday, he thought.

Whoa!

That woke him up, and he realized he was smiling. He stood up slowly and made his way into his closet to wear normal civilian clothes for tonight.

He willed himself not to think about Texas.

So he found himself woolgathering about his last

assignment in Afghanistan and all of the normal-looking villages and huts and mountains he had captured on that powerful, paparazzi-style camera. Justin had shot some really great images of children playing soccer and the Afghani women cooking dishes that smelled so delicious, he wouldn't be surprised if those two dorky CIA bubbas actually smelled food as they previewed the pictures.

Not to mention gorgeous sunsets.

Justin would love to have those images framed and placed around his apartment. He yawned as he got dressed and then left his apartment.

So why did his company commander do what he did? What was so important about those photographs?

Chapter Nine

"So, ARE YOU ready?" Nebraska asked two days later in Justin's tiny apartment kitchen, a turkey drumstick in his hand. A thick eyebrow rose, asking, "Are you going to be a dipshit?"

Saturday.

Dear Lord, it was Saturday. He had survived the family dinner. Food had covered five huge tables. Chicken potpie, fried catfish, three roasted turkeys, deer chili in crock-pots —and that was just one of the tables. The other four consisted of various holiday side dishes and gobs of desserts, even candied Easter Eggs. His family, bless their crazy hearts, cooked every single holiday meal that he had missed while in Afghanistan.

Justin had no doubt gained ten pounds from that meal alone. The chair creaked as he shifted.

He remembered it all too clearly as he looked into the refrigerator and most of the leftovers—stuffed on the shelves and packed tightly in overly bright plastic containers—stared back at him. He didn't know his fridge could hold that much food. It would take him a month to eat all of it... but, with Nebraska's help, maybe a week.

"Ready for what?" Was he referring to Texas? Julia? The hearing next week?

He rolled his shoulder. It felt stiff today and he wondered if it was because he was nervous.

"Jesus Christ," Nebraska muttered. "You like to play dumb sometimes, don't you? Did you read the script?"

Justin rolled his eyes. "Oh, right, the script for next

week's Good Morning Dallas interview. Let me go get that wondrous piece of fiction." He grabbed it from the living room coffee table, randomly flipped to a page, and read.

" *'No ma'am, I couldn't believe my luck in that Specialist Sean Walker back-flipped over the two unknown CIA thugs and wrestled the gun, a crossbow, and the grenade from our piece of shit company commander.'* "

Nebraska smiled brightly. "It has a certain ring to it, doesn't it? War Hero Sean Walker. But you don't have to say it all monotone like that."

"You do realize we have to tell the truth, right?" Justin browsed the rest, then said: "We did not dismantle a roadside bomb and save a school full of girls."

His friend *pshawed* that. "Since when did you get all noble and shit on me? It will dazzle the news anchor, who I hear is totally hot, and will build up buzz for when I write a first-person, tell-all book."

Justin laughed loudly. That'd be the day. Nebraska barely knew his ABCs. When did he find the time to write this?

Nebraska continued, "Besides, the brilliant part of that script is that you can use it when we have to testify in court, too."

Justin wondered if the two CIA agents would appear at the court hearing. Doubtful.

"I still don't understand why it all happened," he confessed. Strangely, they hadn't discussed that day. It was almost as if they wanted to forget it happened. Otherwise, Nebraska's recounting of events might be a bit more truthful.

"Captain Phillips probably snapped. It happens, buddy."

"But you saw the photos. Well, most of them, anyway, until you lost interest. What would make him act that way? And why the hell did he need two CIA agents?"

Nebraska chucked. It irritated Justin that his friend didn't seem to be worried or even questioning anything.

"I'm just a driver, man. A big piece of lumbering muscle and jokes. After about the tenth sunset, I got bored, dude." Nebraska leaned across the small kitchen table. "But you must have snapped something out there in the mountains. Something that the Captain and those CIA idiots wanted badly. Question is: what was it?"

Nebraska studied him in such a serious manner that at any second, Justin was certain his friend would burst out laughing.

Someone knocked at the door and a knowing grin filled Nebraska's face. Justin suddenly felt like some stupid teenager waiting for a date to show up.

"He's early," his friend said as he got up. "Suppose it's time I headed out. I need to practice talking in a mirror."

Sure, why not? Justin thought. Who doesn't do that?

Before Nebraska opened the door, he said, "Which side is my best side?" and he tilted his head left and then right in pensive expressions.

"Uh..."

His friend waved him off and opened the door.

"No worries. I'll figure it out and then I'll dazzle the world."

Justin looked past him and his face froze. Nebraska noticed.

"What the hell?"

Suddenly the man standing at the door pushed his way in and punched Nebraska in the gut, sending him to the floor.

"That's for injuring my partner, asshole," he said as he straightened up and pointed a shiny, sleek-looking gun at Justin.

"Mr. A, how lovely to see you again," Justin said as he backed up slowly and observed the tall man, his dark suit, and the aviator sunglasses. He had to admit that the agent looked good, even with the gun pointed at them. Actually, he looked good because he had a gun pointed at them. *Did I just check him out?*

So... were they supposed to put their hands up?

Nebraska stood up. "Your partner deserved it."

"You shattered his jaw," Mr. A said. His expression was calm, like maybe he didn't care that his partner was injured, and he only wanted an excuse to punch Nebraska. The agent produced a second gun and trained it on his friend.

"Five-time boxing champion, baby," Nebraska boasted, unconcerned.

Mr. A didn't move, but Justin had the impression that the man wanted to laugh.

"Of what, some pohick county?" Mr. A asked. "You're untrained, volatile, and one day, you'll kill someone. And that would be a waste."

"A waste of what?" Justin asked, curious.

"Conversation's over. Both of you walk to my car or I'll shoot your other shoulder."

Nebraska looked to Justin, a gleam in his eye. The bastard was having a good time.

"Just think about how awesome our interview is going to be next week," he said.

Chapter Ten

WHAT A WAY to miss a date... A few minutes ago, an aging police officer shoved him inside a room marked *Interview Room Three* and locked the door.

The lights were dingy yellow and dim, and one of the fluorescent bulbs flickered on and off irritatingly. It was like the room hadn't been used in the last decade. Even the chair had a coating of dust before he gave up and sat in it.

At least he wasn't chained to the floor. After he sat down, he noticed the drilled-in hook in the floor. His foot played with it now as he counted the scratches on the ugly gray table and waited and thought.

About how pissed Texas would be. About their former commander. About how there wasn't even one of those cool one-way mirrors to look into in this stupid room.

Nebraska, in the next room, was mad as hell; Justin could hear him yelling through the concrete walls as someone finally entered his room. Mr. A, probably.

"What's this? Why didn't you put sacks over our heads? You couldn't bring us to your secret CIA headquarters? I'm dangerous, man! Dangerous!"

That's what his friend wanted: something cool and secret and dangerous. Not this place. This was some stupid police department way out in the country that housed bored and aging police officers. It was rather brilliant, actually, for Mr. A to bring them here. It would show them just how unimportant they were. Funny, they never thought otherwise.

But why kidnap them at all?

Everything was getting weirder by the minute, and by now, he had to acknowledge that Texas would have already come and gone to his apartment, probably thinking the worst.

"The CIA kidnapped me" would not be a believable excuse. Really, the whole thing was rather unfair. Especially to Texas.

There were voices next door, though Justin couldn't make out the words.

Justin tried to imagine all of the scenarios that Nebraska would cook up to make this event a bit more interesting. Hell, at least he had someone in his room. Justin just sat there studying the gray table on a gray floor connected to gray walls. He would never paint anything gray for as long as he lived. It was just so depressing.

The next room was now quiet, and Mr. A stepped into Justin's room.

"You have a very loyal friend in there, Staff Sergeant Hauten."

This was the last thing he expected to hear from the CIA agent.

"Let's cut to the chase," Justin said. "What do you want?"

Mr. A chuckled. "That's what I like about you: you don't like idle conversations. Your friend, on the other hand, cherishes a more cat-and-mouse style dialogue. Gives him a challenge, a fight, something to outsmart his opponent. You two make a good team. Sort of like a buddy cop movie."

"Super. Why don't you two write the movie script? I'd rather leave."

"Things to do? People to see? I get it. I also have things to do and people to see. And one of those things is extracting what you know, and one of those peoples is my boss, and she really hates to be disappointed."

"I'm not concerned with your boss' emotional state," Justin said. "But unless I'm mistaken, you have that camera, not I."

Mr. A moved to the other side of the room. "Let's forget about the camera for a moment. Tell me about Captain Phillips."

"He's an asshole."

"Besides that particular favorable impression, what else?"

Justin crossed his arms across his chest. He had the impression that they didn't know who they were dealing with when it came to Captain Phillips.

"You're the CIA. I'm sure you can figure it out."

The man smiled. "You are too adorable, Sergeant Hauten. Just enough charm to cover up that sarcasm to do any real harm. And I'm not the CIA. Let's go ahead and squash that little bug from your head. It was cute while it lasted."

The hairs on the back of Justin's neck stood up.

"Ah, no response?" the agent continued. "Your brain doing some heavy-duty thinking? What were your orders, Sergeant?" The man's voice lifted and nearly yelled the last.

Nebraska must have heard because his friend yelled back, "You piss-ant! You come here and yell at me and we'll see what happens!"

Then something crashed. It sounded like he overturned the metal table in his room.

"See?" Mr. A said with a sly smile. "He's volatile and extremely loyal to you. Why? What makes you so special and so deserving? Why did Captain Phillips trust you above everyone else for that mission?"

The man leaned in. He was so close. Close enough for Justin to reach out and hit him. Mr. A wasn't dangerous. He didn't want to kill or hurt either of them. He just wanted information and until Justin knew why, he wouldn't trust anyone. But maybe he could cut some sort of truce.

"Give me the camera, let us go, and maybe I'll think about it."

Mr. A laughed, which set Nebraska off again.

"I love it when they play detective," he said more to himself than to Justin. "Sure thing, kid. But one step out of line and I'll shoot you myself."

Chapter Eleven

TWENTY MINUTES LATER, he and Nebraska sat on the crumbling stoop of the police station's front door, wondering how they'd get back home. The sky was gray as clouds and a breeze rolled in. It'd probably rain in the next half hour.

"The desk sergeant said we were in Clovington, wherever the hell that is," Nebraska said. "Nice work in there, buddy." He pointed to the camera now around Justin's neck. "All the photos there?"

"I think so. I did a quick look. At the very least, the last few galleries are there. I don't recall the very beginning photographs."

"We should steal a car," Nebraska suddenly said.

Justin didn't quite follow his logic, but he was used to his friend's strange conversations and decided not to argue with him.

"Sure, why not."

Nebraska stood up. "Is it stealing if I have the key?" He produced a large metal round key ring with fifty or so keys on it.

Justin groaned. They didn't look like *regular* car keys, and surely Nebraska realized that. An odd grin came over Nebraska as he scanned the parking lot. Good lord, he was going to steal a police car.

"Do you trust me, Justin?"

That was a dumb question.

"Are we about to get all personal and shit?" Justin asked instead.

"Give me the camera." Nebraska sat back down.

"What?"

"Maybe I'll see what you didn't. Maybe I'll figure out what these goons want."

He remembered what Mr. A had said inside: *"I love it when they play detective."* It was almost as if the agent wanted them to do their own investigation, which meant they were playing right into his hands, which gave Nebraska a chance to amp the situation into something far worse.

Sometimes, things don't need to be said out loud between friends. Justin handed over the camera.

"All right, now," Nebraska said happily, turning the thing every which way. "So... what do all these buttons do?" He started laughing when Justin gave him a disgruntled look. "Kidding!"

He had nothing to do while his friend looked at the images, so he thought more about stealing a car. Mr. A had already left, laughing as his tires spit rocks at them when he peeled out of the parking lot.

All that remained was three beat-up police cruisers and a newer looking truck... with a person sitting in the driver's side. A person who looked suspiciously like—

"You finally notice him?"

Justin whipped his head to look at Nebraska.

"You knew he was there the whole time?"

"Yup," he said as he continued to look at the photos on the small digital screen. "Wondered when you'd finally see Lieutenant Parris. I'll let you say your hellos."

Justin crossed the parking lot and approached Texas' truck. It looked new and really put his piece-of-shit beater to shame.

"Hop in," Texas said neutrally.

Justin wasn't worried about how any of this looked. As

far as standing someone up for a date, his excuse was pretty outlandish, original—and, well, true. It wasn't like he had volunteered to be kidnapped at gunpoint. If Texas was here, that meant he witnessed it all and followed them.

That, or he was a trained spy and somehow found them another way.

Then another thought hit him: he'd already started thinking about their lunchtime get-together as a date.

"Hi," he said as he climbed into the passenger side. Texas looked good. Real good. Short black hair, nice eyes. Pleasing mouth...

Okay, stop!

"You don't look any worse for wear." Texas' voice had a soft twang to it.

"Oh, this?" Justin waved his hands around. "It's a normal occurrence when Specialist Walker is around."

"He seems like a good guy to have on your side. Didn't he fight off a dozen rattlesnakes when they attacked you?"

"Good lord..."

It was a wonder that he was still alive after befriending the tall Nebraska native. Good thing no one really believed Specialist Walker or his tall tales.

"So... you saw us leave my apartment and followed?" *Did you see the guns pointed at us? Did you see the stupid grin on Nebraska's face the whole time?*

"I wasn't sure what I saw, but you didn't look happy. In fact, you looked about as pissed as my grandmother gets when the contestants on Wheel of Fortune mess up when there's that one letter left and they still can't guess it."

"That seems like a valid reason to get mad."

"So, yeah, I followed you."

"And waited for what, exactly, here in the parking lot?"

"Great question, Justin. I was going to go in when you

two came out. And then I waited some more to see what would happen."

His stomach did a funny little flip when Texas said his name, like his inner organs were melting and he couldn't do a damn thing about it. What did that even mean?

"Not much happened. The dipshit tried to scare us into revealing what we don't know in the first place and then he just gave us the camera back."

Texas seemed to think about that for a second. "Like maybe he doesn't know anything either and hopes you'll lead him directly to whatever it is you all don't know in the first place?"

Justin laughed. "It sounds messed up when you say it out loud, but, yeah. I think you may be on to something."

"I like your laugh..."

The truck filled with silence.

It didn't ruin the calm mood. Justin wasn't calm to begin with. He kept staring at Texas' mouth, imagining things. Lots of things that he shouldn't be thinking about; at least, not right now. But Texas brought it to the forefront and made him acknowledge his attraction, and Justin didn't know how to process that.

Texas had revealed himself to Justin one letter at a time and he hadn't even said one kind, or even remotely similar, remark back to him.

"Thank you. I... uh... um... you're... ah..."

Texas smiled. "There's no need to force it. We're just having a conversation. Nothing more. It's something we each do, day in and day out. Don't let the letters bother you right now. I'm not... um... pressing for anything."

"But..."

"You're wondering, imagining, thinking..."

Was it his imagination or did Texas' hand move closer? Did the A/C shut off?

"It's just that you seemed very determined in your letters even though you didn't know how I might react. I could have been disgusted or angry."

"But you aren't. If anything, you're flattered, probably aroused, but you might feel confused or ashamed. You wonder what it will be like to... kiss me." He whispered the last part.

He hand was closer. A finger slightly touched his hand and a shiver vibrated through Justin's body. He felt hot and cold all at the same time. It was like he forgot how to breathe...

His eyes fluttered closed as a hand touched his thigh. Justin could hear his own breathing, once he remembered how to breathe.

"I, uh... can't." He wanted him to go higher up his thigh, but Nebraska would be watching. The hand vanished.

"I understand."

A knock came at the window and Justin jumped. And from Nebraska's shit-eating grin, the man knew what had happened and couldn't be more amused.

"Hell, man, are we going home or what? It's getting hot out here."

The passenger door swung open and Nebraska shoved him into the middle of the bench seat. All of his left side was now touching Texas' right side.

And it wasn't so bad. He could stay like this for a while.

Chapter Twelve

SHE WAS BLONDE, gorgeous, and way out of Nebraska's league.

Ashley Williams, the morning news anchor at Good Morning Dallas, quickly left her news van and approached the truck as Texas' truck pulled into Justin's apartment complex.

"What'd I tell you, man?" Nebraska elbowed Justin in the ribs. "I'm going to marry her one day."

"Yeah, in what universe would that be in?" Texas asked with a grin.

"Kiss my grits, Lieutenant."

"Call me Aaron," Texas said and turned to Justin. "You, too."

There was something the way he said it, whispery, secretively, that made his heart beat faster. He looked over his whole body, inspecting him. Texas, no, Aaron, was tall, lean—a runner—and very attractive.

What would it be like?

To what? Kiss him... explore him... touch him... be touched by him?

"Staff Sergeant Hauten, Specialist Walker. Hi!" The news anchor practically jumped in front of the truck before it stopped. "I got your phone call. I came as soon as I could," she said breathlessly but also with a large, welcoming smile. Justin automatically smiled, too, and could easily see why his friend was head over heels for Ms. Williams.

By now Nebraska had rolled down the window and was

grinning at the woman like he was dying of thirst and she was a tall glass of iced tea.

"My phone call?" Justin asked Nebraska, elbowing him. He grimaced but tried to hide it.

"I may or may not have called her and said I was you," Nebraska said through the side of his mouth.

"You do know that the brigade commander is going to have your heads on a platter for this?" Aaron asked.

"Makes the day more interesting," Nebraska responded and then exited the truck, taking Ashley Williams' hand warmly into his. The camera was still around his neck.

"I've never seen him act this way," Justin remarked.

"I'd say he's smitten."

"I'd say he doesn't have a chance. Let's leave him here."

"Seriously?"

"Look at him. He's towering over her possessively and he's completely forgotten about us. Just let me get the camera."

"Staff Sergeant Hauten!" The news anchor quickly detached herself from Nebraska once Justin jumped out of the truck.

"Ah, pay me no mind, ma'am. I've got a family situation I've got to attend to, so my apologies for wasting your time."

Nebraska stepped in. "I'm happy to fill you in on everything, Ms. Williams." He turned and gave Justin a "you're a good man" look before handing over the camera.

She hesitated, her mouth a perfect O, as if she didn't have a ready response, but her smile reappeared as she gave Nebraska a once-over. As Justin and Aaron pulled away, his red headed friend seemed way too cozy with the anchor.

"I wonder what he'll tell her?" Aaron laughed.

"You mean other than he single-handedly took down a platoon full of enemy soldiers as he performed heart surgery on a camel and simultaneously translated the latest young adult novel into Farsi?"

"Yeah," he grinned. "Other than that."

Aaron turned onto the highway.

"So, where are we headed?" Justin asked.

"Is my place okay?"

Justin thought a moment and watched as a flash of doubt crept onto Aaron's face. Gorgeous men weren't immune to rejection.

"Yeah, that sounds good."

Chapter Thirteen

"DOES IT HURT?" Aaron asked.

Justin had been inspecting his place, the pictures on the wall, the nice furniture, and an impressive entertainment center. The question threw him off.

"What?"

"Your shoulder. Does it still hurt?"

Strangely, it hadn't bothered him since he'd been in Aaron's company; his mind had been on other things. But he wouldn't admit that. Not yet.

"I can't help you move furniture, if that's what you're asking," Justin joked. Absently, he rolled his shoulder; it didn't seem to hurt as much as usual. He clicked the camera on. He wanted to show Aaron something. "I think some of these pictures might look great on your walls. Take a look."

Justin scrolled to the first gallery—all of the images were there, unlike his previous suspicions—and angled the digital display so Aaron could see. At the beginning of their mission, all Captain Phillips had instructed him to do was, "Take pictures, dammit!" and so he did.

Sunsets. Sunrises. Children. Mountains. Animals.

Aaron came in so close that Justin could smell him. He should have taken the camera off, should have just handed it to him. Instead, Aaron had to move in close.

Did I do it on purpose?

He had to lean over slightly to view the images, and when Aaron couldn't quite see the photographs correctly, he quickly moved his hands on top of Justin's to angle the camera just right.

And every touch and every breath felt hot, sexy, and completely erotic. He didn't know what would happen next, but Justin wasn't going to shy away. At least, he hoped he wouldn't.

"These are nice," Aaron said softly as he moved through the photos. "You're a good photographer. The mountains are gorgeous at sunset. In one of them, you see something glimmering in the distance, almost like a huge pile of silver is just waiting for someone to collect it."

"A treasure hunt."

"Exactly. It is odd that Captain Phillips asked you to take these photographs. What do you think he was looking for?"

Aaron didn't seem extremely interested, just innocently curious, but Justin wouldn't reveal that the mission changed over time as Captain Phillips reviewed each gallery. That the target changed at least a dozen times and that by the time their company commander went psycho and shot him in the shoulder, Justin had zero idea of what the man wanted to capture.

"I can honestly say that I have no idea, not any more. Not after what happened."

Justin rolled his shoulders and Aaron must have noticed.

"Can I see?"

"The shoulder? I'll... uh... it's tough to get the shirt over it," Justin said.

Aaron let go of the camera and immediately touched Justin's waist at the bottom of his t-shirt, moving his fingers slightly into the inside of his jeans. Justin sucked in his breath and just... stood there. He didn't know what to do, how to act, what to say. He closed his eyes and swayed a bit, leaning closer to Aaron. Justin opened his eyes, noticed a vein throbbing on his crush's neck and all he wanted to do was lick that spot. Suck on it. Bite on it.

And then explore everything else, too.

Justin took off the camera and tossed it on the couch.

It was slow, and Aaron's hands were scorching hot as he lifted the shirt sideways, keeping his injured shoulder down and neutral.

However, his insides were anything but neutral. Justin had a raging hard-on, and he just didn't know what to do about it.

Finally, the shirt was off and Aaron was gently touching his bandaged shoulder, caressing it, really. It felt so good. Any minute now, Justin was going to wake up and learn that all of this was a dream.

"You probably should be wearing an arm brace," Aaron said, his voice thick.

Aaron was touching him, softly, and in short order, Justin watched as fingers and hands moved away from his shoulder and onto his chest and stomach and his other arm.

His breathing got so shallow that he was in serious danger of passing out.

"Do you want me to stop?"

Aaron's mouth was close. *Just lean in!*

It felt like forever before Justin said, "No," and before he finished the word, before his lips closed, before his next breath, Aaron's mouth was on his.

His lips were soft and then hard and then hungry.

Kissing him felt... exciting, hot, and Justin could not get enough. Butterflies were going crazy in his stomach and it felt like he couldn't catch a breath, but when he felt Aaron's tongue, the kiss turned deeper, hungrier.

Aaron pulled away briefly, pulled his shirt off, and when Justin touched him next, he felt another man's bare skin for the first time. His hands roamed over a strong back and muscled shoulders and a solid, smooth chest.

Aaron broke the kiss but immediately attacked his neck, licking and sucking on him.

"Oh my God," Justin moaned. He was seriously going to pass out. He wanted to touch him everywhere. Kiss him everywhere. Explore... there.

Aaron's hands slipped down and began to unbutton Justin's jeans.

But a small second of doubt came in and Justin froze. Aaron must have felt it because he stopped what he was doing.

How would this work? Who did... what? God, what would it feel like for Aaron's mouth to be on him there? His tongue licking him? His body fitted against him?

And for Justin to go down on him. Would he even know what to do?

"I..."

Aaron, breathing heavy, leaned forward and touched Justin's forehead before placing gentle kisses on his lips.

"We'll go slow. I promise."

"I..." *want you so bad but I fear that I'll be a terrible lover, that I won't be able to do that,* is what he wanted to say.

"You don't have to do anything," Aaron said as he kissed Justin's neck, reading his mind. "Let me..."

"Let you... what?" his voice was heavy.

"Touch you, explore you, just... God, you taste good."

The kiss deepened, turned somewhat harder, Aaron's tongue more urgent.

"Okay." Justin was powerless against him and when Aaron pulled him into the bedroom, he didn't protest, but followed willingly. "You feel wonderful, too."

"Jesus," Aaron growled into his neck as they tumbled

onto the bed. The bites turned sharper, but Aaron was careful to avoid the injured shoulder. He licked Justin's nipples, bit them, sucked on them and then came back to his lips, which felt swollen by now, almost like they were stung by a bee.

A hand cupped his crotch and rubbed, and Justin very nearly bucked up.

"Ahhhh…"

"I can't wait to taste you, Justin. I've dreamed this for so long…"

His pants were suddenly off and he was naked while Aaron kept his jeans on. For a moment he watched as Aaron just took him in, his eyes filled with lust and maybe even traces of love. Had Justin ever felt this way? Had anyone ever looked at him that way?

Aaron moved and suddenly, his mouth closed around Justin's cock. It was hot, hot, hot.

"Ahhhh… God. God. God."

He watched as the man devoured his cock and never, ever, had it felt this good. Aaron's tongue swirled around, flicking the tip as he came up. No inch was spared his loving.

It didn't take Justin long to climax and when he did, it felt so special with Aaron that Justin couldn't help himself when he pulled his lover up and kissed him passionately.

"I had no idea," Justin whispered as they lay on the bed together.

"I did," Aaron said, tracing patterns into Justin's chest. "Because I'm in love with you."

HUNGRY FOR YOU
A Male/Male Military Romance

-VOLUME TWO-

KELLY WASHINGTON

Chapter One

JUSTIN HAUTEN WAS a son of a bitch. He fled Aaron's apartment like the wrath of God was nipping at his feet and spent the next three days remembering the look on Aaron's face. The hurt, the humiliation, the defeat after Justin mumbled some lame excuse about needing to be somewhere.

Jesus, I'm an asshole. Confused, yes, but a confused asshole.

Hurting Aaron was the part that bothered him the most. Perfect, wonderful Aaron. It was the first time something good happened in his life and Justin fucked it up. *I don't deserve him.*

On Monday morning, Nebraska came over in order to rehearse for the Good Morning Dallas interview, handing him version two of the fifty-page script.

"But it's a ten-minute segment," Justin remarked as he flipped through the dense, scripted dialog that Nebraska came up with.

"And your point is?" Nebraska asked. Justin had never seen his friend act so determined. It was pretty obvious that he really wanted to impress Ms. Williams. "I wonder if they'll let me bench-press her."

"Wait, what?" Justin dropped Nebraska's script on the coffee table.

"You know, lift her in the air. I'm pretty sure they'll let me do that," Nebraska said with a stupid grin, lifting his arms for effect. "She's a tiny thing, so it won't be a big deal. I can totally lift three or four times her weight, easily."

Justin laughed, which he desperately needed at the moment. "You will do nothing of the sort. Besides, I doubt you'll even have the opportunity. Once the brigade commander finds out about this, he's going to pull the plug."

"Oh, how he doubts me," Nebraska muttered to himself. He then pointed to the script on the coffee table. "Study that before tomorrow morning. My sister's giving us a ride, so be ready by eight. I don't think I need to remind you that she'll help herself if she has to come in and get you."

Justin shuddered. "Don't worry, I'll be outside waiting."

Once Nebraska left, Justin realized that he never got the chance to talk about Aaron. Either Nebraska could sense that there was a problem and decided to stay mum on the topic, or he was too wrapped up in his desire to impress Ashley Williams to notice, or care.

And Justin wanted to talk about it as much as he *didn't* want to talk about it. He was embarrassed, confused, and he needed to talk about it with someone. Naturally that someone should have been Aaron, but Justin couldn't bring himself to call or go over that night. So Justin busied himself by cleaning his lousy apartment and, as much as he was loath to admit it, he read Nebraska's script. Actually, it wasn't bad, but that didn't make any of it *true*. It read more like fiction than what *really* happened.

He pulled out the camera and studied each and every digital photo. After a while his vision turned blurry.

What was he looking for? Good question. Justin recalled how Aaron had casually mentioned that some of the photos glittered in the mountain areas, suggesting that a treasure was just waiting to be plucked. It was cute when he said it, and Justin's mind had been more on Aaron than the photos at the time, but the more he thought about it, the more he wondered if Captain Phillips had been looking for some sort of treasure.

Oh, not gold and silver bars. But something else. Like unusual technology, weapons, or compounds. His former company commander had become increasingly agitated in the days before the ambush.

Captain Phillips would stab a finger at various plot points on a map and angrily shout, "Get this, but at dusk. I want this image from high-up, pointing down. Be the fucking paparazzi." Something had set him off and whatever it was, apparently it was enough for Captain Phillips to enlist the help of two unknown agents from an unknown agency.

Or was it the other way around?

+++

At a quarter till eight the next morning, Justin, decked out in his Army Service Uniform, stood outside his apartment complex as a stretch limousine pulled up beside him. The back window rolled down and Nebraska thrust his head out, grinning ear to ear.

Justin took a long blink, hoping it was a mirage, and when he opened his eyes again and found the ridiculous vehicle still in front of him, he asked, "Seriously? I thought you said your sister was picking us up."

The driver's side window rolled down as he asked this, and the driver whistled at him. "Hey sexy," a growling-female voice said. It was one of Nebraska's sisters, but he wasn't sure which one. When Justin didn't move right away, the sister just laughed and said, "I like my men a little on the slow slide, darling."

"Pipe down, Tessa," Nebraska ordered with a hearty laugh as Justin climbed in beside him. "Sisters," he said by way of explanation. "Tessa's my baby sister."

Tessa turned around and adjusted her driver's cap. She looked very official, Justin thought. She was the spitting image of Nebraska, but in female form.

"*You* don't get to call me Baby, Sean, not after I beat your ass in our last arm-wrestling contest," Tessa said to her brother before turning her eyes directly on Justin. "You, my tall'n'scruffy man o'beef, can call me Baby and any other four-letter-word from the dictionary. Why don't you come up here with me?" She purred, patting the seat beside her. "I have apricot-scented massage oil."

It took every ounce of self-control for Justin to not laugh out loud. "Thanks, but no thanks, Tessa. It would stain my uniform."

"Oh, you wouldn't be wearing it, but... suit yourself, sexy." She winked, righted herself in the seat, and drove the limo out of the parking lot.

Justin turned to Nebraska, who also wore his formal Army attire, and asked, "Why are we in a limo?"

"My sisters' own their own limo business," Nebraska answered proudly. "For the record, the only reason she beat me was because I was sick with the flu."

"Was not," Tessa interjected.

"Did Tessa drive this all the way from your home state?" Granted, the state of Nebraska was only two states north of Texas, but it still had to be at least 850 miles away. Justin was fairly positive that the limousine's gas mileage sucked.

Tessa chucked. "I convinced mom that there was a limousine convention near Fort Hood this week. As it so happens, I've already booked four jobs in the last twenty-four hours. As soon as I drop you two off, I'm staying in Dallas to chauffeur a girl's sweet sixteen birthday party. Easy cash, plus there will be cake. You'll have to find your own way home."

"Don't worry, buddy," Nebraska chimed in after rolling his eyes at the back of his sister's head. "I spoke to the Good Morning Dallas production manager and she said not to worry it. They'll provide transportation."

Justin spent the next two hours listening to Nebraska and Tessa bicker about everything, from the meaning of vanity license plates, to who was stronger, the ill-fated arm-wrestling contest, and on which brand of breakfast cereal had the most protein in it. Justin allowed his mind to wonder and most of his thoughts centered on Aaron.

It was a welcome relief when they pulled into Good Morning Dallas' lot. For the first time in his life, Justin was rather glad to have been an only child.

Chapter Two

APPARENTLY THEY WEREN'T good-looking enough because once the escort brought them into the studio, they were given a once-over and told to visit the makeup department. "Production lights will wash you boys out. Tell Hector to put bronzer on Sergeant Hauten. He's looking a little pale."

No kidding, Justin thought. *I was just told to wear makeup, of course I'm going to go pale at the thought.*

An assistant took their Army jackets—for safekeeping from the makeup—and Hector, a tiny Hispanic man with expressive eyebrows, went to work on prepping Justin's skin. Pomegranate acne facial wipes, then a clear gel that Hector promised would banish shine for twenty-four hours, a light application of foundation which was then set with translucent power and, finally, Hector applied the bronzer and stood back to observe his work.

"All done, Mr. Justin. I didn't touch your eyebrows. Normally I fill them in, but you have the eyebrows of a bull. *Muy macho.*"

"Ah, thank you, Mr. Hector." *Eyebrows of a bull, huh?* He'd have to remember that one. Justin watched as Nebraska underwent the same procedure, though Hector was loathe to conceal Nebraska's freckles.

"I will now add lipstick, Mr. Nebraska," Hector said. "Your lips need outlining."

Nebraska nodded, unfazed. "I prefer cool tone colors, but sadly with my red hair, my skin tone is warm, not cool. Give me your best nude lipliner, Hector."

Hector smiled like it was his birthday. His steady hand was quick about the business and it wasn't long before they had their Army jackets back on and they were waiting in the green room for their segment. Hector's last instructions were to inform them that they were not allowed to eat anything, lest they destroy his artwork.

Once out of earshot, Justin said, "I'm not sure how lipliner can be considered artwork, but I for one plan to listen to him. So stop eyeing those donuts, Nebraska."

"It's so cruel how they put food in here if we're not allowed to eat it. Am I right, or what?" Nebraska asked the room in general, which had a few other guests, including an up-and-coming actress starring in the latest vampire television series that Justin's mom was gaga over. The young actress looked like she wanted to interact with Nebraska, but the lady beside her—her publicist?—nudged an elbow and whispered something. From that point forward she avoided eye contact.

Fortunately, they did not stay in the green room long. An assistant, wearing a thick headset, came to collect them five minutes later. The donuts were safe for now.

+++

Ashley Williams met them off-stage. "Staff Sergeant Hauten, Specialist Walker, thank you for being here today." They shook hands. "Your segment will not be taped live, gentlemen. Our last interview went a bit long, so I will interview you on another stage and it will air at the end of today's show. I hope that's okay."

Nebraska took the lead, which was fine with Justin, though it wasn't necessary for Nebraska to push him aside like yesterday's newspaper.

"We're just happy to be here, Ms. Williams," Nebraska

said, stepping in front of Justin.

The news anchor looked pleased by Nebraska's marked adoration. *Another loyal follower*, Justin thought.

"Wonderful. If you'll follow me, please." After a few turns, she led them to a corner studio outfitted with three cream-colored chairs, a dark coffee table, and multiple potted plants in the background. Justin got the impression that this interview wasn't the station's top priority. Two individuals—one studio hand and the cameraman—were setting up in front of them. It was a bare-bones production.

Ashley Williams sat in the left-most chair, which faced their two chairs, as Justin and Nebraska did their best to look—and act—comfortable in front of the camera. Even though they were not being taped live, Justin had never felt so nervous in his life.

What were they there for again? Oh, right. Captain Phillips.

She began asking questions, none of which Justin fully heard or understood. After a few minutes it became clear that Justin was just along for the ride. Nebraska had everything under control as he retold the story without too much embellishment. His friend was a natural. Justin noticed that he completely omitted everything about the camera.

"Do you think Captain Phillips was suffering from Post-Traumatic Stress Disorder, Sergeant Hauten? And if so, what might have triggered his actions?"

That woke Justin up. "It's possible. Being deployed to a war zone isn't an easy thing for most, even those fully trained to be there. However, I'm just a soldier. I'm not qualified to make that type of assessment. What triggered his actions? I truly do not know and I wish I did. I wish I could have made a difference before it happened."

She smiled at his answer. It was too politically correct. Justin wondered if the station would even run their five minute clip.

"Thank you both so much for being here. It was a pleasure talking to you. Before we close out, I want to congratulate Sergeant Hauten on his nomination for the Army's Non-Commissioned Officer of the Year award. All of us here at Good Morning Dallas wish him the best of luck for a healthy and speedy recovery."

Nebraska turned suddenly, his eyes full of confusion. "Is that true?" he whispered. "When were you going to tell me?"

Shit. "I didn't know the nomination had been accepted until she just said it."

Nebraska's eyes turned cloudy, like maybe he wanted to believe Justin but his stubborn nature wouldn't let him. Ms. Williams looked slightly uncomfortable, but she kept the microphones and the cameras rolling in case she captured a great news story out of them rather than the dull one they just had.

"Can we talk about this later?" Justin asked.

"Hmm. We'll see." Nebraska stood and moved away from Justin. "May I ask you a question, Ms. Williams?" She was already standing. She was very poised in her designer pantsuit.

"Of course."

Justin watched in amazement as Nebraska pulled a ring from his pocket, knelt down on one knee and confessed, "Ashley, the moment I met you is the moment I believed in love at first sight. Will you marry me?"

Chapter Three

THE NEWS STUDIO was in a state of chaos after the proposal when Justin decided to slip out. Nebraska was pissed at him, so it wouldn't matter if he left without saying anything. Besides, after Ashley Williams said "yes" to Nebraska's marriage proposal, Justin didn't think he'd be missed.

True to their word, the production manager had a town car waiting for Justin. It was a quiet ride to his apartment outside Fort Hood and after a few minutes onto the highway, Justin was sound asleep.

It felt like only a few minutes passed when the driver announced it was time to get out. Justin thanked him, left a tip, and entered his lonely apartment.

He shed his Army Service Uniform—careful to not overstretch his injured shoulder—and hung everything in the closet. He looked up and eyed the camera on the top shelf and wondered if he needed to safeguard it.

"That's silly," he said out loud. "What am I going to do, hide it under the bed?"

It's the mission, the camera, or what's on that camera, that got you shot in the first place, pal.

He was such a numbskull. It was only a matter of time before everyone he knew hated his guts.

He thought instantly of how he had fucked things up with Aaron. Would the man ever speak to him again? Justin had barely gotten to know him, and there was so much he wanted to learn. He felt like punching the closet door and he almost did when a noise jolted him from his thoughts. Someone was in the room with him.

"Hi," a sultry voice said from his bedroom doorway. It was Julia. She wore a thin, yellow sundress that hugged her curves. "Look at you." She gave him a thorough once-over. "Not much left to remove."

Once he realized that he could see *through* the sundress, Justin's erection was immediate, and he felt a surge of excitement and guilt all at the same time.

Her body was hot, and the sexual heat she radiated practically blinded him with the need to have her, consume her, claim her. Justin's mind was overloaded. Obviously his body and throbbing erection wanted her, but his mind... well... to say that he was conflicted would have been an understatement.

His thoughts turned to the night he shared with Aaron. Their lovemaking never once felt forced or faked. Being with him felt natural, but after Aaron's declaration of love, it scared the shit out of him. Maybe he wasn't attracted to men. Maybe it was just something about Aaron. Or maybe he was afraid to admit the feelings that had been there all along, just deep, deep down, and never acknowledged.

"I thought you might like some company," Julia said, stepping away from the doorframe hastily. She was trying to hard to act sexy. Justin was struck with the thought that she was doing this because she could and not necessarily because she wanted to. She made a point of lifting her hand, showing that she carried a grocery bag. "I brought chicken soup."

"Julia, you're an amazing person, but I can't do this. Not right now."

Justin was a lot of things, but he wasn't a jerk. Well, he was, but he wasn't one on purpose. A small look of surprise stole over Julia's face.

"Did you already make plans? That gorgeous

Lieutenant Parrots was at your door when I arrived, but I sent him away. Wanted to make sure we wouldn't be disturbed."

"It's Lieutenant *Parris*, and you did what?" *Aaron was here.* Justin wiped his face; he was suddenly sweaty. He grabbed a pair of jeans from his closet and jammed his legs into them.

"Don't be jealous just because I called him gorgeous," she said and grinned mischievously. She came closer, inspecting the clothes in his closet without much true interest, though there was something of an odd look on her face. An expression he couldn't quite decipher. Justin stepped around her.

Julia sighed. "Where are you going?"

He ran out of the apartment, onto the landing that overlooked the parking lot. Aaron had just reached his truck, turned around, and looked back at the apartment building. A chill zapped through Justin. Even from the slight distance, he could tell that Aaron's eyes were narrow slits and that if looks could kill, Justin would have been flat on the landing.

Julia joined Justin on the landing. *Jesus Christ,* he thought as he looked at her and then at Aaron. *Why is this happening to me?*

Aaron shook his head, directed a look of contempt at Justin, and climbed into his truck. The door barely closed before he sped away.

I've lost him. Justin felt sick to his stomach. He was in serious danger of throwing up. He might as well throw his heart in the trash. He didn't need it. He didn't want it.

Julia was still beside him and, instead of comforting him, she watched him with weary, exhausted eyes. What did she have to be tired about?

When Justin looked back out at the parking lot, in the

same spot Aaron angrily tore out of, an official-looking black SUV pulled in and parked. Justin sighed. He watched as an unknown figure stepped out—at least it wasn't one of the agents—but he still had a feeling the next twenty-four hours wouldn't be kind.

The camera. He needed to hide the camera.

He turned to Julia and softly grasped her shoulders. Her hair bounced.

"Will you do something for me?" Julia nodded as he asked her to hide the camera. Surprisingly, she appeared to understand his instructions completely.

Maybe he was wrong about Julia.

The driver of the black SUV reached the floor below them. He could hear her careful, non-hurried footsteps, as if she knew she already had a captive audience, and then the top of her head came into view.

She was practically the size of a child, but this was no small girl playing dress-up. Her jet black hair was short; the asymmetrical bob framed her ageless face like the deadly ended side of a pair of scissors. With a scowl firmly in place, her dark, emotionless eyes were trained on him and if he so much as moved a fraction, Justin wondered if she would pounce.

Her dark gray suit was impeccably powerful looking and her high heels added a good five inches in height. The woman wasn't beautiful or young or even remotely attractive. But she was confident, probably dangerous in a "my brain can kill you" sort of way, and it was extremely evident as she walked the last few steps to the landing. Julia stiffened against Justin.

"There was no need to dress up for me, Sergeant Hauten," the woman said calmly. Her voice was throaty, like she had just smoked thirty cigarettes simultaneously. "I'm Mary Lovecross," she said by way of an introduction without disclosing *who* she worked for or *why* she was there. Mary Lovecross inspected Julia briefly before dismissing her.

"I like to present my best side at all times," Justin said. If there was ever a time to impress a lady, now would be that time. With his bare chest, firm abs, and strong shoulders, Justin could have sold a matchbook to Satan for triple to going rate.

Justin didn't know how the woman could possibly scowl deeper at him, but she did.

"Charming," she drawled as an eyebrow rose in an impatient manner. Clearly she wasn't easily impressed. "Get dressed. You're coming with me."

So the woman didn't come by just to say hello.

Mary Lovecross must have been a death-eating soulsucker in another life because she scared the crap out of Justin.

"And if I say no?"

The eyebrow rose again. "I have a distain for the word *if.* It implies indecision. And I really don't like that in the person I am giving orders to."

"I think you should do what she says," Julia whispered.

At least they didn't have a gun pointed at them. Mary Lovecross didn't need a gun as an enforcer. Her eyebrows worked just fine.

"Can we hit up a drive-thru?" Justin asked. He now wished that he had eaten a few of those donuts. "I'm starving."

Chapter Four

SOME SURPRISES ARE nice: like someone bringing cupcakes into the office, getting asked out on a date, or finding money.

Justin, dressed in a black t-shirt and dark-washed jeans, jumped into Ms. Lovecross's fully decked-out, state-of-the-art SUV, and felt that whatever surprises she held in store for him would *not* be the nice kind.

She drove the SUV past every drive-thru restaurant, out of the city, and into an area that might be described as the Texan Badlands. Dust. Tumbleweeds. Large swatches of sunlight blazing down. Justin, through the haze, could see abandoned cars, trucks, and trailers, as well as dozens of sinewy, wild dogs. His stomach somersaulted.

Two things happened in places like this.

Someone dumped your lifeless body here, or you attended confidential meetings.

They were silent at the beginning of the drive though he felt her looking at him at times, like maybe she was trying to make up her mind. Justin, for his part, wasn't exactly in a talkative mood. So he sulked in his seat, stared out the window, and wondered what the lady wanted. Because she wanted something.

Once they reached the badlands, she casually mentioned, "I'm not going to kill you."

"Uh...likewise," he responded dryly. That elicited a bark-like laugh from Lovecross. He realized that he had started thinking of her as just Lovecross. She was one of those genderless comic book badass characters who never required an introduction.

"Listen, kid. You're in way over your head." She cracked the window and lit a cigarette.

"What am I in, exactly?"

"You stepped in a very tall pile of shit, I'm afraid. I'm shocked you still have that camera." She glared at him as if he were suddenly stupid. "How is it that you still have the camera?"

"Mister A gave it back to me after a small, detention-like meeting. Strange, but I'm getting a feeling of déjà vu."

"Gave it back to you, huh?" she asked cryptically, giving Justin a wolf-like smile. "I take back what I said. You stepped in *two* piles of shit. Adam Asshole—yeah, that's our nickname for him—is more of a minor irritation in my book, but not someone to fuck with. He likes to toy with people. I hope you didn't make a deal with him." She looked him over. "No deal? Good, but you need to be careful, kiddo."

Justin felt very uncomfortable, as if she'd turned on the heat.

"I'm not exactly well versed in the art of espionage, ma'am; not like some in this vehicle apparently are."

She ignored the comment. "Cameras are stupid things that will land you in hot water. The boiling type that melts the skin and muscle off bones. A camera means evidence, even if it's taken out of context. And evidence, in the wrong hands, means someone's taking a dirt nap."

Justin shuddered. "Evidence of what?"

She took a long drag of her cigarette. It was almost gone. She lit another one with the smaller cigarette butt and then tossed the first one out the window. The Texan Badlands are also full of cigarette butts.

"You can't sweet-talk me, kid, not like you and your friend did on Good Morning Dallas this morning. Which, by the way, was like watching a train wreck. Highly amusing, though." Justin groaned loudly. "You gave your little girlfriend the camera, right?"

"She's not my girlfriend," he said stiffly. "And the interview wasn't that bad." His mind went back to the spot in the interview when Nebraska spontaneously proposed to Ashley Williams. The fact that she said *yes* stunned Justin.

"I practically abduct you and that's what you get uptight about? You've got your priorities screwed on all wrong, kiddo."

"I just think you should get your facts straight."

"Listen, kid. My facts are straighter and longer than your dick. You need to be careful. As we speak, your place is getting tossed. It's not just the camera. If it was just about that, then I would have had it before you left Afghanistan, none of this would be happening, and you would have returned to being some regular soldier living out his crappy life, waiting for things to improve."

"Who's in my apartment? *Who are you?* Turn around. Now!" He grabbed for the door handle. Good Lord, was he actually thinking about jumping out of the SUV?

"And you'd do what, exactly? Take off your shirt and model for them? I've seen better. You don't strike me as the suicidal type." She lit another cigarette and looked him over as if she were taking stock of him. "An idiot, yes, but definitely not suicidal. Your girlfriend is fine. Let's just say she's in good hands."

"What about Nebraska?" With any luck, his best friend was none the wiser.

"I wondered when you'd ask about your trusty sidekick. Didn't you find it strange that he wasn't waiting for you after the interview this morning?"

"No." He wasn't about to admit that he and Nebraska

weren't exactly on good terms at the moment. "Let me guess," Justin said, "You've already picked him up."

"He's a feisty one!" She laughed so hard that it sounded like a lung might fly out of her mouth. "Specialist Walker isn't as docile as you, so I had one of my deputies arrest him. At the moment, your friend is sitting in one of my jail cells."

Jesus. Justin took a deep breath. "Who exactly are you?" he asked.

"I'm from a department you've never heard of, kiddo," she responded without elaborating further.

"You're just rolling out the red carpet for me, aren't you? I don't know what you want and I don't trust a word that comes out of your mouth."

"That's the smartest thing you've said. It's simple: don't trust anyone."

Justin rolled his eyes. "That's super helpful. Thanks."

The SUV slowed down. That's when he noticed a lean-to shack up ahead. One strong wind and it would topple over. But there was another car there, one of those long town cars that could either be an unmarked police cruiser or some rich dude's car looking to score drugs.

His shoulder began to ache as tension and adrenaline kicked in.

"Are we expecting friends? I still have no idea why I'm even here, what's going on, or why I'm mixed in all of this... stuff."

Lovecross killed the engine as two military guards approached the SUV. "You want to find out?" Justin nodded. "Then get out of the car."

Chapter Five

ANTICIPATION'S A BITCH. The dusty, howling wind stole Justin's breath the instant he opened the door. It was hotter than hell and the hazy sunlight combined with the wind made seeing anyone fairly impossible. He could have been looking at the Loch Ness monster for all he knew.

He felt a hand dig into his back and shove him forward toward the tiny shack. Its door smacked open with a loud crack and instead of landing on steady floorboards—as he expected—Justin nearly lost his balance as he learned that no, it wasn't a floor; it was a staircase that sank into the earth.

"Keep moving," a raspy voice croaked from behind him.

Justin couldn't see a thing, but he was hyper aware of his surroundings. Lovecross was in front of him, smoking what would be her sixth cigarette in an hour. There was a soldier in front of her and a soldier behind him, both of whom were fitted with protective vests and armed with semi-automatic rifles.

This was either very good or really bad.

Justin was at a loss as to what to think. Not a single soul knew where he was. There wasn't a postcard for this type of situation. Not that anyone would come running to aid in his escape; Aaron hated his guts—with reason—and Nebraska was in a jail cell. That left his mom, and in that case, it was better to leave her in the dark.

The air abruptly turned cold. Justin wasn't being led into the fiery pits of hell after all. Either the room they would descend into was very, very deep, or it was an established underground bunker building with air conditioning. He wasn't sure which he might prefer. At any rate, the total darkness wasn't doing him any favors.

The steps were concrete and the railing was metal. Someone had gone to elaborate lengths to build this facility. It reminded him of the time he visited Luray Caverns and how engineers had built out walkways and stairs and artificial lighting to see the stalagmites and stalactites. However, now, as he stepped lower and lower, his uneasiness was as thick as the concrete steps below him.

Keys jangled ahead of him and instinctively, Justin knew to stop moving lest he knock Lovecross down. She'd stab him with one of her pointy high heels.

Light, combined with the sound of a rusty metal door opening, greeted the four of them. And what he walked into was the stuff of movies.

It was a wild, yet controlled, cavernous underground chamber outfitted into some sort of high-tech military bunker.

Against a lower far wall, in a room that looked like an amphitheater, a huge knowledge wall was plastered with news feeds, maps, satellite images, and scrolling presentations. Justin's eyes focused on the thick glass that separated the amphitheater from the man-made, carved-out hallway. He felt like he was looking down on a NASA control room. It was all clean lines, stainless steel, and rope-lighted walkways. Computer terminals dotted the floor below, occupied by fast working technicians doing God-knows-what.

It was almost as if someone found a cave and jackhammered their way around it and built out this structure. It was utterly brilliant, but not enough for Justin to forget why he was here.

Finally, he noticed the other soldiers. He couldn't believe that he had missed seeing them in the first place.

Dozens of armed soldiers—some patrolling, some stationary—lined the large hallway. Justin observed them observing him. Then he noticed that the armed soldiers were also staring at Lovecross.

Unless he was mistaken, the soldiers seemed to tidy themselves up. Those standing appeared to stand taller. Those patrolling seemed to walk in sync, like a small parade materialized out of nowhere.

He stepped into a world he knew nothing about or how to untangle himself. The door behind them shut and Justin, without having to ask, knew that he wouldn't be able to walk out of here on his own. Now that he was here, he might as well learn what Lovecross knew—or at least what she was willing to tell him—and then come up with a plan.

Justin was used to thinking on his feet, but his feet had never been in a place or situation like this.

Lovecross lit another cigarette. One of the soldiers calmly instructed her to snub it, but the look she gave him could have melted the skin off his body. He apologized almost immediately. Whoever Mary Lovecross was, she had clout and balls and something else... power.

Justin didn't trust her, but he also didn't have much of a choice.

"This isn't an amusement park," Lovecross barked at him as he stood there stupidly. "Let's go."

They left the observation deck hallway, and Justin followed Lovecross and the two soldiers down a dark corridor that was also carved out of the rock. Soft-lighted sconces and rope lights cast eerie shadows as they walked. Carved further into the side of the rock were solid metal doors, sequentially numbered and spaced out every twenty feet. Justin counted his footsteps. The older soldier unlocked door eight, stepped aside, and motioned for them to enter.

Lovecross went in without hesitation. And why not? The woman wasn't afraid of anything. He took a deep breath, unprepared for whatever he might encounter, and crossed the threshold. His muscles ached. His shoulder throbbed. His mind felt like it was going around a racetrack, over and over.

Justin looked around and had to blink about a dozen times. The room looked like a studio apartment; couches, a bed, a large flat-screen television, and even a coffee table. Then he noticed someone else was in the room.

Nebraska sat on the leather couch, eating. He looked horrible. It looked like someone had used his face for a punching bag. His knuckles were red and scabbed up, too. So whoever he scuffled with probably ended up far, far worse.

Nebraska looked up and anger flooded his bruised face, but he finished chewing and stared at Justin with narrowed eyes and an ice-cold expression. Nebraska was not happy to see him.

"I failed to mention that Specialist Walker was in one of my jail cells," Lovecross said. Her voice was light and airy, as if she couldn't wait to see what happened next.

The door clinked loudly behind him as Nebraska put the plate on the coffee table. The three of them stared at each other. Or, rather, Nebraska starred at Justin, and Lovecross observed them.

"Oh, it's you," Nebraska said coldly. Justin wasn't sure if he was referring to him or Lovecross.

"What the hell happened to you?" Justin asked.

Nebraska frowned slightly. "Oh, this? Simple misunderstanding."

"Nothing about you is simple, my friend."

"I may or may not have been arrested. I hear it depends on who you ask." Nebraska looked pointedly at Lovecross.

"And if I ask Lovecross?"

She raised an eyebrow but otherwise didn't indicate she was displeased with the lack of a title in front of her name.

Nebraska lifted a hand and began to tick-mark fingers. "Resisting arrest and disorderly conduct."

"Nebraska!" Justin groaned.

But he wasn't finished. "Assaulting an officer, destruction of public property, and public nudity. Like I said: depends on who you ask. It may all go away if..." Nebraska trailed off.

"If what?"

"If I give them what they want: Captain Phillips' orders."

Which one? Justin wanted to ask, but he didn't have time.

Nebraska jumped up from the couch quicker than a striking scorpion. His upper body reared back and, without provocation, he punched Justin in the side of the face. Stars exploded and it felt like the universe imploded on itself.

"That's for lying to me, you son of a bitch," he heard his friend yell through the ringing in his ears.

Justin should have known. Really, was there any other outcome?

Chapter Six

"I THINK YOU broke my cheekbone." Justin palmed his face. It felt like something sharp was still implanted in his face, like the pointy edge of a hammer. "Jesus Christ," he said through gritted teeth. "Even talking hurts." He moved to the couch, intending to sit up, but the room started to spin, so he lay down instead.

"Builds character," Nebraska said. "Besides, your face is too pretty and whatever comes out of your mouth is going to be a lie."

"Perhaps you could have said something sooner and not decimated my face in the process."

"And ruined the satisfaction? No thanks," Nebraska said. "Listen, lady, give this dipshit his own room. He can really stink up a place."

Justin couldn't see Lovecross, but she was still in the room, in the corner, observing. And smoking. The woman defined chain smoker.

"I'm not particularly fond of this game," she said calmly, but Justin could hear the edge in her voice.

"He's the one playing games here," Nebraska said. "I can't believe you didn't tell me. I'm your best friend, for christsakes."

"I didn't think it mattered," Justin answered pitifully. Really, it was more of a mumble than anything intelligent.

"That you were nominated for Noncommissioned Officer of the Year? Of course it matters."

Silence. Justin wasn't sure if he wanted to admit the next bit, but he did anyway. Screw whoever was listening.

"Captain Phillips is the one that submitted my packet. After everything that's happened... well, I doubt my name will stay in the running. Besides, I still have to compete in the Best Warrior Competition."

"But you didn't tell me," Nebraska said. "I had to hear about it from someone else. I bet you told Aaron." His voice was dejected sounding.

"No," Justin said. "He didn't know, either. You know how awards and stuff like that don't really matter to me. Besides, Aaron isn't talking to me, either."

"Well, that's convenient, isn't it? You can concentrate on being my friend now." His voice turned heated. "What else haven't you told me? Hmm? Like why we were taking all of those pictures? You stopped telling me what Captain Phillips wanted after the first few weeks. I saw how the two of you talked. Short, heated words every time you gave him the camera."

Nebraska's words stung. It was like another punch in the face. "It wasn't anything. Well, nothing important. Just guidance, really." He held in his suspicions about their former commander. Little things that didn't make much sense at the time. Like his lack of knowledge in proper protocol, command, and control, and other smaller infractions that most officers were trained on. Captain Phillips, at the time, came across as clueless.

There was a scrape against the wall. The strong scent of sulfur hit him as the third person in the room lit a match.

Surprisingly, Justin had forgotten all about Lovecross. So when she spoke, it was like a small jolt went through his body.

"You'll be happy to know, then, that you will not be receiving an award today," Lovecross said in a placid tone, as if she didn't care one way or the other. Justin knew better. She had been studying their every move, word, and expression. "I am curious to know what your guidance was, Sergeant," she said with a great deal more interest. Her eyes narrowed and she stared at him like he was a hardened criminal.

Justin looked up. "I didn't say *I* was giving *him* guidance," he lied.

Nebraska scoffed. "You and I both know that the Captain was a bit on the clueless side. You're just being modest."

Lovecross smiled artfully. "I think you may be right, Specialist Walker."

"Huh?" Justin asked, not trusting the woman's next words.

"What was that?" Nebraska said heatedly at the same time.

"I do wonder what else he hasn't told you," she said with a knowing smile tugging at her lips.

She thought she was so clever, Justin mused. Sadly, it might work. Nebraska looked at him expectantly, as if by doing so, Justin might bust open like a piñata and information would fall out like candy.

"She's playing you against me, Nebraska," Justin said quickly. The chair he was sitting in felt very confining, like it was sucking him in. He stood up but the room spun, and he sat back down just as Nebraska grabbed him with the strength of ten men and flung him across the room.

The flat-screen television crashed to the floor with a loud and deafening crack.

As the television emitted sparks and popping sounds, two large hands clamped around Justin's neck, choking him. He wrapped his own hands around Nebraska's wrists and pushed and shoved and did everything else in his power to try and remove the pressure from his neck.

It wasn't working. His body automatically fought back

by kicking as hard as he could, over and over.

Black edges framed his vision. The rest was filled with the contorted, sour expression of his best friend hell-bent on teaching him a lesson.

Then he felt Nebraska's grasp lessen. Justin reared up and head-butted his friend and kneed him in the groin. They both collapsed to the floor, side by side, breathing heavy.

"Our nation's army is made up of goddamn idiots!" the petite woman hissed as she stalked out of the room.

"Are we alone?" Justin mumbled. His head felt like it had gone through a meat grinder and his voice sounded like a strangled mouse. His eyes refused to open. He heard shifting noises beside him. "Holy shit, man. What was that for? Seriously, I think I may need a doctor."

"Yeah," Nebraska moaned in a higher-pitched voice. His arm flung out and crashed against Justin's stomach. Justin's upper body bounced up and all of the air hissed out of his lungs.

"It's better off this way; them thinking that we hate each other."

"Them thinking it?" he wheezed. "Hell, you convinced me. Why was that necessary?"

"They won't try to break us."

"No, you already did that. Jesus, help me up."

But neither moved and when someone came to collect them two hours later, they were found exactly like they were.

Chapter Seven

IT WAS TIME for a shift change.

Justin felt about a million years old. He could barely see with the one eye swollen shut, but he refused to hold Nebraska's hand when they entered the hallway following the soldier escorting them. "Fine, be that way," Nebraska joked and then winced as he looked at his friend's destroyed face. He apologized for the twentieth time. "I think you'll need to delay that Noncommissioned Officer of the Year photo shoot."

They joined dozens and dozens of soldiers, civilians, and other uniformed individuals in the hallway. They garnered a lot of attention.

"I was going to tell you," Justin croaked. It felt like he swallowed liquid concrete and it was now solidifying in his throat.

Justin looked to this left and realized that he was looking down at the darkened amphitheater. When he and Nebraska got to the bottom, the escort deposited them at a large conference table.

Their names were prominently displayed in front of two chairs at the main table.

"Even my own mother doesn't let me sit at the main table," Nebraska said as he picked up his own nameplate, waving it around cheerfully.

The control room was now full of people and their chatter, but all Justin could see and focus on was the woman standing at the lectern.

"Alright, quiet down everyone," Lovecross announced

over the room. Collectively, about a hundred people turned their attention to the tiny woman up front. She didn't appear to need a microphone. "We've had the images loaded into our Datamine Location Software, aka DLS, and our intelligence analysts have had about two weeks with them. Staff Sergeant Hauten and Specialist Walker are with us today. They took the photos you are about to see."

"Two weeks?" Nebraska asked in Justin's ear.

Justin shrugged. Not much surprised him anymore when it came to Lovecross.

The large knowledge wall behind her flickered on, and the first image that Justin took three months ago popped up on the thirty-six by forty-nine-foot screen. This was considerably better than the tiny preview screen on the camera.

He immediately thought of that night in Aaron's apartment, standing beside him, their bodies, hands touching, previewing the same images, but then he pushed the thought away. Justin needed to focus on the present situation. Ruminating on Aaron wouldn't help.

"Now, the first few photos are fairly useless, no offense to Sergeant Hauten. But he did what any good photographer does: he took test shots of sunrises and sunsets in and around certain mountains and hilltops. Even without a date or timestamp on these images—" *she clicked through them at a fast rate* "—we were able to determine latitude and longitude and the date and time that they were taken. Some of these images are lovely and while they do not directly aide in our investigation, they do corroborate sequence and location, and we can map the image itself and where the photographer was standing when he took the shots."

The last image turned into a sophisticated digital

illustration as the intelligence data was layered over the photo. Things were labeled, like the mountain range, its elevation, and the date and time the image was taken. Then the image zoomed out into a panoramic cityscape view and a red X indicated where Justin was standing as he snapped the photo. Cities and regions were labeled, too.

Justin was extremely impressed with Lovecross' team's abilities until she solemnly stopped on the first photo of a small girl smiling shyly into the camera.

Justin wasn't positive, but he thought he heard Lovecross sigh.

He remembered girl and her family vividly. They fed him and Nebraska—the food was absolutely delicious and Nebraska had eaten everything—shortly after the image was captured. The girl's family, their house, and small patch of land were the focus of the next few photos.

Suddenly and without reason, Justin felt a sense of dread. He was also sweating even though the cavernous room was freezing.

"This is eight-year-old Smyeena. Sergeant Hauten photographed her and her family on June seventeenth. Here is the cityscape of her location in relation to the images thus far. The intelligence layers will build as we progress through the hundred or so images. Unfortunately," she hesitated briefly, "three days later, Smyeena's family fled for their very lives, their two-room hut was burned down, and Smyeena was kidnapped by an assailant now identified as Objective Snatcher."

The room felt devoid of oxygen as every organ in Justin's body plummeted. Nebraska sat stock-still and silently turned his head to Justin.

"I'm going to kill Captain Phillips if he had anything to do with this," Nebraska said through clenched teeth.

Lovecross continued, "However, tribal factions, civil

wars, and other intimidating actions like this happen all the time all over the world, not just in active war zones. But, preliminarily, we believe that this family and Smyeena are the first victims of Objective Snatcher. The overlay will show a pattern that I trust will corroborate my theory."

She moved to the next series of photos: a group of kids playing soccer. Justin's hands formed into fists under the table.

Please let them be okay. Please let them be okay.

She didn't have commentary on the soccer photos, not until the close-up of a young woman. Justin remembered that she was in her early twenties and just as beautiful as they come. At the time, he was instantly smitten with her and couldn't stop taking her picture, asking her questions, or just staring at her. She had been planning her wedding and had taken a small break to watch the children play soccer. He remembered that she spoke in broken English.

Even now, through the digital photograph displayed on the screen, her beauty and vibrancy filled the dark room.

"Leia Woondiour, twenty years old. You'll see, as the overlay maps itself, this image was taken on June twenty-fourth at four in the afternoon. These dates are important, people." Lovecross paused here. "Three days later, Leia's family and her intended groom reported that three masked men abducted her. State Department contacts report that Leia was last seen on a flight with a known human trafficker, heading to the United States. Her whereabouts are unknown at this time and the United States may not have been the final destination. Human trafficking is a global problem. Regrettably, she could be anywhere."

"This has to be a coincidence," Justin said to Nebraska. "There are only two people who saw the photos: me and Captain Phillips."

"I think I'm going to throw up, man." Nebraska's face was an ashy green, and it made him appear smaller, weaker.

Mary Lovecross didn't stop. "Seven days after Leia's photograph was taken, Sergeant Hauten took this image of his squad as they bought a goat from a local farmer. You know where I'm going with this, though this incident appears to have been escalated. Three days later, on July fourth, the farmer, Amad, and his family were killed execution style. Their ten-year-old son was *not* among the dead. A boy matching his description is seen on airport security footage several hours after the massacre. He appears to be with a suspected trafficker—a motherly aged woman that gets a cut of the sale."

Justin remembered the goat; it was a silly day, but he couldn't recall the farmer too well. He could hardly breathe and had to physically unclench his fists before his short fingernails cut through his skin. His body was wound up tight and any second now, he would burst out like a bullet. He had to get out of there.

By looking at his friend, Justin could tell that Nebraska was also having an extremely difficult time processing everything.

All of this was Justin's fault. The killings. The abductions. How could Lovecross stand up there and calmly dictate this information without any emotion? Did she expect him to sit there and not be affected?

Why his photographs? Justin remembered that it was early July when Captain Phillips changed the mission. "No more damn people, Sergeant," his former company commander ordered at the time. Did the Captain know? He must have. And still he sent them off each day to take photographs.

"It appears that one of our own is responsible for this,

though I have my own suspicions," Lovecross said loudly. Shocked sighs echoed around the room. "Oliver Michael Phillips has been charged with treason against the United States for selling confidential information to a relative in Great Britain. A relative alleged to be involved in not only human trafficking, but terrorism as well. Do you want to see what selling information to our enemies looks like?"

She didn't wait for an answer.

She clicked through the rest of the images, which were of the scenic variety: roads and convoys; mountains and abandoned buildings and military compounds, including the glittery photos that Aaron had commented on; and destroyed homes, IED craters, and dismantled mines. The last image was of a dark building, tinted with blushes of red from the setting sun. That was the night Captain Phillips ambushed him.

The final overlay compiled every image and every Datamine label into one very large cityscape image.

"Here we go: the red line indicates the exact path points for Sergeant Hauten and Specialist Walker. The blue dots show us the victims' location in relation to known military operations labeled in the green dots—this is all classified, folks!—as well as non-military operations in orange dots, such as those conducted by the State Department and other Agencies, in purple dots. What does our diagram look like, folks?"

A small flame flickered in front of Lovecross's face as she lit another cigarette. Justin guessed why she needed the cigarettes: to keep her sanity.

Several personnel chimed in at the same time. It was a heart.

"Operation Snatcher has turned into Operation Heart."

The screen went off and the room was cast in darkness briefly until someone turned on a few overhead lights.

Lovecross was suddenly inches from his face.

"You won't understand or believe me right now, Sergeant, but none of this is your fault. From here on out, Captain Phillips, that camera, and these images do not exist. Get some rest. I'll have someone drive you and Specialist Walker home in the morning."

Chapter Eight

THEY MUST HAVE been escorted back to Room Eight, but honestly, Justin didn't now how he got there or when he sat on the couch or when he lay down. It didn't matter if his eyes were opened or closed; all he saw were the images of Smyeena and Leia and the farmer and their families.

"Do you think this room is bugged?" Nebraska asked, breaking the silence. It sounded like he was lying on the bed behind him.

"Does it matter?" he asked hoarsely.

"I don't trust the Lovecross lady. Everything seems too tidy. Too wrapped up in one package."

Small doubts crept into Justin's mind. It seemed too perfect, and they had everything pinned on Captain Phillips. Case closed. What was it that she had said? *A camera equals evidence, even if taken out of context.* Had something been taken out of context?

Something about her statement nagged at him.

"At least we aren't in some federal jail cell awaiting treason charges," Justin reasoned.

"Look around you, buddy: we *are* in a jail cell. A comfortable one, but we're locked up, that's for sure."

"Yeah, I guess you're right."

"Shit, man. I don't want to be right, I want to know why. Why were those kids snatched? Captain Phillips had no way of knowing who you were going to snap on any given day with that camera. I didn't know, and I was with you. It was random. And why all the drastic actions just to get us here? It's like a charade: my being arrested, that intelligence overlay, Mr. A kidnapping us, and don't get me started on this Lovecross character. I doubt that's her real name."

"They want something," Justin said. His old Army notebook materialized in his mind. How could he have forgotten it? He kept all of his notes in it, even some stupid doodles. Aaron's letters were tucked inside of it, too. If he were lucky, it would still be in his duffle bag back at his apartment.

"Or someone."

"Obviously, Captain Phillips is keeping his trap shut. Otherwise they wouldn't keep bothering us."

Nebraska seemed to think about this before he said, "Well, you two were sort of close. He listened to you. Perhaps he said something that wasn't meaningful to you then but it might be now, given the incredible circumstances we're in."

When did Nebraska start sounding like the voice of reason?

"Maybe," he agreed half-heartedly. "Can we talk about something else? I want to know how on earth you grew the balls to propose to a woman you've only met once."

Nebraska chuckled. "Apparently it's one of the biggest news stories of the day. It was the third trending topic on Twitter. I'm sort of a Big Deal now."

"Haven't you always thought of yourself in that way?"

"You know me too well. I'm telling you, man, it shocked the hell outta me when she said yes."

"And the nation, apparently. Obviously I've missed a lot," he said lightly. He decided not to bring up the fact that Nebraska kept this a secret from him. "So, tell me what led up to this and where did you get the ring?"

Nebraska told him about his grandmother's wedding ring and how he begged his mother to give it to him yesterday. It was great hearing the happiness in his friend's voice as he spoke about love at first sight, even as their current nightmare entangled in his thoughts.

Chapter Nine

THE PROPER PAPERWORK hadn't yet been processed for their release first thing in the morning. Nebraska was right in one respect: they certainly hadn't been guests. Lovecross failed to make an appearance, which wasn't surprising, and when a uniformed soldier purposefully approached them, keys in hand, Justin and Nebraska—exchanging curious looks—followed without question.

The drive away from the bunker, through the badlands —Nebraska thought the name was fitting—and into the recognizable neighborhoods that they knew was quiet and uneventful. The only cool part was how the bunker's garage was ten stories below ground—Justin counted each landing—and the myriad of vehicles, tanks, sports cars, decked-out vans, and military Jeeps that peppered each level. He wanted to know more about the facility and its function while at the same time, he couldn't wait to get as far away as possible.

The soldier never asked for directions, a fact that should have angered Justin. Instead, along with a lack-of-sleep hangover, an aching body, and a pissed-off attitude, he decided to let it go when the soldier dropped them off not only at Justin's apartment complex but also right in front of his stairwell.

It wasn't the soldier's fault; he was just doing his job. But Justin knew what was bothering him, in addition to everything else: Lovecross and her cronies had tabs on him.

Mary Lovecross was right in at least one thing: Justin's apartment was a complete mess.

"They certainly did a number on your place, Hotten," Nebraska said unnecessarily as they warily entered—the door was wide open—and inspected the damage. "What I don't get is why they literally dump everything, even your crappy silverware, on the floor. You think they'd be worried about stepping on a steak knife or something."

Justin immediately went to his bedroom closet and confirmed the inevitable: the camera was gone, though he had no way of knowing if Julia did exactly as he asked or if she had run for dear life after Lovecross collected him the previous day. He wouldn't know the answer until Julia popped back up in his life. Justin should try and figure out where she lived.

Nebraska joined him as they searched high and low for Justin's cell phone, but it was nowhere to be found. "It was a crappy phone anyway, Hotten," his friend said with a chuckle.

He wasn't an expert, but as he looked around his small one-bedroom apartment, it felt like the place had been tossed on principle.

Intimidation? Fun?

Other than the camera and his cell phone, he had nothing of value or importance. No weapons. No military equipment. The furniture, dishes—everything—were second hand; ready to be given to other soldier when it was time for Justin to transfer out.

"Let's get out of here," he said through gritted teeth.

He grabbed his dusty and scuffed-up duffle bag and shoved in a couple of uniforms, clothes, and his toiletries. He found Aaron's letters tucked inside his notebook, undisturbed, and placed the whole thing gently inside the bag, but not before touching the corner of each one. Aaron's letters weren't a secret and it wasn't like he was ashamed of them, but if he couldn't have Aaron, then he wanted the letters to remember what he'd lost and what an idiot he'd been.

From the corner of his eye, he saw that Nebraska was watching him. Justin should have been embarrassed, but he didn't care. All he knew was that he'd never felt this way before, like he had lost something wonderful before it was even his to begin with, and right now, that was about as far as he was willing to go to define his emotions.

It was only once they were outside, standing beside Justin's crappy car and in the stale hot air, that they realized they hadn't found Justin's car keys. Together, they groaned.

"You know," Nebraska said with a breathy sigh, "normally, we're not this stupid or clueless or utterly helpless, but the last few days..." He shrugged as if he couldn't quite explain the last few days in one small sound bite.

The parking lot was empty. He didn't even know what day of the week it was anymore.

"There's a pay phone up the road, near the gas station. We can call your sister."

"Naw, she's still in Dallas, remember?"

"Crap, that's right. Must have been a killer party if she's still there. Do you have Ashley's phone number?" Justin asked.

Nebraska's face lit up like a puppy. "Do I? I've got it tattooed on my ass, buddy."

Chapter Ten

THERE WAS ALREADY trouble in paradise.

Earlier, after walking almost nearly a mile to the gas station and making several collect calls to Ashley's cell phone—neither had quarters for the pay phone—she finally agreed, very begrudgingly, to pick them up just as soon as she could.

She didn't sound pleased to hear from them, which annoyed Nebraska to no end and he wasn't in a good mood when Ashley's tiny Smart car pulled up.

Justin stuffed himself in the extremely tight back seat as Nebraska sausaged into the passenger seat. It was like watching cows squeeze into a Barbie car.

Justin had to do a double take when he finally got a good look at Ashley. She was beyond gorgeous and dressed up for a formal event. Her hair was pulled up elegantly and her dress was so sparkly that it reminded him of a disco ball as the sunlight flicked, reflected, and bedazzled tiny rainbow dots all over the car.

Her blue eyes inspected them like a janitor might inspect days-old gum residue on the floor. She drove them to the north side of the county, where the houses were as big as hospitals and Texas money flowed up, not down.

The lovebirds in the front seat were acting more like angry children. Their shoulders were stiff and the air was filled with so much tension that Justin asked Ashley to crack a window. Justin being crooked, tangled, and crushed in the back seat wasn't helping matters, either, and he wanted to say something to break the ice, but he was prevented from doing so once the little car pulled into a gated entrance and crawled along a driveway and up to a house so enormous that he couldn't see much of anything else from where he sat.

"Do not talk to anyone," Ashley hissed at them before the valet approached. Nebraska looked incredulously at his bride-to-be and stifled whatever it was he was going to say. His door flew open and he tumbled out, startling the valet. Justin grabbed his duffle bag and climbed out of the tiny passage unassisted. It felt like both of his shoulders were dislocated.

"Welcome back to the Parris residence, Ms. Williams," a deep voice said from the house doorway.

"Thank you, Doug," she replied as she collected a shimmery clutch that matched her long, flowing dress. Her voice was light and airy, as if she were unaware of the two scruffy men emerging from her car.

He approached her with an appreciative look and something of a swagger in his step. He was handsome, tall, formally dressed in a tuxedo, and he held out a champagne glass. She took it and smiled up at him. Doug placed a hand on her lower back and together they walked in without so much as glancing back at the two of them.

Nebraska suddenly looked capable of murder.

"Did he just say the Parris residence?" Justin asked, turning to the valet. The color drained from Justin's face. It was probably just a coincidence.

The valet nodded. "Major General and Mrs. Parris."

Justin took in this information along with the vastness of the Parris residence. He felt a touch of vertigo. It was a mansion. Did Aaron grow up here? Did they even have anything in common?

"He touched her back as if he owned her," Nebraska said heatedly. His eyes narrowed and his fists clenched and unclenched over and over.

"It's probably nothing," Justin offered as calmly as he could. The thought of Aaron being inside of this house made his heart beat erratically. "Perhaps Doug does that to all of his guests. Let's keep our mind on the reason we called and asked to see her. She can help us unravel the pile of shit we landed in."

The parking attendant stood there awkwardly, observing them, waiting for someone to do something. When no one came to escort them into the house, the valet, with an uncomfortable-sounding sigh, he stepped into Ashley's car and drove away.

A small cloud of dust plumed and the afternoon sunlight trickled through it lazily before they walked to the door and slipped inside.

Chapter Eleven

IN THE SAME way that the bunker amazed and astounded Justin, the bright entrance was staggering in its opulence, and that was just the foyer. It was bigger than his apartment. Everything glittered and gleamed, and the rest of the view was what he imagined the insides of a mansion would look like: polished furniture, cultivated artifacts and decorations, and clean. Even the air felt posh and purified.

Justin dared not utter a sound; the place felt like a library or museum or a funeral parlor. And poor Nebraska, with the rage building inside him, stood stock still like a concrete statue, probably thinking that one minor touch would shatter everything around them like dominos.

However, it was surprisingly devoid of people. *Where was everyone?*

All that was missing was a small army of servants, but that didn't take long to change.

A small woman, stout, grandmotherly-like but with harsh features, quickly descended upon them from the right stairwell.

"You will follow me," she ordered in an accent Justin couldn't place.

Nebraska shed the statue-like appearance and shrugged, trying not to look like he cared one way or the other, but Justin wasn't fooled. His friend was trying to contain the beast inside.

They climbed up a set of stairs that curved and hugged the walls. As Justin and Nebraska followed the small woman, they heard intermittent flashes of music, as if a door somewhere was being opened and closed frequently. The servant walked onto the third-floor landing, down a carpeted hallway filled with museum quality military artifacts, and abruptly stopped at a cream-colored door.

"You will go inside this room and wait for the man of the house to address you," she ordered just as another block of music wafted down. She left them so quickly, and without waiting for a reply, that Justin wasn't sure if she needed to be somewhere else or if she just couldn't stand to be in their presence.

Justin observed that Nebraska's face was turning purple with his attempt to contain himself, and the two of them stood in the hallway rather stiffly. While Justin was unsure of himself at the moment, he didn't feel any sense of danger. Perhaps annoyance and worry at knowing that at any moment, he might turn and see a tuxedo-wearing, champagne-drinking Aaron staring him down.

He heard the music again. And laughter. It sounded like it came from the floor above them.

"I wonder what's going on and when we'll see Ashley? She did agree to talk, right?" Justin asked, looking up at the ceiling like it might answer him. The third floor was dark and deserted, but he wasn't in the mood to explore or look for her. He turned, expecting to hear Nebraska's response. Instead Justin was alone in the hallway.

"Look at this!" Nebraska said from inside the room they were ordered to wait in. "Ashley won't be able to resist me in this!"

Justin walked in the bedroom and was struck with how masculine it appeared. Dark wood paneling covered the walls and brown-black-tan bedding looked like it cost more than a new car. However, what his eyes really focused on was the stuffed grizzly bear in the corner of the bedroom. It wore an oversized World War I olive green army uniform. He could not fathom why such a thing would be there. He would never be able to fall asleep in a bedroom that had a stuffed bear in the corner.

Nebraska didn't appear to even notice the grizzly bear. His attention was captivated by whatever was on the bed. It held two black tuxedos, crisp white shirts, and other formal accessories, including matching black skinny ties.

"Do they just keep clothes like this lying around?" Justin asked.

"Actually, we do," a voice said from behind them. Justin twirled. "We get so many party crashes that we need to clean them up before they are ready for polite society." It was Doug, leaning against the doorframe, a bored expression pasted on his face even though the insult was clearly aimed at Justin and Nebraska and their state of dress and injury.

"Sounds like a personal problem to me," Justin said easily. He studied Doug, looking to see if there was a resemblance between him and Aaron. They had the same lean, muscular build, dark hair, and Grecian nose, but where Aaron had a smile, Doug had a sneer.

"My father has spoken highly of you, Sergeant," Doug said, his voice expressing the opposite. His countenance changed into something slightly less hostile when he added, almost as an afterthought, "As does my brother, Aaron."

Aaron talks about me? There was nothing to say to that. Justin couldn't remain neutral or casual if he discussed Aaron. His heart lurched happily. So he swallowed hard and nodded instead. The other man seemed to accept that.

"I am Doug Parris," he said. "Ms. Williams will join you upstairs after my father's speech is over. It is an exciting day. As you may have heard earlier today, my father, the General, intends to run for Governor of Texas next term. This is a party in his—"

"How do you know my fiancé?" Nebraska asked. His face was purple again. It was an unattractive look.

Justin groaned and looked heavenward. "I'd advise you to leave," he said to their host and turned to Nebraska. "Cut it out! We don't have time for this." The last thing they needed was another argument. Couldn't he have one day where nothing stupid happened?

Doug didn't seem alarmed. In fact, he looked downright excited, as if the party had been extremely boring until now.

"Fiancé?" Doug crooned, an eyebrow arched. "Is that what you call what you did yesterday? A proposal, roughneck?" He laughed. He played with something in his fingers: a cigarette lighter.

"In case you're in denial, Ashley agreed to marry me," Nebraska said just as artfully. "Perhaps she's interested in a real man and not some rich, pretty boy."

"Yes, well, perhaps you should think about what brings in television ratings. Soldier Proposes On Live Television! Ms. Williams is a savvy businesswoman and after yesterday's stunt—yes, I said stunt—her name is on everyone's lips." He smiled victoriously.

Justin didn't want to admit it, but he had the same thought, too, not long after the news anchor actually accepted Nebraska's proposal. His friend didn't see the calculated expression on Ashley's face yesterday but he wasn't about to corroborate Doug's theory, either.

He heard Nebraska's intake of breath, saw the flare of his nostrils and the sag in his shoulders, and knew what would happen next. Justin noticed the flicker instantly—the tick in Nebraska's jaw, the quirk of his lips, the clench of his fists, the stance of his legs just before he lunged at the door like a wild animal.

"Go!" Justin yelled at Aaron's brother. Doug made a jolting noise, a sound that was a combination of a scream and someone clearing their throat, and fled like a startled mouse. He dropped the cigarette lighter in the process, and Justin picked it up. It was silver and oblong, with some sort of emblem engraved on it. He shoved it in his pocket.

In the sudden stillness, a snippet of music and laughter and voices wafted in. Was Aaron's voice mingled in? Was he having a good time or was he trying to forget Justin?

"It's not true," Nebraska said.

At first, Justin wondered if he spoke his thoughts out loud but realized that Nebraska was talking about Ashley's motives in agreeing to marry him. He studied his friend and realized that beneath Nebraska's tough-man exterior, he was a hopeless romantic.

Justin, keeping his thoughts to himself, smiled mischievously. "Let's get cleaned up and prove it to him and everyone else upstairs."

Chapter Twelve

IT WAS A perfect fit. The tuxedo clung to Justin's body in all the right places. It chiseled his waist, yet the cloth was generous around his broad chest and shoulders. Aside from the swollen, purple eye and bruised cheek, Justin, with his dark, serious eyebrows, defined nose, bronze skin, and the beginnings of a scruffy beard, could have stepped out of the pages of a men's fashion magazine.

Aaron, eat your heart out.

Nebraska cleaned up nicely, too. He jumped in beside Justin in the huge marbled bathroom and studied himself in the full-length mirror. It was tough to take the lumberjack look out of Nebraska's normal style, but his bright orange-red hair, fair, freckled skin, and asymmetrical facial features—due to his former profession as a boxer and a troublemaker—contrasted nicely against the dark, form-fitting suit.

Nebraska praised his own reflection. Justin thought his friend looked roguish, dangerous, and playful, all at the same time.

"I look like James Bond," Nebraska said.

"Maybe James Bond's second cousin."

Nebraska scoffed. "You don't get to be Bond."

Justin thought for a moment and then did a quirky turn in the mirror, as if he were modeling. "Naw, I'd rather be Buckaroo Banzai."

"Ooh, good one."

They left the room, went up a flight of stairs, and met an unexpected person lingering outside a set of double doors.

"Julia?"

She turned and glared at them, as if they had interrupted some big plan, but then she smiled up at them so quickly that Justin had to do a double take. Her blonde hair was pinned up and the baby-blue doll dress she wore made her look younger and innocent.

Nebraska seemed instantly smitten with her, or maybe he liked the color of her dress, or maybe he was too upset at Ashley to remember that he was engaged to her. Whatever the reason, he appeared happy to see her, quickly scooped her up in a big hug, and held her there longer than necessary.

"What are you doing here?" he asked.

"You know me. Always ready for a party. I heard that you guys would be here." She pulled out of the hug, looked up at Nebraska oddly—her eyebrows knit together and her lips formed into a small pout—before she cleared the expression. "Looks like you two have been through hell and back."

Her speech felt forced, like maybe she wasn't happy to see them. Which wasn't like Julia at all.

"So you decided to crash Major General Parris' party?"

"It's a great house, isn't it?" she said with a slight slur in her voice, which caught Justin off guard. Her eyes were clear and focused, her stance steady, so he wondered why she was trying to act intoxicated. He didn't know her game or why one would act this way.

"Julia, are you feeling okay? I'd like to get the camera. Do you still have it?"

"Yes, of course," she said absently, "but there's something else you should know." She kept shifting her weight between her feet, like maybe her heels were bothering her. He'd never understand women and their need to punish their feet.

"Okay."

Before Julia could say anything, the double doors jerked open and Doug stumbled out. He was definitely unfocused until he zeroed in on them. His eyes narrowed and he laughed like a drunken baboon.

"Well, look at who it is!" Doug said. "Ashley's lapdogs." He howled loudly.

"Ashley Williams?" Julia asked.

Doug whipped his head around at Julia's voice. "You fucking bitch!" he screamed. His whole demeanor changed, like he was looking at something so foul, so revolting, that his face contorted into a red mass of ugliness. "How dare you show your face in this house, you whore!"

Justin expected her to cower behind him or Nebraska, but she stood her ground, her backbone rigid and proud.

"Watch yourself, buddy," Nebraska said in a low, ominous tone. He stepped in front of Julia. It seemed that at any second, Doug would strike like a snake, but he was drunk, and that made him especially unpredictable. He might attack with force or he might sit down and start crying about a terrible childhood. In the military, Justin had seen it all.

"This doesn't concern you, Nebraska," Julia said as she moved out from behind him, hands on hips, her eyes full of daggers for Doug.

Justin starred at Julia, wondering if he even knew her at all.

"I swear to God, bitch, that if you're not out of this house in ten seconds, I will throw you over the rail."

Nebraska looked casually over the ledge. Justin did the same. It was a forty-foot fall to the foyer below.

Seconds ticked by, and it felt like some great battle was about to begin.

Doug growled and rushed toward Julia like a brick flying through a window, but he didn't succeed. With a badassery move Justin had never seen in person, Julia, like some ninja-ballerina, jumped up, executed a full-body rotation and kicked Doug square in the chest.

"Holy shit!" Justin and Nebraska uttered at the same time.

Doug flew backwards and tumbled unceremoniously to the floor with a thud. His champagne glass flew from his hand and shattered against the double doors. He didn't move.

Other than the blur of music and laughter from inside the party room, there was complete silence as both Justin and Nebraska looked at Julia with awe until one of the double doors opened and a stout woman stepped out. It was the same woman who had been their escort earlier. She looked at them, stopped short, noticed the direction of their fixed attentions, and her eyes rounded when she saw the man on the floor.

The woman sighed loudly, "Oh, Mr. Douglas, not again," she muttered. "I'll get Mrs. Parris."

Once she was out of sight, Nebraska picked up Doug, hauled him over a shoulder, and without the slightest hesitation, walked down the stairs.

"What are you doing?" Julia whispered heatedly. Her face was flush and her mouth was in a tight grim. "Did you check for a pulse? Are his pupils dilated?"

"Are you in college or something?" Justin asked. "Where did you learn to do that?"

She looked at him annoyingly, as if the questions were so absurd, they didn't require an answer. They were carrying an unconscious body through a house that none of them had been invited to, and she was annoyed with him for asking a few simple questions? Unreal.

Nebraska opened the bedroom on the third floor and tossed Aaron's brother on the bed. Doug's body bounced a couple of times and he made a few grunting noises. This must have been enough of proof of life for Nebraska because his friend waved his hand in a dismissive fashion and said, "He'll be fine."

"He'll be fine?" Julia mimicked. "Are you insane? He needs a doctor."

His friend looked eerily calm but Justin knew otherwise.

"He crossed a line that most men know not to cross," Nebraska said through clenched teeth. "I'm sure that when he wakes up, he'll understand the situation and the man-code universe will continue on without question." He looked at the two of them and shook his head. "Anyway, I need to find Ashley, and it sounds like you two need to talk, too. I'll catch up with you later, Hotten."

With that, Justin was alone with Julia. Well, not precisely alone. Doug was there.

"Did you want to stay in here with him?" Justin asked. He didn't need to wonder at the anger displayed upstairs. Unless there was something else to explain it, Justin was confident that Julia and Doug had some sort of relationship that recently went sour. Really sour.

Julia glanced over at Doug, his snores were now extremely loud, and something passed over her face: regret, shame, sorrow?

It was a moment before she said, "No."

They stalled in the darkened hallway after closing the bedroom door behind them. Justin thought of only three things: did Julia have the camera with her, could she teach him how to do that ninja-ballerina move, and was Aaron upstairs?

"Are you going to tell me what's going on?" he asked.

"I don't know where to start."

"Let's start with the camera. Where is it?"

He couldn't see her expression so he didn't know if she was being serious when she said, "It's in a five-drawer cipher combination locked safe, which is behind another locked door that requires a pin code and a badge to swipe in."

She sounded serious. The hairs on his neck stood up. Her voice was different; the tone was solid, real, and authentic.

"Why do you sound different?" he asked. He couldn't place how it used to sound, only that it was now altered. Less whiny.

"Probably the champagne," she said without much conviction. "Do you want the camera back or did you want me to hold on to it?"

"If I could forget about that camera, then my life might be a little less stupid right now. But I'd like it back. Anyway, before that jerk interrupted us, you said you wanted to tell me something. What was it?"

Julia sighed, turned away from him, walked down the hallway, and climbed the stairs. Justin followed in silence. Bits of music wafted down.

He saw that her shoulders were so tight that he worried about her, and he wondered what she might be thinking about. Did Lovecross' people rough her up, too? God, he hoped not.

Julia hesitated at the top step, turned, and looked down at him with the most vulnerable, saucer-sized eyes possible.

What was going on with her? One second, she had a backbone of steel, standing up to a pompous asshole, and the next, she looked about as strong as a wilted flower trying not to cry. Her emotions seemed to be happening in the wrong order.

"I'm pregnant. That's what I wanted to tell you."

Whatever Justin thought she was going to say, this wasn't even remotely close.

"Wait, what?" he asked just as a figure appeared out of the corner of his eye. Someone had just come out from the party and walked to the stairwell.

It was Aaron, impeccably dressed in a black tuxedo. A political button hung on his lapel, proclaiming *Texas Needs Parris*. His tall, lean body and handsome face was a sight for sore eyes, and he looked completely edible. The shadows gave him a mysterious air that Justin found incredibly appealing.

The ties in Justin's heart yanked free and he was hot, cold, breathless, and incapable of a coherent thought.

"I'm tired of all the lies," Julia said, unaware of the emotions going through Justin or the fact that Aaron was standing directly behind her. Aaron's eyes locked on his with surprise, a smile almost at the ready, like he was almost ready to forgive him. "Yes, I'm pregnant, Justin, but there's more. I'm not who you think—"

Aaron's smile vanished as he sucked in his breath.

Julia spun around and tumbled into Justin's arms. Her hand flew to her mouth and Justin felt her whole body began to tremble. *Why would she be scared of Aaron?*

Aaron's stare was hard; his brown eyes were like ice.

"Aaron," Justin said pleadingly.

His lover's silence was deafening and his face hardened before he took on a placid expression. That look must run in the family since it reminded him of Doug. Aaron looked down at them as if they were nobody to him and not worth his attention. Then, he quietly turned on his heel and walked away. From a short distance, the music wafted in a decibel louder and then the door clicked softly, its echo as hollow as Justin's heart.

Chapter Thirteen

THE EVENING WAS full of heartbreak and guns.

Nebraska, having been inside the party doors, came out several minutes later, oblivious to Justin's pain but carrying his own in the form of a small object cradled in one of his hands.

"Ashley won't talk to me," Nebraska announced, his voice sounded like acid as he said her name. The three of them sat in a grouping of cushy couches on the second landing far away from the Parris family and their guests. Julia sat in the furthest corner, deep in her own thoughts. Justin felt badly for her, but he was happy to keep his distance. His blood pressure was already too high.

In terms of seeing everything but not being seen themselves, they had the advantage. Several of the guests had already left, and a pretty blonde was looking for Doug with unsuccessful—though humorous to them—results.

"She doesn't believe a word," Nebraska continued. "She was already pissed off at how *fucking shitty* we looked, her words, not mine, saying we must have climbed out of the sewer instead of a *secret government bunker.* The woman did a finger-quote around secret government bunker, can you believe that shit? Military Correspondent, my ass. She's never heard of Mary Lovecross, doesn't know a thing or have inside contacts and that she'd be laughed out of a job if she took our word for it. Geez. I'll be damned if she didn't look beautiful as she insulted us left and right, Hotten. And..." He hesitated before thrusting something in Justin's face. "She gave back the ring; said it was all a mistake. That she was sorry and shit and asked if I could keep our break-up a secret for a few months."

"The engagement ring?" Justin asked. The ring was tiny compared to the rest of Nebraska's hand but it was still a beautiful engagement ring and, as Nebraska had told him the night before, as they sat in Lovecross' bunker, it once belonged to his grandmother.

"I'm sorry," Justin offered sincerely.

Without warning, Julia stood and he visibly flinched. He felt Nebraska's sharp look. How could Justin begin to explain the situation with Aaron and how her announcement had incalculable results? Why the hell did she even tell him she was pregnant?

"I'm starving," she said with as much conviction as someone who had already eaten a nine-course meal. "I'll grab several plates."

"Yeah, uh, thanks," Nebraska murmured. He cleared his throat after she left. "Okay, that was weird. Obviously I missed something..."

"I saw Aaron," Justin said.

"Well, that's good, right? You wanted to see him."

"Julia's pregnant," Justin said instead of answering. In his mind, the connection made sense.

Nebraska blinked a couple of times, trying to make the two statements fit together. "Not working for me, buddy. Wait, did you two..."

"No!" Justin said with more force than was necessary. "A couple of years ago, maybe. I'm not sure, to be honest."

"You're not sure?" Nebraska asked incredulously, shaking his head. "How can you not remem—*ohhhhh*," he said cutting himself off in mid-statement. "Doug. He's the father. That's why Julia's here. It had nothing to do with us."

Justin had been so preoccupied with seeing Aaron that

it should have been an obvious connection. Now that Nebraska said it out loud, it made complete sense.

"I don't give a crap who the father is. I don't see why she had to announce it to me right in front of Aaron, giving him the impression that the baby's mine."

"Holy shit, man. Is that what happened? No wonder he looked furious when he came back into the room. I figured someone found Doug, so I left sooner than I had intended to."

A feminine figure in a dark suit approached them, carrying several trays of food. Justin looked up to thank her, only to realize that it was Julia. Her blonde hair was pulled back into a tight ponytail, her face looked like it had been scrubbed free of makeup, and the baby-blue doll dress was gone. In its place, she wore a charcoal-colored pantsuit and a crisp white, collared, button-down shirt.

What. On. Earth? Earlier, while they were still on the steps, what was Julia interrupted from saying? *I'm not who you think I am?*

"And the night continues to add puzzles," Nebraska said, a wide grin growing as he starred at Julia. "Was that outfit laid out for you in one of the bedrooms, too?" Julia opened her mouth to respond to his sarcastic question, but he held up his hands in surrender. "I am starving, so let's wait for the twenty-questions round until after we're done."

Julia huffed but sat down and also ate.

The plates of food she brought were piled high with just about every type of food that they couldn't pronounce—or afford—and they quenched their hunger right about the time Aaron stepped on the landing below them and held a conversation with someone who could only be his mother.

Mrs. Parris was elegantly dressed in a flowing black gown. It gave her small, plump figure a slimmer look. But it was the look on her face that drew Justin in. It was the face of a mother looking up at her son with so much love that even the nearby shadows seemed to fade.

"I'm not staying," he said to her in an exasperated, yet tender, tone. "Doug probably left with some blonde, like he always does. He'll turn up in a day or two with about three shades of lipstick on his collar and a shit-eating grin, and everyone will pretend it never happened."

Justin observed that Julia tensed up during the conversation. If Doug was the father of her baby then, one, he pitied the baby, and two, what Aaron was saying would be cutting her to the bone. He tried not to feel sorry for her, but he did.

Mrs. Parris sighed but didn't disagree with him, which was telling in Justin's mind.

"What about your friends?" she asked, and Aaron looked startled. "I thought I saw him and the tall one with red hair, though they didn't stay long, did they? Ms. Williams mentioned something about a follow-up interview with your friends after the General finished up. If you ask me, the General did a good bit of over-preening. Anyway, your friends looked great in their tuxedos. You were right about the Sergeant. I'm glad you thought about the suits."

Justin's ears burned. What was he right about? And how did he know they'd be here tonight? They didn't know they'd be here tonight. How was it that everyone else knew what they would be doing?

Aaron hesitated, looking over his shoulder several times, and said in a despondent tone, "I think I might have been wrong about him."

His mother reached up—she was a tiny woman—and kissed him on the cheek. "You just wait, deary," she said with just the right amount of cheerfulness that only a mother could get away with. "He'll surprise you yet. After what you've told me about him, he'd be a fool to walk away from you. I'll be at your apartment later tonight, after the party's died down, and sleep there. If I stay here, the General will want to describe, in excruciating detail, how the interview went, all of which I was, of course, present for. You know how he is, deary."

Aaron went downstairs and out the front door as his mother climbed upstairs. Julia downed a glass of water, set it rather forcefully on the table, and pulled a gun out of some pocket that wasn't apparent to the naked eye.

Nebraska groaned and Justin rolled his eyes.

"What, did the gun not work with your dress? A fashion faux pas?" Justin asked sarcastically. "I think the man you want to aim your weapon at is incapacitated on a bed on the third floor."

"You can say the baby's mine," Nebraska offered with surprising glee. Justin rolled his eyes again. He knew how much his friend enjoyed it when the unexpected happened. Or maybe Nebraska thought women holding guns were hot.

"This isn't about the baby, dammit," she spat. "Now that Lieutenant Parris is gone, it's time you two come with me to the station. I have a few questions."

"Why was that the tipping point?" Justin asked.

"Station?" Nebraska asked at the same time. "You own a station?"

"I knew you wouldn't leave if lover boy was still here. It's your nature to be a hopeless romantic."

"Don't be insulting," Justin said, but he stood up anyway.

"Actually," Nebraska cut in, "it's not insulting. It just means you're holding out for one true love."

"I wasn't talking about that," he said. "She called Aaron 'lover boy.' It's insulting."

"See? He proved my point," Nebraska told Julia. "He's very romantic. It's one of the many things I like about him."

"Shut up and get moving," she said, jerking the inky black firearm to the left toward the staircase.

Chapter Fourteen

EVEN PRETTY FACES can be misleading. Julia, with the skill of a seasoned drill sergeant, marched them out of the Parris mansion, into the backseat of a dark red SUV, gave them a stern *Move And I Will Kill You* look, and, with the loudest silence Justin had ever felt, drove them into a township named Evergreene.

Nebraska, lounging back in the seat with his eyes closed, appeared rather nonplussed as Julia pulled into a gravel lot and parked in front of a brick building. Squinting, Justin read the letters on the glass door: Texas Bureau of Investigation.

Why the hell was she bringing them to a TBI office?

"Out," her voice cracked over her shoulder.

Justin watched as Nebraska came to life and tried his door handle; and then watched his friend's stumped reaction when nothing happened. He tried the handle a dozen times. Then, leaning over, he tried Justin's side, too, but he was a little too vigorous and it broke off in his hand.

"She put us in a car with child locks," Nebraska said with the right amount of humor that it brought a smile to Justin's face. Now if he could view the world like Nebraska did—everything was always an adventure—then he'd be able to laugh every time something abnormal occurred.

Within a minute Julia opened the passenger door.

"Um, you'll need to get this fixed," Nebraska told her and placed the broken off door handle in her hand. Justin climbed out into the humid, dark night as his friend looked around, whistled, and said, "Texas Bureau of Investigation, huh? Is this the station you were talking about earlier? Could use a little sprucing up, if you ask me. My brother's in construction and I'd be happy to call him up for you."

"Why I'm sure I'd be delighted, sir," Julia said with a mocking southern accent, but Justin noticed that she was trying to hide a faint smile. She didn't hate them, he thought, but she certainly wasn't some ditzy, party girl, either. He was curious to know her story. "Now if you don't mind and if you're done inspecting the grounds, Specialist Walker, perhaps we can go inside. I'm sure you have a lot of questions."

"I only have one question," Nebraska said as he raised his hand like a schoolboy. Julia starred at him.

"Just one?" Justin asked when she didn't say anything. He could easily think of a dozen off the top of his head.

"Yeah." Nebraska smiled. "Are you going to change back into that light blue baby doll dress?"

"Don't make me shoot you," Julia quipped before ordering them inside the building.

The bright ceiling lights nearly blinded Justin as he took stock of the open floor plan. Desks were arranged in pairs, most of them empty, and he noticed that two desks —in different parts of the room—were occupied and in use. Two people—uniformed officers—immediately jumped to their feet and some sort of commotion caught him off guard. It took a moment to realize that what he heard was a series of hoots, hollers, and catcall whistles.

"Got you some good looking johns there, Detective Fenske," a beefy officer called.

Justin and Nebraska exchanged looks.

"Detective Fenske?" his friend mouthed.

Justin searched Julia face for a reaction, but she didn't

seem fazed.

Johns? What the—? Oh, right. He forgot that they were still in the tuxedos. But johns? Seriously? Why wasn't she correcting them?

Julia appeared to be ignoring the two officers and continued to lead them further into the room.

"Where did you find these pretty boys?" a tall black female officer asked. "A bachelor party? I'm happy to take one of them off of your hands, Fenske. The tall one."

"We're not johns," Justin said through clenched teeth, lifting his hands, as if showing them that they weren't handcuffed would clear up the misunderstanding. He didn't know why he cared about what they thought. Obviously, his new hobby was befriending folks who wanted to shoot him, detain him, arrest him, or, in general, make his life hell.

Nebraska shaped his hand into a phone, put it to his ear as they walked by, and said, "Call me!" to the female officer, who laughed even louder.

Julia, with a straight-faced expression, opened a door on the far wall and ushered them inside. Any hint of vulnerability or pain about being pregnant was gone. It was like she was a completely different person.

She looked strong, determined, and official. And, as Justin walked passed her into the room, she smelled clean, like Ivory soap and cherry Chapstick. She was a beauty without any makeup.

So why the act all these years?

The room she brought them into was an interview room. It was small, but not confining, and infinitely more inviting than the station Mr. A hauled them to. The beige walls were filled with framed photographs of the Alamo and the State's capital, Austin.

A medium-sized box at the end of the rectangular table

piqued Justin's curiosity. He looked at it multiple times as they sat down, hoping Julia would explain if it pertained to them.

"So..." Justin said tonelessly. "You're a detective." *Hurray! What else can go wrong tonight?* He folded his fingers together on top of the table. Julia had done such a good job of making him—and everyone else—believe that she was this stupid, blonde, brainless bimbo that Justin could not fathom that she was anything else. He was still upset about the pregnancy announcement thing, too.

Actually, he had a lot to be upset about, if he thought about it.

"It's kind of hot, if you ask me," Nebraska said. Julia's eyebrow rose assertively, as if she was asking him to reconsider his statement. "Actually, I take it back. All of it. Whatever I said." He tugged at the tie around his neck. Justin noticed that Nebraska's face was flushed. Any minute now, he and his red hair would burst into flames.

"Yes, I am," she answered without divulging anything further. She grabbed the box, pulled it over, removed a manila folder, and slid it across the table. Neither he nor Nebraska rushed to open it.

"What's this?" Justin asked.

"Open it, Sergeant Hauten."

So he was Sergeant Hauten now?

Nebraska rolled his eyes and roughly opened the folder. Whatever they expected, whatever thoughts were going in their heads, were quickly erased when they viewed the single photograph.

It was of the beautiful, smiling Leia Woondiour—and it was the same photo from Justin's camera. He hadn't expected Julia to show him a picture of one of the victims. His heart constricted and he felt lightheaded. Why was she showing them this?

Nebraska was breathing heavily beside him. "Are you trying to rub salt in the wound?" he asked heatedly.

Julia tilted her head slightly and narrowed her eyes, like she was trying to decipher his meaning but didn't want to ask.

"Do you know this woman?" She tapped the photo. There was something in the way that she asked, like she desperately needed to know or a part of her would fall apart. Some of her blonde hair fell in her face and she quickly tucked it behind her ear.

"I took this picture of her in Afghanistan about two months ago," Justin answered. "Why are you asking?" Did she print out every photo? What he really wanted to ask was, *What do you know?*

"How did she get into the United States? Did she marry a service member?"

"Wait a minute," Nebraska said quickly. "Are you saying you've seen her?"

Chapter Fifteen

JUSTIN BIT THE inside of his lip, hopeful. He stole a glance at his friend.

"Yes," Julia said in a somewhat guarded manner. "Did your unit bring her back to Texas?"

"Of course not," Nebraska said. "What does our unit have to do with any of this? Where did you see her?"

"She's safe. That's all you need to know."

Justin breathed a tiny bit better. He considered the information from the Lovecross brief and now Julia's— what? Investigation? Research?—had somehow intersected. Now she had the photo of Leia Woondiour and was fishing for information. At least Leia was safe, or so Julia said. But what about the two children? Did Julia know about them?

"Why did the officers out front think we were johns?" Justin asked. "Furthermore, why were you in my bedroom yesterday?"

Nebraska looked like he wanted to add to the conversation, but he shut up, turned to look at Justin, then back at Julia, and kept going back and forth like a tennis match.

"Answer the question, Sergeant," Julia said, each word tinged with a low timbre of anger.

"I'd be nice if you answered mine, too. I don't understand how an *undercover* agent can do the things you did. Because that's what you are, right?"

"It's simple, really. You were not one of my original targets and I liked what I saw." Her tone was unapologetic. Justin understood; she was just doing her job.

"What's going on here?" Nebraska looked taken aback. "Targets for what?"

"You *used* me is more like it."

And now she had the camera, which might not have been a good thing after all. Lovecross' words echoed in his head: Trust no one. Not even Lovecross.

Julia had either been investigating their unit or she was investigating him. That's why she acted and dressed the way she did around not just them, but everyone.

Julia shrugged and muttered, "Not that you let me get far."

"What's that supposed to mean?" Was his voice an octave higher? The conversation was getting out of hand.

"Because you're..." she hesitated and shrugged. She looked to his friend for help.

Nebraska was on the edge of his seat, either getting ready to bolt or break up their fight. He'd probably bet on Julia.

"I'm what?"

"Gay," Julia answered.

"Confused," Nebraska said at the same time, but nodded in agreement with Julia.

"I am not—" Justin sighed and rubbed his scratchy beard and thought of Aaron. He couldn't finish the statement. It didn't matter, and it wasn't any of her business. So he said instead, "How long has our Army unit been under investigation?"

Nebraska blinked about a dozen times. "We're under investigation?" He gestured between him and Justin, then shook his head. "You know, I'm seriously beginning to question why I ever joined the military. I could have been a washed-up semi-professional boxer by now."

Julia exhaled a large breath. Her eyes held Justin's glare long enough to win a staring contest. But some sort of silent truce occurred between the two of them when she cleared her throat and she pulled another folder out of the box. This one, however, was deep blue and embossed with the large letters of TBI and its seal. She did not slide it over for the men to see.

"The military isn't exactly the most prestigious institution." She held up her hands to stop them from verbally attacking her. "Before you crucify me, you have to admit that there are bad apples in every profession, including those in our military ranks. I know what it's like to serve, and I've seen some of the worst crimes you can imagine. I was a criminal investigation sergeant in the Marine Corps for eight years before joining the FBI. I transferred to the TBI two and half years ago to run my own operation when one of my targets moved here. So," she paused. Justin thought she looked tired. If he were investigating an entire unit of Army soldiers, he'd be tired, too. "Prostitution may not seem like a debilitating type of crime, but it is and is generally funded by hard criminals, human traffickers, drug smugglers. Its fingers web throughout an underbelly of crime. It can feed political corruption, and it shatters the lives of so many innocents, including children. And it happens right next door. Your neighbor. A buddy at work. That lady you see each week at the grocery store. One prostitution or drug conviction can unravel a ratline of money laundering, child-selling operations, pedophilia, and even counterfeit prescription drugs sold on the Internet. And, sadly, some of this happens in the military."

"And this brought you here? You're saying that our unit is involved in prostitution, drugs, and human trafficking?" Justin asked coldly. If he acted like none of this affected him, maybe he'd believe it, too. This was how the two women's investigations intersected: human trafficking. If Leia was abducted for the prostitution trade and she was in the area, the chances were high that Julia and her team would have learned about it. That didn't exactly explain who her original target was or why she joined herself to his hip years ago to further her investigation.

It really meant one thing to him: Justin must know her target. And not just know, but also be friends with. It could be any number of people.

"The harsh realities of life are, well, harsh and I don't believe in brushing it under the rug. But things haven't been adding up, not since your return stateside. In fact, things have been somewhat interesting over the last two weeks."

"Like how?" Nebraska asked.

She slid another photo across the desk. It was Captain Phillips' official military photo. He stood proudly in front of the American Flag in his ceremonial uniform. He was a handsome man in his mid-thirties with dark black hair and light blue eyes. He seemed so brand new and shiny, like a young boy joining the Boy Scouts. Naïve, almost. Justin was taken aback by this quick assessment as he studied the photo. It was something he had always thought about the Captain, though he never voiced that impression.

Justin shook his head. Captain Phillips just didn't seem capable of any crime, much less one that involved selling women and children to criminals. But his judgment was forever altered when the man put a bullet in his shoulder.

He rolled his shoulders absently at the thought. Was Captain Phillips her target? The timing seemed on par.

Justin looked up and found Julia studying him hard, like she was waiting for him to crack or disagree with her or even hypothesize on how things were somewhat interesting.

"I'd like to know," she said ominously, "why almost every agency in this country, Great Britain, and Afghanistan want this man's head on a platter." She leaned into the table, bringing her closer to them. "Considering the fact that the military has only charged him with *conduct unbecoming an officer*, I find it interesting that this man has suddenly accumulated so many enemies. Don't you?"

"Was Captain Phillips your target?" Nebraska asked.

She leaned back, crossed her arms across her chest, and shook her head. "He wasn't even on the list," she said as both of her eyebrows rose in a *I don't know what else to tell you, but isn't that an interesting bit of information?* way.

"This is like some stupid cop show where one side of the government doesn't talk to the other and the bad guy always ends up being one of its own. I'm not interested in becoming a cliché or doing your job for you, Detective Fenske."

"Nor am I. You'd just fuck everything up. And believe me, I understand your hesitation in trusting me. Yes, I can tell," Julia smirked at him. "Do you know what else I can tell?" She paused, but Justin didn't answer. "I know that you know more than you're revealing, but I know something that may unravel that. You're conflicted about many things and that you have no clue who to trust. However, I am asking you two as a favor because, one, I don't think you're involved in the crime; two, there might be more victims; and three, I don't think we have much time."

Justin read the worry, frustration, and edginess on her face. Sadly, he mused about her last two points, she was correct.

He and Nebraska shared a look. Not a word passed between them, but they were on the same page.

"Much time for what?" Nebraska asked.

"It's only a matter of time before some insanely powerful people start walking through my front door, asking questions. Four hours ago, I found this woman," she pointed to the photo of Leia. "Captain Oliver Phillips was hiding in her closet, armed to the hilt, and very nearly killed Ms. Woondiour." She paused, but they were too stunned to say anything. "He's in a cell fifteen feet away from here."

Chapter Sixteen

IT'S NOT EASY to face a monster even when you know what to expect. It's worse when that monster might not be who you think it is.

However, Justin didn't envision Captain Phillips would look so pathetic sitting hunched over in Julia's temporary jail cell. His hair was longer. His face displayed fresh cuts and bruises, and it appeared he hadn't shaved in weeks. His eyes were red rimmed, puffy, distant and closed-off looking, as if he was imagining himself elsewhere.

"You've got five minutes, Sergeant, to figure out why he's not in military custody," Julia said sternly.

She left the holding room and suddenly Justin was alone with his former commander, confidant, and mentor. He hadn't talked much about Captain Phillips to anyone; not even Nebraska. It was tough to see him like this. Dejected. Abandoned. Alone. Scared.

How would he look in the same situation? Justin firmly believed that he would never look that desolate. But, he reminded himself, he wasn't wanted for treason and other nefarious crimes.

"Hello, Captain Phillips," Justin said loud enough to be heard. He walked up to the bars that separated them. The bay was pretty dark and the shadows were deep enough to hide someone. A blinking red dot in an upper corner of the room flashed at him intermittently.

They were being recorded.

"Hotten," was the mumbled response. He sounded drunk, but he looked scared, the kind of scared a man gets before he meets death reluctantly. Why wasn't he fighting or begging to be released?

"You are a popular man these days. Seems like you're on everyone's most wanted list. Why is that?"

"That would depend on who's asking," Phillips said, lifting his head, and looked at him—really looked at him—for the first time since Justin walked in. The man wasn't just scared; the shadows hid so much. There was something more there that gave Justin a chill, like maybe he wasn't even playing the same game anymore.

There was a depth of cunning intelligence in his light blue eyes, shining brightly back at Justin. Captain Phillips had always seemed out of his element in Afghanistan. It wasn't that he couldn't adapt the harsh realities of deployment—the commander had come across as being oblivious to standard Army Operations—but Justin had the impression that the Captain viewed it as a brief assignment that would end on his own terms and not because the tour was over. Like he was always on his own mission.

"I'm asking," Justin said.

"How's the shoulder?"

Justin gritted his teeth and worked his jaw. "It's been better."

"It was a rather unfortunate event, Hotten, but a necessary one." He looked appraisingly at Justin's tuxedo. A small smile tugged at his lips. "Doesn't seem to be slowing you down, though."

It was necessary to shoot me? Justin wanted to yell at him. *Do you have any idea of what you've caused?* The way Julia described it earlier, heaven and hell was about to descend upon this man from every department and bounty hunter in the country. "There's a two million dollar reward on his head," Julia had informed him moments ago. "So far, no one knows he's here, but it's just a matter of time."

"I know about the abductions," Justin said. Tints of red began to cloud his vision and his body shook with ill-contained rage. Screw this asshole.

Captain Phillips laughed. "I've always admired you, Hotten. The way the other soldiers looked up to you. You're a natural leader, but don't make me knock some common sense into you."

Justin hit the bars so hard with his knuckles that a metallic ding rang out, followed by several tiny pops. Something inside him welcomed the pain.

"Where are the children?"

"Poof! Into thin air like a well-played magic trick."

"I don't give a shit about a magic trick or whatever little game you're playing. Why were they taken? Who took them? And why the fuck am I mixed up in all of this?"

Captain Phillips didn't answer right away, and silence and crackling tension filled the room. The camera's blinking red dot distracted Justin—or rather, its *lack* of blinking. Had someone turned it off? It was then that he realized the Captain's body was positioned so that his back was facing the camera and it had been since the moment Justin walked in.

"You won't understand my actions," he said in the barest whisper, his head hung even lower, as if he was interested in his feet.

"I trusted you once. Help me understand."

The Captain mumbled something that sounded like "Ask Leia" before he started screaming like a maniac. The handcuffs and the chains at his feet clattered almost as loudly.

Julia rushed in, keys jingling at her waist, and ended the meeting by pulling Justin out of the dark bay. She locked the metal door behind them and showed him into a medium-sized office. A name placard etched with JULIA S. FENSKE sat at the front on the desk, next to the box from the interview room. Nebraska, filling up a chair too small for him, sat in the corner, twirling the returned engagement ring.

"Get anything?" Julia asked Justin.

"Only that I'm tempted to collect that two-million-dollar reward on him myself," Justin said in a monotone voice. He decided not to reveal the part where Captain Phillips said, "Ask Leia."

He cupped his fist in his other hand and cradled it. His right hand throbbed with the pulse, the skin was cut and bloody around the knuckles, and the whole damn thing felt about twice the normal size.

She didn't hide her disappointed sigh.

"You need to get out of here," Julia said. "Maybe he'll calm down. Otherwise, it will be one of my guys that calls in his whereabouts. As it is, I'm not exactly following proper protocol by not reporting him to the higher authorities. I haven't even booked him. I just hope my instincts are correct."

"You honestly think he's innocent?" Nebraska asked as he stood and shoved the ring deep into his front pocket.

They towered over her. Justin hadn't realized just how tall her high heels had made her appear. In flats, she seemed so tiny.

"No. Not even close. He's certainly guilty of something, but my gut tells me that there's more to the story. I need to find a translator before I can interview Ms. Woondiour. I don't have time to deal with you two right now. Just... go."

"So I'm back to being Justin again?" He raised an eyebrow, but she missed his expression and he wondered if she even heard him. She had the weight of the world and an unexpected pregnancy on her shoulders.

Nebraska leaned against the desk and grabbed something. Julia didn't notice and Justin couldn't tell what it was, but a satisfied grin flashed across his friend's face.

The small station was deserted on the walk out. No catcalls and obligatory insinuations to cheer up his friend's gloomy mood. Even Captain Phillips had quieted down— or Justin couldn't hear him anymore.

Julia paused at the front door and manually unlocked five deadbolts of various sizes. The door was as thick as a tank. No one was getting in or out of this place unless permitted. He was surprised that he had overlooked it on the way in. Justin supposed that, at the time, he was too pissed at Julia to take notice of anything.

Which reminded him: he was still rather pissed off at her. He had some serious damage control to fix with Aaron.

Gravel crunched under his feet and he took a deep breath as he stepped out into the night air.

"Oh, and Justin," she called a second later. He turned. She looked so beautiful standing in that doorway that it almost took his breath away. Even Nebraska gawked. He expected her to elicit promises from them to not leave the area. Instead she said self-consciously, "Let's just say you were the best part of the assignment."

Chapter Seventeen

IT WAS SO late and Justin was so tired that he no longer cared about the fact that Nebraska was driving them around in circles as they searched for Aaron's apartment in a stolen car. They'd been detoured so much over the last few days that Justin had to remind himself that his original plan had always included seeing Aaron.

"Remind me again how this isn't illegal?" Justin asked from the front passenger seat. They were in the same vehicle Julia drove them to the TBI station in.

Nebraska looked extremely comfortable behind the wheel, steering with one hand, tuning the radio to a classic rock station with the other.

"The keys on Julia's desk practically begged me to take them. But I can let you out so you can walk, if that's what your dignity calls for."

"Yeah, no thanks. I think Julia's going to be pretty pissed when she finds out her car is gone."

Nebraska chuckled, and Justin had the feeling he missed the joke. "It's not her car. She drives a white Honda. Really, didn't you ever pay attention to her? I swear it's like I know more about her than you do. And I don't think she's going to be going anywhere until she figures out what to do with her prisoner."

"I don't think anyone knows who Julia really is."

Justin felt Nebraska's stare. "Actually," Nebraska hesitated, his tone serious.

"What?" He had a feeling he wasn't going to like where this was going.

"I don't think anyone knows who Captain Phillips really is. You told me that he looked like shit and scared like a baby in there. Which is—"

"Completely uncharacteristic of him," Justin finished.

"And after everything Lovecross revealed during that oversized presentation and how Julia found him in Leia Woodinour's closet... it's like a movie."

"This is all twisted, that's for sure." The conversation was turning him into an angry mess. He felt like an utter failure, which was unnatural. "I don't know what to think anymore. Everything is so confusing."

Nebraska made a sharp left onto Birchwood Avenue. In response, Justin grabbed the roof handle "oh shit" bar with his right hand and immediately regretted it. Pain shot through his hand, arm, and up into his shoulder and neck.

He swallowed down the wave of nausea that instantly hit him. "Was that necessary?" he asked through gritted teeth.

"Sorry," Nebraska offered up a grim smile. "I thought you were about to fall asleep and, well, I don't know where the hell Lieutenant Parris lives. My sisters don't leave until Sunday. I don't think they'd mind if we crashed with them at the hotel. It has an indoor pool. I think they're excited to see you in swim trunks."

"So they can sexually assault me? No thanks!" Justin laughed.

"I resent that. But that doesn't mean it isn't true, so you better figure out pretty quick where the lieutenant lives."

Sadly, Justin couldn't quite recall which apartment complex he lived in, and he didn't have Aaron's phone number. And he knew he wouldn't be at the Parris mansion since he watched him leave.

Justin smiled. It was fairly obvious that Nebraska

aimed to take their minds off the Captain Phillips' situation. It was working.

"The walls were red brick and his apartment was on the second floor."

"Right," Nebraska scoffed, "because that helps out a lot. Which apartment number?"

"It was on the left hand side."

"That trip to my sisters' hotel is looking more and more promising," Nebraska threatened.

"Let's reverse this: what if we were on our way to see Ashley Williams?"

His friend scowled. "Attempt one didn't work out so well. I suppose for attempt two, I'd sing Journey songs to her at the top of my lungs until she let me inside. I'd recite poetry in French and compose sonnets about the color of her eyes."

"I didn't know you knew French."

"I don't," he chuckled. "But I'd be counting on Ashley not knowing French in order for it to work. As fun as that imaginary exercise was," Nebraska pointed out with a sad sigh, "we aren't on our way to see her."

"I think he lived near one of the golf courses," Justin said. The night that he fled Aaron's apartment, it was a warm and sweaty night, and nearly dark; but he thought he had passed a golf course. Since he didn't have his car—he had been a passenger in Aaron's truck that night—he walked to the nearest bus station and took the bus home.

Nebraska nodded, made a U-turn at the next intersection, and turned up the radio to listen to a Creedence Clearwater song.

Thankfully, the nausea had passed and Justin watched as they drove by trees and houses, all lit up from the inside. Then his thoughts turned dark. He wondered about the families whose lives were shattered and destroyed back in Afghanistan all because of one man's selfishness, treason, and... well, it baffled him as to why something as innocent as a photograph could drastically change so many lives—and not for the better.

Justin did not want to be alone and, as much as he cared for Nebraska, his friend could not provide the type of comfort Justin wanted. Needed.

He wanted Aaron. He wanted to make things right between them. And it wasn't the lust or the body chemistry—no, that pretty much scared the crap out of him. It was how he felt so comfortable with Aaron. Nervous, yes. But being around him felt like home. Someone to come home to and be with. To share with and laugh with and love.

That's why he needed to find Aaron in the middle of the night as the world slept and the good guys battled the bad guys; Justin wanted to close off the world and sleep. Next to Aaron.

"I'm glad you like Lieutenant Parris," Nebraska added as he turned into an upscale apartment complex that might or might not be Aaron's. "It took you a while to figure it out, but he wasn't so obvious about it."

"What are you talking about?"

"Dude, I can practically read minds. It's just called body language by non-believers. Anyway, his eyes used to follow you everywhere. I could tell that he wanted your body!"

"Don't be crass," Justin admonished as he looked out of his window, but secretly he was pleased. He wouldn't have acted offended otherwise. "I think this is the right apartment complex." Nebraska parked, and they stepped out into the hot night air.

In his nervousness, Justin almost forgot his duffle bag. With a bad shoulder and an injured hand, it wasn't easy to swing the bag over his good shoulder. It really clashed with the tuxedo, too.

Nebraska was giving him an odd expression, like maybe he could tell that Justin was anxious.

"How do I look?" Justin asked.

"It's possible he may not recognize you."

"Close enough."

His body tingled as they climbed to the second floor. There were two apartment doors on the left hand side and he honestly did not remember which one was Aaron's. But he was too close to turn away now.

"Choose one," Nebraska suggested. "Maybe you'll get it right."

"Or maybe we'll get a shotgun pulled on us."

"How's that different from any other day this week?"

"Good point. I can see the headlines now, 'Soldier survives twelve months in war zone, is accidentally killed knocking on wrong door.'"

"Just knock already!" Justin tapped on the first door and waited. "Knock harder. He's probably in bed."

With someone else immediately came to mind. What if I am too late? Justin didn't even know what day of the week it was anymore. Anything was possible.

But he knocked harder than was necessary. The sound of a deadbolt slid over, and the door cracked a little. It wasn't enough for Justin to see who it was, though.

"Aaron," Justin started. "I am the world's biggest idiot. I am so sorry about what happened the other night and then what I think you may have seen yesterday afternoon when Julia was at my apartment. It isn't what you think, not by a long shot. Actually, nothing is what it seems anymore. Not that you think things that appear completely obvious as wrong. You were right to think it, but it turns out that Julia is an undercover police officer posing as a prostitute and Nebraska and I were sort of detained—"

"Don't bring me into this," Nebraska muttered.

There was a gasp behind the dark door and it nearly closed. Justin wasn't even sure who he was confessing to. Was his voice a little bit too loud? It sounded so loud in his head.

"Wait! Wait. That came out wrong. She was just trying to steal the camera, I think, but that isn't something you'd be investigating two and a half years in advance. So that's odd. I'm still questioning everything I thought I knew about Julia. And that pregnancy announcement, wow, I mean, what a thing to have happen, right?"

"You're dragging on, buddy," Nebraska said.

"I know I look like shit. The face is a by-product of a combination of many things. One of which is that I'm a jerk and I hurt you and I've realized that I never want to hurt you again. If... if you'll let me make it up to you, I promise that I'll—"

"Justin?" Aaron was standing halfway outside the *other* apartment door, leaning against the doorframe. "I think you've traumatized my neighbor enough for one night."

Nebraska started laughing, which he tried to cough to cover up.

"Uh... Oh, good Lord," Justin groaned as the door he had just been confessing to shut with a loud snap. Three locks subsequently turned against the door.

"Who lives there?" Nebraska asked as if it wasn't Justin's single most embarrassing moment.

Aaron completely stepped out of his apartment. He was shirtless and wore light blue pajama bottoms. His hair was disheveled and sticking up in certain places, his smooth chest begged to be touched, and his bare feet completed a desirable domesticated look. Aaron couldn't have looked more appealing to Justin even if he was wrapped in bacon sandwiches.

"Mrs. Tigo," Aaron said and crossed the few steps between him and Justin. With each step, Justin felt warmer. "What happened to you?" His hand reached up and almost touched Justin's face, but Aaron let it fall just before doing so. He inspected Justin fully: from the now-wrinkled tuxedo, to the bruises, to his bloody, swollen hand.

Aaron shook his head.

"It's a long story," Justin answered with a heavy sigh. Aaron didn't seem happy to see him—and why would he be?—so it was probably a good idea to apologize and then leave.

"Why are you here?" Aaron asked. His voice was low. Any minute, Justin expected to be yelled at. He was entitled to no less.

"You deserve an apology and an expla—"

A female voice echoed from inside Aaron's apartment. "Aaron? Is everything okay, honey?"

Justin backed up, tore his eyes off Aaron, and stared at the open door. His mind whirled. "I, uh, you sound busy, so I think we'll go," Justin said. He was too late, obviously. That it was a woman did surprise him.

"Don't go," Aaron said in a somewhat amused tone. "That's my mother. Besides, I think you two might need medical attention."

The stress that was wound up tight inside Justin's chest released, and it was like he could finally breathe again. Aaron let them inside the apartment.

"What's this about Julia being a prostitute?" Aaron asked Nebraska.

Chapter Eighteen

SLEEP AND A one-on-one conversation with Aaron did not come easy for a multitude of reasons. One of which was that Aaron's mother turned out to be a registered nurse and took it upon herself to give Justin a full physical at one in the morning. Somehow, Nebraska easily extracted himself from the same physical, declaring he wanted to possess a few more scars.

Aaron's mother pulled Justin aside.

"Internal bleeding is no joke, young man," she told him calmly. She wore a flowery robe and white slip-on clogs and acted as if strangers routinely came into her care this late at night. Justin wanted to make a joke and mentally acknowledged that it was completely the wrong time. She observed their tuxedos and tsked and clicked her tongue at them, as if remembering what they had looked like earlier in the day. Which, if Justin wanted to even think about it, felt about a thousand years ago. "If you're shy about disrobing, Aaron or your friend can attend with you."

"Count me out, buddy," Nebraska said before Mrs. Parris stopped talking. He shucked off the tuxedo top, sat on the couch, and within a minute was snoring loudly.

"It's been a long day," Justin offered by way of an explanation.

Mrs. Parris smiled. "Yes, I can see that." Her tone was kind and motherly, but Justin could tell that she was analyzing everything about him. He wondered if he met with any approval. "You seem to wear your day somewhat worse than your friend there. Come, come. Into the bedroom for your examination."

Fifteen minutes later, Justin emerged from the bedroom with an uncomfortable grin, a patched-up cheek, a bandaged hand, and a lovely bottle of painkillers. Apparently most registered nurses kept such medication on their person. "Just in case it's needed, young man," Mrs. Parris quipped. "And lucky for you I did. You young men think you're invincible. Off you go. Off you go." And she shooed him out of the bedroom that happened to be hers for the night.

Justin's eyes adjusted to the darkness. Aaron's bedroom was down the hallway. A light brightened the space as the door opened soundlessly. Actually, it could have been as loud as a freight train—all Justin could hear and feel was his heartbeat.

Aaron stood in the doorway. Behind him, a soft bedroom lamp cast his frame in an artistic, sensual silhouette that made Justin's mouth water. It was about the sexiest thing he'd ever seen. He wanted to reach out to Aaron, to pull him in close. Smell him. Taste him. Touch him. But it wouldn't be that easy. *Aaron* wasn't that easy. At the moment Justin would settle for not being thrown out. At any rate—perhaps this was in his favor—it would be nearly impossible to rouse Nebraska from the couch.

As if on cue, a loud snore rumbled from the living room.

"What are the nurse's orders?" Aaron asked in a guarded manner. Justin deserved that.

"Rest and one of these every four hours." He shook the pill bottle. "I'm sorry... about everything," he whispered. He took a few steps toward Aaron. "You deserve to know what's going on. I know it already seems apparent, but I don't want to assume that we can stay the night. But... can we stay the night?"

Aaron, with an expressionless face, stood there for a

moment without answering. Then, his lips quirked into a semi-smile, he pushed himself off of the doorway and moved aside.

Justin didn't hesitate. He walked into the bedroom.

READY FOR YOU
A Male/Male Military Romance

-VOLUME THREE-

KELLY WASHINGTON

Chapter One

GIVEN THEIR PREVIOUS parting, Justin felt that it was best to clear the air. He dropped his duffle bag unceremoniously to the ground.

"I'm sorry," he said after the door closed. "They are the two words that could never adequately explain away what a jerk I've been. I panicked and instead of acting like an adult and discussing it with you, I ran off. My feelings for you scared me, and that's tough for me to say. Even after the craziness that's followed me around these last few days, I found that I constantly thought of you to get me through it. I don't know what all of this means. I can't describe how I feel. All I know is that when I wake up in the morning, I want to wake up next to you."

Aaron pulled Justin into him and hugged him. Aaron was warm, and it was easy to sink into him.

"I understand," Aaron said. "For the record, what you just said is a lot better than the rambling apology you gave to Mrs. Tigo outside. I fear the woman is permanently scarred after hearing the word *prostitute*."

Justin smiled as Aaron moved back slightly until they were face to face.

"What am I going to do with you?" Aaron asked.

"I'm more trouble than I'm worth," Justin warned humorously. "I've got a stray named Nebraska, an ex-girlfriend that's an undercover detective, and some sort of powerful head honcho whose claws are firmly implanted in my ass. Not to mention two other secret agents that may or may not work for the U.S. Government. At the moment, frankly, I'm shocked that they haven't made an appearance."

Aaron laughed softly. "I guess there's always tomorrow. But... I was thinking more along the lines of a shower. I'm not sure if you know this, but you've got blood on your face and all over your clothes."

+++

He quickly learned why Aaron's nickname was Texas.

Justin started the shower and jumped when he realized Aaron was behind him. He didn't hear him open the bathroom door, but now that he was here—and beginning to undress—Justin had to admit he had secretly hoped this would happen.

His arousal was immediate, though he did try to hide it before finally releasing whatever embarrassment he possessed, and by the look of things, Aaron's thoughts seemed to be headed in the same direction.

Justin stepped in the tub; the hot water was liquid heaven. He slicked his dark hair back.

Aaron hopped in and Justin couldn't help but continually stare at his naked body. He wasn't a novice when it came to showering near other men—he was in the military, after all, and communal showers were the norm—but he'd never been this close to another man's body while doing so. He also didn't think he'd ever seen a cock that large, either.

"I think I understand things now," Justin said with a thick laugh.

Aaron followed his look and grinned. "About the nickname? As in it's the size of Texas?"

"Jesus Christ, you put me and every other man in the world to shame."

"Not even remotely true," Aaron said mischievously. "I'm not interested in every man in the world. Just one."

He reached up and adjusted the shower head to turn the water into a fine mist, which heated the air in the bathtub. Justin's body tingled as Aaron lathered a washcloth and gently cleaned off the blood. Then he used his hands to soap and caress the rest of him. When strong fingers dug in to massage his neck, Justin felt most of the stress rinse away.

Aaron washed his hair and was extra careful on his face and injured shoulder. They weren't completely leaning against each other, but Aaron's leg would press against his thigh or calf, and Justin would shiver and take gulps of air. Lots and lots of gulps of air.

It felt wonderful, and Justin couldn't imagine any other way of taking a shower from now on. He noticed things he had previously missed: like the fact that Aaron was taller than him and had tattoos on his shoulders and upper back. There was also a small scar on his chin that he felt the urge to run his tongue over.

The anticipation of being so close to Aaron nearly killed him and he saw the same look on his lover's face. When Aaron's mouth finally crashed on his, he felt like he could die a happy man. Justin hungrily kissed him back, his hands digging into Aaron's back, neck, and head. His lips and tongue explored Aaron's mouth, jaw, neck, and that delicious little scar.

Aaron's kisses turned as gentle as butterflies, and Justin savored every kiss, suck, and nibble. But Aaron didn't push too hard for anything. It was a shower, and Justin knew that's all it was intended to be.

That is until Aaron's slick hand rubbed against his erection and he very nearly exploded.

"Jesus Christ," Justin moaned against Aaron's mouth.

Justin's back was suddenly pressed against the tiled wall as Aaron slowly stroked his lover's cock.

It was measured and controlled and perfectly done.

Justin came undone over how great it felt and how Aaron's erection was scorching hot against his leg, too. Justin was sure that his insides were melting. He'd turn into a big puddle soon.

He wanted his own hands to be doing something, anything. At first, they were on Aaron's shoulders and back, but gradually Justin's hands trailed down Aaron's smooth chest and stomach on their own volition. He had never touched another man like this and since Aaron was stroking him, Justin found it somewhat difficult to focus on anything else at the same time.

"Please," Aaron hissed into his neck, biting him. "I'm dying for you to touch me."

Justin's left hand was at his lover's hip.

Inches. Mere inches.

And then his hand wrapped around Aaron's gorgeous, thick, red cock. He pumped jerkily, not quite getting the rhythm down at first. Then Aaron slowly thrust his hips against Justin's hand and was essentially fucking his hand. Soon he was in sync, and he loved feeling every inch of his lieutenant's cock.

The sight was... glorious, and he watched as Aaron's gorgeous body swayed back and forth and how his eyes fluttered open and shut and how his mouth looked more delicious than anything else he could possibly name at the moment.

Justin's pleasure didn't diminish just because Aaron's hand stopped stroking him; it intensified as he focused solely on his lover's pleasure. He caressed his back and kissed his lips and sucked on his neck.

"I'm close." Aaron sucked in his breath and closed what

little gap remained between their bodies. "Oh, my love. Oh... Oh..." His thrusts became fast and shallow and then Aaron crashed into him and kissed him hard, grunting and moaning during the last few thrusts.

"You are so sexy," Justin said.

Aaron shifted between Justin's legs and leaned against him, kissing him, firmly trapping Justin's erection against his stomach. But then Aaron slid down slightly and then back up, all the while pressing his body against Justin's.

"Damn, that feels good," Justin moaned.

"How did my mouth feel the other night?"

My God, the man is killing me. "Hot, soft, phenomenally good."

"I want to taste you again," Aaron said.

"I want all of you all over me. That's what I want."

Chapter Two

AARON SHUT OFF the shower and together they tiptoed into the bedroom and fell into the bed, soaking wet.

"We'll regret this when we can't sleep tonight," Justin joked, a nervous edge to his voice.

"Consider this the education of Justin Hauten," Aaron said. "There will be no sleeping tonight."

Aaron climbed on top of Justin, and suddenly, his hands and mouth were everywhere. When his mouth closed around Justin's cock, Justin blew out a breath and nearly cried out.

He tried to shut everything off. His thoughts. His worries. And in the darkness, he watched as Aaron devoured him and then move on top of him. Aaron was straddling him.

Oh, dear God. If he was going to panic, now would be the time. But he didn't. Justin smiled in the darkness.

"I want you so bad, I'm nearly blind," Aaron whispered into his mouth. Justin's hands grabbed Aaron's hips. "But I need you to make the decision."

He didn't think. He pushed Aaron aside and immediately pinned him against the bed.

He kissed and bit hard down on Aaron's chest and stomach and finally, only after a minor debate within his own mind, Justin took him in his mouth.

Licking. Sucking. Swirling his tongue around him. And as much as he tried, he couldn't fit all of Aaron's gorgeous cock in his mouth. But his eagerness—and both of his hands—made up for his deficiencies.

He felt Aaron's fingernails dig into his skin, and his moans were like poetry to Justin's ears.

"My God, I need you to fuck me right now or I swear I'll die," Aaron confessed heavily as Justin felt his hair getting pulled. "Lay on your back, Justin," Aaron ordered.

He wrestled Justin down against the mattress, straddled him, and before his next cognizant thought, Aaron sat down on his cock.

"Fuuuuuuuck!" Justin nearly bucked him off as Aaron rode him.

Hard.

Like his life depended on it.

It was hot, scorching hot, watching their dark silhouettes rhythmically fuck.

Aaron, one hand on Justin's chest as the other stroked his own cock, slowed his movements to a nice, unhurried tease. Up. Pause. Down. Up. Pause.

Justin heard the faint sucking noise that accompanied their lovemaking. He wanted more of Aaron. He wanted harder, faster, deeper. He wanted control.

So he took it.

Justin leaned up, embraced Aaron in a fierce bear hug, seared his mouth against his luscious lips as he stood—still deep inside Aaron—and pivoted against the edge of the bed.

He was on top now, Aaron's legs spread, welcoming, as Justin's cock worshipped him. He was demanding, punishing even, but his lover begged for each and every one of his thrusts. Their lips and tongues met often as Aaron's arms and legs pulled him in deeper. In between kisses, Justin's mouth was at his lover's neck, biting, licking, grunting.

This is what he wanted. Needed. The build-up, the tension, the emotion rocked his world. Everything burst inside of him, fireworks detonated behind his eyes, and he couldn't breathe as he made his last few thrusts deep inside Aaron. He came like the world crashed around them and this, right now, was the only thing that mattered.

Justin adjusted slightly before collapsing beside the man who destroyed the walls around his heart. He clung to Aaron, their sweaty bodies fitting perfectly as they kissed softly, hands roaming over skin, detailing, remembering.

And then they slept.

Chapter Three

KNOCK. KNOCK. KNOCK.

"Is that in my head or is someone knocking on your bedroom door?" Justin asked hoarsely against Aaron's temple. Legs intertwined, arms thrown every which way, Justin had a difficult time determining which body parts were his. They hadn't moved since their lovemaking, and if he had just one wish ever in his life, he would wish to stay like this for a very long time. He glanced at the windows. Still dark. Very dark. They hadn't slept long.

KNOCK, KNOCK, KNOCK.

"Definitely the door," Aaron groaned and then let loose a string of profanities. "What?"

"Uh, guys," a groggy voice said through the door. It was Nebraska, and he didn't sound like he was in a good mood, either. A sliver of light came through the bottom of the door. "You might want to get dressed and come into the living room because things just got mighty fucked up out here."

Justin groaned. *Just waking us up was mighty fucked up.*

It was either those two agents or Mary Lovecross. Either way, it was terrible timing, he thought.

Without warning, Aaron was no longer beside him, and his entire right side felt cold. The bedroom light switched on, and Justin found a naked Aaron hunting through the closet, grabbing clothes. The clock on the nightstand read two a.m. Then he noticed red marks all over Aaron's neck and chest as he pulled on a soft gray t-shirt and a pair of distressed blue jeans.

"Did I do that to you?" What he didn't ask was, *Was I too rough?*

Aaron smiled and nodded, but playtime was over. "Anything I should know before we go out there?" he asked. He seemed ready for just about anything.

"I don't even know where to begin," Justin answered as he rummaged through his duffle bag and pulled out the only clean clothes he had: an old concert t-shirt and dark-wash jeans. "Only to ask if you're sure you really want to date me."

Aaron smiled. "I reserve the right for a thirty-day trial period first."

"I think you'll know after the next twenty-four hours, actually," Justin said seriously. Shoes. He needed shoes. And maybe a gun. He looked in the closet. "Do you have a gun?"

"That bad, huh? Nope, it's still at the base armory."

Justin nodded and reached for the door, but Aaron stopped him.

"Wait," he said softly, embracing him. "Whatever happens," he hesitated, perhaps rethinking what he might say, "I meant what I said the other day."

I'm in love with you. It hung there. Aaron remembered. Justin remembered.

KNOCK, KNOCK.

"Guys?" Nebraska asked through the door.

"We'll be right out," Justin said and turned back to Aaron. He didn't know what to say. He wasn't quite ready to return the statement. But it wasn't doubt—there was no way in Hell he wanted to hurt Aaron again—it was owning up to his own acceptance of it before he could say it. That might take time. Aaron's eyes told him that he knew this and that he accepted it already. He wasn't going to push. Justin leaned in, his lips touched Aaron's briefly—fleetingly—and it felt right. And that was enough for now. "I know," he whispered.

They left the bedroom.

Mr. A and Mr. B stood calmly by the front door, casually chatting with Mrs. Parris, who had her nurse satchel in hand. She didn't seem alarmed that a strange assortment of characters were in her her son's apartment. Justin wondered if she thought they needed medical attention, too. Mr. B's face was still pretty messed up, his jaw wired shut. Justin didn't miss the smug look on Nebraska's face, since he was the one who had shattered the man's jaw.

Overall, it was quite the domestic scene unless one counted the number of weapons the agents were displaying.

Aaron nudged Justin in the ribs. "You certainly have interesting friends. And I was right, though now it's the wrong context: I don't think there will be any sleeping tonight."

Chapter Four

JUSTIN'S FIRST THOUGHT upon seeing the two secret agents filling up Aaron's apartment was that at least the men weren't aiming their weapons at him. He couldn't compete with guns or the fact that at any minute, they could take Mrs. Parris hostage. They were blocking the door, however, so that was a bummer.

Granted, the scene before Justin was somewhat disturbing. In fact, it was downright cozy. The two secret agents appeared to happily chat with Mrs. Parris, Aaron's mother, about this and that, and "You poor dear!" she said to one of the agents, Mr. B, offering him a small vial of medicine to relieve the pain of his broken jaw.

"Mom" Aaron said, "it might be best if you stepped back this way." He indicated a spot behind him, Justin, and Nebraska. Effectively, the back of the hallway. But she ignored him and continued to give instructions to the injured agent: "Yes, that's it. Drink it up. My Aaron certainly has interesting friends," she said proudly.

Mr. A locked eyes on Justin and lifted an eyebrow. "Yes, indeed," the agent agreed. "Nothing but a bunch of friends here."

It was two-something in the morning; these guys had interrupted their night, and the agents didn't seem to be doing anything remotely badassery.

Er, nor was he.

"Now might be a good time to tell me what's going on," Aaron said out of the side of his mouth.

"Why are both of you wet?" Nebraska asked at the

same time, looking back at forth at Justin and Aaron's damp hair.

It was one thing to be prepared for every single outcome, to outsmart one's opponent without the aid of a real weapon and look good while doing it. It was another thing to stand there and look simpleminded.

But he had his friends. Aaron was the only normal looking one around, though a stupid, confused expression mixed with an "Are you afraid to answer Nebraska's question?" was aimed at Justin.

It was very well deserved, though ill timed.

Which question was he supposed to answer first? Was he embarrassed, or was it because two agents were standing ten feet away from them? Or was it because he'd just experienced one of the best sexual encounters of his life and hadn't recovered yet?

And Nebraska... what was there to say about the man? He was a towering giant with bright red hair, about a million freckles, quick with the jokes, a mean right hook, and loyal to a fault. So loyal, in fact, that he had beat the shit out of Justin two days ago because Nebraska thought it would make the situation they happened to be in better.

It didn't.

So Justin looked like—and felt like—a breathing carcass. One eye was, for the most part, swollen shut and his face was a round canvas of bruises. It was a wonder that Aaron even found him attractive.

"These are the two assholes I saved Justin from two months ago," Nebraska said, answering Aaron's question.

"Was that before or after you did several backflips and snatched their weapons at the speed of light?" Aaron asked with a smile.

"Let's not quibble with the specifics," Nebraska said. "But if you must know, *Lt. Smartass*, Justin might have been reading one of your letters at the time."

"You're not helping," Justin groaned.

Aaron's mother approached them, effectively sealing off whatever discussion that might have taken place. But the look that Aaron gave Nebraska was nearly murderous.

"He knew about the letters?" Aaron whispered heatedly.

"It's nice to see that you're all cleaned up, dear," Mrs. Parris said to Justin. She patted his cheek. "Though I had hoped that a good cleaning would have cleared up your face. But I see that all of the marks are bruises. No worries, deary, those will fade in time. You don't mind the bruises, do you, Aaron? Riveting friends you have. The one with the shattered jaw isn't interested in a physical. So, I'm off to the kitchen to make tea."

"Your mother knows?" Justin turned to Aaron.

"Really, why are you both wet?" Nebraska asked again. "Even your clothes are damp." He pushed a finger into Justin's back, supposedly to point out a sweaty spot.

"Don't be dense, man," Justin said to Nebraska. "It's called a shower." *The most delicious shower ever!* He turned to Aaron. "And how it is that your mother knows?"

"Why are you so worried?"

"I'm not."

"Dude, it's obvious you are," Nebraska offered. He pointed at his own head and said, "Body language."

One of the agents cleared a throat. "Have we come at a bad time, hm?" Mr. A asked. He had moved away from the door while the other agent stayed in place. Mr. B looked odd, like he was wobbling.

"Of course not. We were in serious need of comic relief," Justin answered. "Timing, however, doesn't appear to be a strong suit for you."

"Dude, you seeing what I'm seeing?" Nebraska asked

under his breath. Mr. B swayed.

"Then how's this for comedy? The most intriguing information has reached my ears, Sergeant Hauten," Mr. A said as he glanced sharply at his partner. "Is Captain Phillips under the protection of the Texas Bureau of Investigation?"

"I thought Captain Phillips was in a military prison," Aaron said.

"Thoughts are funny things, Lieutenant," Mr. A said. "They are unreliable." He sat on the couch, looking unconcerned.

"We don't know what you're talking about," Nebraska all but growled at the man.

If the agent knew who Aaron was, then how much more did he know? Would he know about Julia, her undercover prostitution sting, and that she was the one who found Captain Phillips? The other agent continued his post at the door, but he appeared to lean against it for support.

"I'm impressed with your loyalty, Specialist Walker." Mr. A nonchalantly pulled out his revolver. "Never like sitting down with this thing. Always pokes me in the side."

"I'll have you know that I'm very nearly a Sergeant."

"When do you go before the promotion board, Nebraska?" Justin asked and then whispered to Aaron, "What did your mom give to the other agent?"

"Any number of things," Aaron replied. "You don't become a general's wife and not pick up a few things over the years. I have no doubt that she read the men for what they are. Which means she's about five steps ahead of me."

"Same."

"I go before the board in a couple of weeks, buddy."

"Is this particular conversation necessary?" Mr. A seethed. "And what are you two whispering about? Ah... defiance, I see. I assure you, it's not necessary. I'm on your side. I promise."

"In my experience, if someone has to tell you that, then they are definitely not on your side," Justin said.

Mr. A smiled. "You said you needed comic relief. I suppose it wasn't that funny." He didn't exactly train the weapon on any of them, but the implied threat was there.

Just as Mr. A stood up, there was a sudden crashing noise at the door. The small table next to the door, filled with a few picture frames, keys, and small odds-and-ends, shattered.

Mr. B was sprawled on top of it, blocking the door with his body.

The other agent looked heavenward and sighed. "I really need to get a new partner."

"Now *that* was funny," Nebraska said as his laughter filled the living room.

Chapter Five

"WHAT DO YOU think Mrs. Parris is going to do when she sees that we're gone?" Nebraska asked from the front passenger seat. He was turned around as much as the seatbelt would allow him.

"She might be slightly alarmed," Aaron said. "But then she'll see that she has a patient at her disposal. Mom really loves her examinations."

"I wish I had seen Mr. B fall," Nebraska mused. "Your partner wasn't looking too good there at the end, if you know what I'm talking about, buddy. I also wish we didn't have these zip ties around our hands."

"You all really have the strangest conversations," Mr. A said from the driver's seat. From the looks of it—and Justin's memory was a bit fuzzy—it appeared that he was taking them to the TBI office. The same office that Julia had brought him and Nebraska to yesterday.

"Just ignore him," Justin said. "What's your mom going to do to the agent? Horrible things?"

"Nothing like that. She takes her nursing job seriously." Then he lowered his voice. "And... my mom knows about you because I confided in her."

"Today?" Justin asked.

Nebraska was straining to listen.

"Sit straight, Specialist Walker, or I'll put you in the trunk," Mr. A ordered.

"Get a lobotomy. Oh, and as cozy as that sounds, I wouldn't fit."

"Seven months, I think," Aaron said. "She's the one

that encouraged me to give the letters to you."

Seven months ago, the three of them were still in Afghanistan and Aaron, presumably, had already written many of those love letters.

"Why did you write the letters? And why to me?"

Aaron hesitated at first, then said, "Have you ever met someone special and you felt that they could make you into a better person?"

"Uh…" It was these types of conversations that normally had Justin mumbling like an idiot. It was probably best if he kept his mouth shut.

"I have. And that's how I felt when I met you. I wanted to know what made you smile and then that turned into me wanting to be the person that made you smile."

"What if they don't feel the same?"

There was a sad smile on Aaron's face that Justin desperately wanted to erase. "You can't force it." Aaron paused, his eyes low. "What did you think when you found out that it was me?"

"We are here," Mr. A announced.

"At first, I was just glad that it wasn't a joke." Justin smiled, but when it looked like Aaron wasn't amused, he quickly added: "I was shocked. Confused. Excited. Nervous. It was a thrilling thought."

"He was a little slow on the intake," Nebraska added.

"Time to go, gentlemen," Mr. A said again.

"How did you—" Aaron asked Nebraska.

"Body language never lies, my friend."

"He used to be a boxer," Justin explained.

"What does that have to do with anything?" Aaron asked.

"Everything," Nebraska said.

A clicking noise interrupted them. The handgun was at

Nebraska's head.

"Is that really necessary?" Justin asked. He looked outside the window and saw that they were at an abandoned-looking warehouse. "All you had to do was tell us."

"Out. Of. The. Car." The agent's face was bright red. "Jesus, it's like rounding up toddlers."

Chapter Six

IT WAS A building within a building within another building, and it turned out to be a pub called The Itchy Nail. By the time they reached the place, it was easy to see why everyone would need a drink. The place was dark, dank, and equal parts seedy and upscale, with a slight musky odor that couldn't be checked at the door.

Not surprisingly, Nebraska loved everything about it.

An eye panel slid open and before the agent could breathe a word, the bouncer said, "Oh, it's you." A thick, solid slab of a wooden door creaked open.

Justin looked around the dimly lit pub. Most of the booths were occupied by an odd mixture of people: businessmen and women in designer suits; vagabonds dressed in homeless couture; and then there was the guy with the pirate eye patch. Pirate guy was sitting alone.

All at two-something in the morning.

No one seemed to pay them any notice and apparently it was fairly normal to escort individuals into The Itchy Nail with their wrists zip tied together.

It wasn't a reassuring thought. Nor was the joint's name, if Justin were being honest. He had images of hands nailed to tables and other torture techniques.

"Can we sit with the pirate?" Nebraska asked. His face was equal parts delight and amusement. His freckles danced, the surest sign Justin had ever seen that his friend was eating this up.

"Shut up," the agent said.

"Remind me how we got into this situation," Aaron

said.

Nebraska raised his cuffed hands. "Do you mean before or after this jerk tossed these here zip ties at our feet and ordered you to secure our wrists?"

"He had a gun to Justin's head," Aaron said. "What was I supposed to do?"

"The man wouldn't have done it, and you know it. I'm beginning to think Mr. A has a crush on Justin."

"That's not a flattering thought," Justin added. "Any new injuries would probably improve my looks at this point. Seriously, I can't feel much of my left side anymore."

"You're trying to piss me off, Nebraska. It won't work," Aaron said.

"I already know what's going to happen here," Nebraska said. "You two are going to become thick as thieves and I'll be pushed into third-wheel status. Also, you didn't have to make my zip ties so tight."

"Lover's quarrel?" the agent asked.

"What is this place?" Justin asked.

"It's the place where I ask questions and you provide answers." Mr. A pushed them into a booth located in the back corner of the pub.

"Like Jeopardy?" Nebraska asked. Justin wondered if the agent was falling for any of this.

Mr. A rolled his eyes.

"I love Jeopar—" Aaron stopped when a huge man with a hunchback suddenly appeared from nowhere and quietly asked for their drink order.

"One Itchy Nail, Geoff," the agent answered. The hunchback disappeared just as quickly.

"Why do I get the impression that we aren't going to like this drink?" Justin asked. He was squished in next to Aaron and under the table, Aaron's hands found his and squeezed. Justin had to remind himself that all of this would be new to his lover. He and Nebraska were old pros by now.

Justin gave a quick, reassuring smile to Aaron, whose return smile didn't quite match.

"You aren't," the agent answered. "Ah, thank you, Geoff." The one shot glass filled with shiny, silver liquid was deftly placed in the middle of the table.

Nebraska, for his part, seemed to be looking everywhere, probably trying to memorize it all. Justin wasn't sure, but it was entirely possible he heard Nebraska say something to the effect of, "I'm totally having my bachelor party here."

"Are you going to pour this drink into our mouths, too?" Aaron asked as he leaned forward in an authoritative manner. "I really don't see how you have the upper hand here."

Mr. A smiled. "I'm so glad that it was you, Lieutenant Parris, that asked me that question. It always feels weird to me when I have to bring it up. You see this phone?" He held up an ordinary-looking cell phone. "It's a remote control, much like the type that opens garage doors or makes those little RC cars zip around the house. That's all nice and fun and harmless. However, it's also the type that detonates certain remote-control-triggered explosive devices. I may have *accidentally* left a suitcase bomb in your apartment. Oops." The agent shrugged as if this wasn't a big deal to him. "One of you will drink this liquid. The decision is yours."

"I swear when this is all done, I am going to kill you," Aaron seethed. His hands erupted from under the table, pointing at the agent across from him. He tried to pull his hands apart, but only succeeded in making the zip ties dig deeply into his wrists.

"You are so adorable. I can see why Sergeant Hauten likes you."

"What do you want?" Justin asked as calmly as he could. He placed his hands over Aaron's and gently pushed down. "Don't let him get to you," he said quietly to Aaron.

"You'd blow up your own partner?" Nebraska asked incredulously. "Completely uncool and highly doubtful. I call bluff."

The agent started pushing numbers on the phone.

"Wait!" Aaron yelled, and the agent looked up. "I'm not willing to take that risk, guys. We're talking about the woman that gave birth to me twenty-six years ago!"

Aaron shoved Justin's hands aside and scooped up the shot glass. But he held it there, the metallic-looking liquid sloshed around slightly.

"You're only twenty-six?" Nebraska asked. "How old are you again, Hotten?"

"Thirty-one. Aaron, you are not drinking that," Justin said. "The man's a federal agent. They don't do these kinds of things."

"Who cares how old they are? Jesus Christ," the agent said. A vein in his forehead was visibly pulsing.

"I don't know, buddy," Nebraska said. "I don't think he's a legitimate agent of anything. More like a rogue asshole that does assholery stuff with stupid cell phones and shit. I bet it's a pre-paid phone that can only dial 911, a local pizza joint, and one of those hair transplant businesses. Receding hairlines are an epidemic in this country."

The agent rolled his eyes and pushed another number on the phone. "In two numbers, the sequence will be complete and the signal sent. Drink up, Lieutenant."

"We're too far away for that to be effective," Justin

said, but he wasn't certain anymore.

The agent just laughed and pressed another number. "One more number, gentlemen."

"Give it to me," Justin told Aaron. "All of this can be blamed on me."

Nebraska snorted. "Seriously? Don't be such a fucking martyr, buddy. If you want to blame someone, blame the bastard rubbing my thigh right now. Besides, we all know that I'm the biggest, brawniest, and, frankly, the best-looking one here, and whatever that shit contains will do less damage on me."

Nebraska reached over, grabbed the shot glass out of Aaron's hands, and downed its contents in one motion. The agent deleted whatever he typed into the phone and put the device in his pocket. The man looked satisfied with himself, but Nebraska summed it up rather nicely: "Doesn't he," he pointed to the agent, "look downright smarmy and smug? It isn't a good look on anyone, even smarmy and smug assholes."

The agent fumed when they chuckled at Nebraska's comment.

"What happens now?" Justin asked. He found Aaron's hands under the table and squeezed.

Mr. A smiled crookedly. He seemed more in control now, like maybe from here on out, the rest would be easy.

"Now... we wait."

Chapter Seven

IT TOOK TEN minutes before Nebraska turned loopy, and in that time, hot coffee was delivered to the agent. Justin and Aaron declined, not trusting much of anything, plus it was doubtful that they could properly hold a coffee cup with the zip ties around their wrists.

Nebraska rambled. About the pirate guy ("He's so tiny!" and "Can we invite him over?"). Jelly beans ("Pina Colada is the best!"). Proposals gone wrong (Unintelligible sobbing). And puppies ("You should have seen how the Bassett Hound puppies kept stepping on their own ears.").

"The future Mrs. Walker isn't going to be happy about this," Nebraska said in a clear voice. He shook his head as if to clear it free of cobwebs. "She's gorgeous and tall and smart and her breath smells nice and her hair is so long and strong, it could strangle a man."

"You got close enough to smell her breath?" Justin asked. "Why is he talking like this?"

Nebraska continued: "I said she had something in her teeth and I got close, and I really like the color of this table. It's so brown and it holds things really well, like straight and all. Not like those slanted tables over there. It's dark in here."

They turned to see what it was he was talking about.

No slanted tables, but the wall lights were low, yellow, and dingy. The pirate guy, evidently feeling observed, gave a toothy smile and waved.

"Mind-altering liquid," the agent said. "In a few minutes, he'll answer any question I ask him, and there's nothing you can do but watch."

"Like what?" Aaron asked.

"I can't believe Aaron's only twenty-six years old," Nebraska said. "Because he's tall and stuff and... trees are tall and stuff. Oh, my God! Aaron's a tree. Hotten! Hotten! Aaron's a tree!"

"About Captain Phillips, naturally. Where's the camera?"

"Didn't you sack my place looking for it?" Justin asked through clenched teeth. That part still irked him needlessly; like someone invading his privacy.

"Silverware! Undercover Detective!" Nebraska yelled out like a drill sergeant. There was a sudden hush in the place before various conversations started again. Justin felt eyes on them now.

"What's so important about this camera?" Aaron asked.

Again, Justin had to remind himself how bizarre the last few days had been for him and Nebraska. Kidnappings. Mary Lovecross's bunker. The pseudo-detentions by Mary Lovecross and Julia, aka Detective Fenske. Now, this. Not that The Itchy Nail wasn't his cup of tea—it was certainly an interesting place—but he wasn't fond of any type of confinement.

Aaron was like a newborn babe compared to what he and Nebraska had encountered lately.

"An undercover agent, huh?" The agent mimicked. "Fascinating. It's not the camera itself, but the photos it contains—and the Captain's orders."

"I've seen the pictures," Aaron said. "Didn't seem too important to me."

"Other photos! Other photos on there!" Nebraska yelled. "Yellow daffodils are pretty."

"Besides," Justin said. "You gave it back to me. Can't

be all that important if you were willing to let it out of your possession."

The agent smiled. "I was most curious to see how many hands it passed through, Sergeant."

Justin suddenly felt very cold. "Were you the one giving the orders to Captain Phillips all along? What about the children?"

Nebraska squealed in delight. "Yes, I do want to order. A cheeseburger, onion rings, and a cherry-vanilla Coke. I'm so hungry."

"I don't know about any children." The agent's face clouded and oddly, Justin believed him. What if this man didn't work for the United States Government? What if Captain Phillips was mixed up in a covert type of operation and it got out of hand? What if someone intercepted and it changed everything? And those children were innocent victims of some stupid operation?

"The future Mrs. Walker wants children," Nebraska sang. "Dozens and dozens of them."

Justin felt like he was right, but he didn't have any type of proof. The question was: who was who, and who could he trust?

"Oh, my God," Justin breathed. "You don't know at all, do you? Captain Phillips wasn't just working for you, was he? That's what you want to know. You want to know who else he was working for."

The agent's face changed and he turned abruptly to Nebraska. "I'm done with these stupid games. Where is Captain Phillips, Specialist Walker?"

"In a... cell... a... cell phone with Julia," Nebraska answered, his face looked child-like, like there was nothing in this world that could bother him. "A cell phone!" Then he looked down. "What are these?" He tried to pull his hands apart. "Ahhh, it's okay. The future Mrs. Walker must have done this. She'll be back any moment. Though I'm rather shocked that you're in our bedroom right now."

"What were Captain Phillips' orders to you and Staff Sergeant Hauten? How many times did his orders change? Who else did he communicate with?"

"Hotten, my man? You there? He got shot in the shoulder and birds flew out of the bullet hole. It was surreal, man. Like, why were birds there in the first place and how did they get inside that tiny hole and why didn't the bullet kill them?"

"I don't think you're going to get the type of answers you want from him," Justin said.

"Don't make me shoot your friend, punk. You have no goddamn idea of who you're messing with. What were Captain Phillips' *original* orders?" he yelled.

"Shiny stuff," Nebraska answered gleefully. "Find shiny stuff."

"What does it matter? The man is in jail. Find him and ask him," Aaron said loudly.

"You think that because your father's a two-star general that you'll get any kind of favorable treatment from me, you pissant? I know all about you, Lieutenant Parris, about your parents and how your father plans to run for governor in two years but he has doubts about running because of you. I know that you came out of the closet three years ago and that your father didn't speak to you for six months. Even now, he has a difficult time looking at you without a tinge of disappointment. I know that ten years ago, you fathered a child with a sixteen-year-old girl in your high school and that almost all of your paycheck goes toward child support. And, during your last assignment in Washington DC, your stripper boyfriend was arrested four times for solicitation and for blackmailing you. If you think that everything around you three is unconnected, then think again. The reason that your unit came under investigation is because that prostitution sting followed Lieutenant Parris here."

Justin couldn't believe his ears, and Aaron wasn't disagreeing with anything. Was Aaron the target that brought Julia here?

"Oh, my God," Justin said. "Is it true?"

Aaron briefly closed his eyes before he faced Justin. "All of it, though not the last part, but only because I didn't know about the prostitution sting; not right away, at any rate."

The agent snickered. "How many men have knocked on your door accidentally over the years, Lieutenant?" Aaron didn't answer so the agent continued. "I suppose the real question is: how many did you let inside?"

Justin couldn't breathe. He studied Aaron's handsome profile.

"Only one," Aaron finally answered. "Captain Phillips."

Chapter Eight

JUSTIN SNATCHED HIS hand away from Aaron as if it burned him. *Only* Captain Phillips? What the fuck was going on?

"What?" the agent asked. Clearly he hadn't expected that answer, either. Even Nebraska's zany antics abruptly stopped.

Suddenly, Justin realized that Aaron knew more than he could have known and that maybe—maybe—everything was a ruse. The letters. The images on the camera. The scary Lovecross woman. Julia. Was there even a TBI? Was their lovemaking tonight a pretense? It certainly felt real.

"I know everything," Aaron said. "The orders, the images, even the children Justin mentioned. Captain Phillips was my..." Aaron hesitated and looked down briefly.

"He was your what?" the agent and Justin asked at the same time.

Nebraska started making odd noises, and were his hands... loose?

"My lover."

The agent drew his weapon and pointed the muzzle an inch from Aaron's head. He wasn't watching Nebraska, who wore the biggest shit-eating grin ever.

"Bullshit, Lieutenant," the agent yelled. "You better tell me something that's true."

"Only that you're fucking gullible," Aaron said as he cocked his head and looked at Nebraska.

Nebraska, even without ample room, reared back and

swung both of his fists into the agent's temple. A loud crack echoed in the room as Mr. A slumped sideways and then slid out of the booth with a *thud-thud.*

"Ouch!" Nebraska cradled his hands and swung them back and forth, as if cooling them off would help dull the pain.

"Grab him up, quickly!" Justin ordered. Nebraska slid out of the booth bench, roughly shoved the crumpled agent into the corner of the booth, then sat back down and glanced around. Although it was witnessed, no one did anything about it. Maybe they just didn't care. Or maybe this was a normal event.

"How long will he be out for?" Aaron asked. His eyes were wide, and his lips were thin and white, his body shaking. Justin wondered if he was in a bit of shock from it all.

"Couple of hours, buddy. Nice work!" Nebraska gushed at Aaron as he searched Mr. A's pockets. A small pile of things ended up on the table: car keys, the blasted cell phone, a Ruger SP-101 revolver, even pocket knife with mini-scissors, which Justin and Aaron used to cut off their zip ties.

Justin then ejected the rounds from the gun as Nebraska found a small notebook that seemed to be written in code. And then other scraps of paper with all of their names on it, along with facts about each of them.

Justin couldn't face Aaron just then—and Aaron was looking at him hard—so he studied the cell phone instead.

None of what Aaron said was actually true, he told himself as he absently looked at the phone call history. Aaron had wanted to distract the agent, that's all. It worked. He scrolled through the tiny display. There were no incoming calls, and every number dialed out was the same. Was the agent receiving orders or giving them? Mr.

A didn't seem orchestrated enough to run an operation. Nor did Captain Phillips, for that matter.

Justin pressed the redial button, wondering, hoping that it might tell him something. It was to a computer generated voice mailbox, *Please leave a message. Beeeeeeep.* Frustrated, he hung up and slammed it against the table.

Aaron looked like he wanted to say something, but Nebraska beat him to it, "That Itchy Nail drink didn't do crap," he boasted just before he started hacking and coughing and making gross growling sounds from the back of his throat for a full minute. "Well," he said as he cleared his throat, "let me amend that slightly: my throat feels like I literally swallowed a shot glass full of nails, but it did make me feel all warm inside, like whiskey. I wouldn't mind another one, actually."

"No!" Aaron and Justin said at the same time. Then Aaron's hand was on Justin's leg and there was a look. An apology? An explanation?

Nebraska put his hands up as a peace offering.

"I'll, uh, find the men's room and give you two a few minutes to sort... this... out." He made a show of shoving the revolver into his waistband. Justin wasn't worried that he'd shoot his pecker off; it wasn't loaded.

Chapter Nine

JUSTIN FACED AARON fully. "What was true and what was false?" he asked with a challenging tone to his voice.

"If I said 'all of it,' would it make sense?"

"Elaborate."

"The girl from high school was my best friend, but the child isn't mine. It's a long story, and it would take a lot longer than we have right now to explain it. Diana, that's her name, is still a very good friend of mine and her son is a great guy who's about to go into the fifth grade."

"Fair enough. What about the prostitution thing?" He recalled that Julia's job had brought her here when one of her targets moved here. She had to have meant Aaron. But that was ridiculous, right?

"I didn't know enough about Stephan before I got involved with him. He was new, sexy, wild and very different from anyone I've ever known. It's not always easy to navigate when you're figuring out what it means to be gay, especially in the military. It was my first assignment out of the Military Academy, I met Stephan at a bar, and unfortunately, I found out too late that he was a prostitute. When I tried to leave the relationship, he threatened to tell the military that I was gay. There was an investigation, and thankfully, I was cleared of all wrong doing."

Justin nodded. He could understand that. "Have there been men knocking on your door?"

"Yeah, I don't even know what that part was about. That whole 'who's been knocking on your door?' thing that this jerk said—" Aaron kicked the unconscious man propped up across from them. "—is completely fabricated. I have no idea what that was about, or my mom's been opening the door to a lot of unknown men—which might explain a couple of the odd things that's she's been saying over the years." Aaron shook his head and laughed. "Anyway, so I just rolled with it since that was about the same time I noticed Nebraska's hands were free." Aaron smiled. "I'd like to point out that it worked."

He should have trusted Aaron. Instead, his mind had immediately turned traitor, requiring proof. Justin smiled back. Aaron was a quick study, quicker than he was in this instance. Justin had been so focused on Aaron that he hadn't noticed that Nebraska had worked his zip ties free.

"So the thing about you knowing everything about Captain Phillips..." Justin trailed off.

"I know only what you two have told me, which is surprisingly little. If I'm going to be a member of this posse, it might be about time for a back brief once we get out of here."

"I think now sounds pretty good," Nebraska said once he rounded the corner. There was a buzz about the place. "I think folks are starting to notice that we're moving about freely. I'm kind of sad that pirate guy disappeared, though." He picked up the rest of the stuff from the table and pocketed it, including the empty shot glass. How many pockets did Nebraska have?

"I'll take the cell phone," Justin said, holding out his hand.

Nebraska handed it over and then held up the ignition key to Mr. A's car.

"Time to get going, friends."

"What do we do with him?" Aaron asked, pointing at Mr. A as he and Justin shimmied out of the booth.

"I've got an idea. Is there a pen in his pocket?"

Nebraska rummaged around. "Here. But we need to get going. I think that hunchback is coming this way."

Justin reached over, uncapped the pen—which was a nice black ink—and wrote a derogatory word on the man's forehead.

"Dear God, Hotten. If the man didn't already hate you, once he sees that, he's going to hunt you down until you both reach the gates of Hell."

"Let's focus on the positive, shall we, and just enjoy the moment?"

Collectively, they stood back and looked at Justin's handiwork.

"Okay, let's go. Give me the revolver, Nebraska."

"Is he always this bossy?" Aaron asked.

"I'm a terrible shot, being left eye dominant and all," Nebraska said as he casually handed over the weapon as if it were an everyday occurrence. "But, yeah, normally. I think he's just trying to impress you now that he's busted up and ugly."

Justin took the lead and rechecked the revolver to confirm it wasn't loaded. "I heard that," he said dryly.

They walked through the dining area and into a grimy-looking bar area. Amazing characters sat atop haphazardly leaning barstools and Justin openly ogled them. Trench coats. Business suits. A glam rock band—a halo of glitter sparkled on the floor around them. A couple of women who looked like librarians arguing the merits of a classic book. All intermixed with individuals who either had to be, or wanted to look like, homeless men and women. The latter furiously and continuously glanced behind their shoulders, as if they wanted to ensure they were not being observed. Behind the splintery-looking counter, a burly bartender polished his mugs with a dirty rag.

Obviously, there wasn't a dress code. Justin wouldn't have been surprised if someone dressed in a superhero outfit waltzed in.

They passed the hunchback, Geoff, who waved and overly enthusiastically asked them to come back again, "If you can find us again, that is," he said with a bark of whooping laughter. Justin hoped he never saw this place again. Nebraska nicked several coasters and a handful of matchbooks with The Itchy Nail's name on them.

"Sweet!"

"I don't think Justin's ugly," Aaron said to Nebraska as the heavy door shut behind them and they weaved in and out of several dank, echoey hallways.

Justin heard that, too, and smiled, but said instead, "I'm hungry. It feels like I haven't eaten in days."

Chapter Ten

MRS. PARRIS WAS still up, waiting for their return, and followed them around like a moth as they searched the apartment for any type of suitcase. Nothing.

Once Aaron's mother had their attention, she presented them with a large bowl of pasta. "In case you were hungry, dearies," she said cheerfully.

You'd think the three of them were on death row, given the amount of food they shoveled into their mouths. Mrs. Parris sipped her tea as they ate.

"I didn't know when you might walk through that front door, so I began to drink all the tea myself. That is, until she showed up."

"She?" Justin asked through a mouthful of noodles.

"Yes, a most impressive young lady. She acted very friendly, as if she knew all of you."

"Why didn't you tell us this when we came in?" Aaron asked.

Mrs. Parris scoffed. "And have you all run right out of here before eating anything? I heard your stomachs coming before you even stepped foot on the stairwell outside. And I just assumed you'd notice that the downed officer, er, agent, ah, person was no longer here. It was quite obvious to me. But you never asked."

She sipped her tea.

"Who was she?" Aaron asked protectively.

"Did she single-handedly remove Mr. B?" Nebraska asked with something like admiration in his voice.

"Was she smoking a lot of cigarettes?" Justin asked

with a groan.

"One question at a time, boys. She didn't stay long, but she did leave a card. I'll see if I can find it." She stood up slowly. Justin could tell that she wanted to be helpful, yet she looked extremely tired. If they were all at Justin's mother's house, she would have kicked them out long ago and bolted the door. Aaron's mother was either a glutton for punishment or a saint.

"Did the woman have short, black hair?" Justin asked.

"Hm? You have someone in mind, deary? No, no. It was brown, I think." She moved to another part of the dining room. "It's not on this side. I distinctly remember telling her to leave her card on the table. She was quite adamant about leaving a calling card and I wanted to make sure to show you."

"Did you two talk?" Aaron asked before turning to Justin. "If my mother is in any danger, I swear..."

"For all we know, it could have been a neighbor," Nebraska offered and gulped his tea. "Man, this stuff is good. What is it?"

"I'm so glad you like it, deary. It's an exotic Indian tea that the General bought for me last Christmas. And of course we talked. I am nothing if not a civilized hostess."

"A neighbor?" Aaron asked incredulously. "That carried a body out of this apartment and then had tea with my mother at—" He looked at his watch. "—three-thirty in the morning?"

"What did you talk about?" Justin asked.

Mrs. Parris chuckled. "Naturally, our first conversation centered on the man who was, at the time of your hasty departure, pushed against the window treatment at a most odd angle. Then we sat with a nice cup of tea and chatted about this and that. Children mostly, but then the man stirred and we felt it was best if she took him with her."

She paused as she flipped through several stacks of paper. "He was heavy. If your father knew, he'd be having fits right about now, but I rather enjoyed myself. I haven't done something like that in ages..."

Nebraska spewed tea everywhere. "You mean this has happened before?"

"Please don't tell me you carried—" Aaron groaned, unable to finish the sentence.

"You called the General?" Justin asked. Part of him kind of hoped that this high-ranking officer would be coming to the rescue. However, Justin changed his mind when he saw Aaron's expression.

"Hm? What was that? No, of course not," Mrs. Parris said absently to the three of them as she moved out of their sight and into the kitchen.

To which question did she answer *no* to?

"I can't deal with the General right now, and I really don't want to know if my mother helped someone carry that man out of this apartment. But I do want to know who that someone was."

"It doesn't sound like it was Mary Lovecross. So that leaves Julia," Justin said. "I think she'd be interested in taking the agent with her and questioning him when he woke up."

Nebraska nodded. "Seems logical. Although I do like the idea that our fan club is growing. Wonder if Julia was able to get a translator for Leia Woondiour's statement?"

"Mary Lovecross? Leia Woondi—who? The agents from tonight? Call me crazy, but I'm not exactly following any of this," Aaron said. "They are like like bad actors trying to portray what a secret agent might do in questionable circumstances. I mean, they seem rather harmless. Like high school bullies."

"High school bullies that visit awesome pubs," Nebraska

said.

"These agents," Aaron said. "I think they are in the military. Maybe Criminal Investigations. How would he know so much about us unless he had access to restricted files and such? Why not just say so, though?"

"I don't know. Maybe," Justin said. "What he thought he knew about you was mostly conjecture. He didn't know the facts behind most of it. Mr. A was only interested in Captain Phillips, the original orders, and how many people or agencies the camera circulated through. He was confused when I mentioned those abducted children."

"Yeah, me, too," Aaron said. "What about these children?"

"Jesus," Nebraska said heavily. "I forgot that you didn't know."

"Do you remember when I showed you the photos on the camera and how some of those images were of children and families?" Aaron nodded. "Some of those families were slaughtered within days of my taking their photos. Three people were also abducted, two children and a young woman, Leia Woondiour. The State Department says that Captain Phillips was involved in treason and human trafficking."

"Holy shit."

"And it appears that three separate agencies are investigating separate parts of this whole thing."

"Right," Nebraska jumped in. "Julia, also known as the *hawt* Detective Fenske, is with the TBI and investigating prostitution in and around the military base. Then, during a sting, she comes across Leia Woondiour and finds Captain Phillips in her closet. Which doesn't make sense if he had something to do with her abduction."

"Okay," Aaron said.

"Mary Lovecross appears to be pretty high up in the

government—or she's so scary they let her have run of the place—and they're saying that he ordered me to take pictures of covert military operations. He then supposedly gave those images to a relative, a relative that's conveniently involved in human trafficking, too. The two don't seem to go hand-in-hand, in my opinion."

Aaron, nodding at Justin, paused for a second. "Suppose it depends on who or what they are trying to traffic or smuggle. And where does Mr. A fit in?" Aaron asked.

"The relative? Or a friend of the relative, maybe?" Nebraska guessed. "He could be the go-between."

"I don't think so. Of the three agencies, Mr. A seems to be the least knowledgeable of the situation. Or he's acting clueless."

"On purpose?"

"Maybe, but only if he thought we knew more information than we do," Justin said. "I honestly don't think he knows the half of it and that Captain Phillips either duped him or completely disregarded what the mission called for."

"Okay, hold on." Aaron stood up and paced. "We're asking the wrong questions."

Chapter Eleven

JUSTIN HESITATED. "SUCH as?"

"We're assuming that Captain Phillips is guilty here. What if it's meant to look that way?"

"In case you forgot, the man shot me," Justin said.

"If Captain Phillips is charged with treason and human trafficking and even conspiracy for murdering those families, then why was he free for Julia to pick up? He should have been locked up in a federal detention center. And other than your interview with Good Morning Dallas, which more or less centered on Nebraska's proposal, none of this has been picked up by the mainstream media. Not the human trafficking piece, at least."

"You've got a point," Nebraska said tightly. Justin expected his best friend to say more, but he didn't. Nebraska wasn't immune to rejection.

"Did you see the photos?" Aaron asked.

"Of course I did," Justin answered. "I took them."

"Not those. But of the murdered families?"

"No," Justin and Nebraska said at the same time. They shared a look.

"What were the orders, Justin?" Aaron asked.

Silence, then, "Move on."

"From everything you've told me, all of this, apparently, hinges on what the original orders were."

"He said to move on," Nebraska spit out.

"Obviously, you have a theory," Justin said.

Aaron's eyes narrowed. "Not really, only that you abruptly closed off the discussion, and that makes me suspicious. Not only am I now involved, however unintentional, you've brought my mother into this. You're not telling me the truth."

"Are you calling us liars? I'm about to throw you on the ground, Lieutenant," Nebraska growled.

Justin gave his friend a stern look. Nebraska looked like he wanted to hit something. Anything.

"I—" Justin started.

"Found it, dearies." Mrs. Parris popped her head around the corner, looking down at a small piece of paper in her hand. Justin wasn't sure, but it looked like she was wearing dish gloves. "So silly of me, actually. I accidentally left it next to the cream in the refrigerator after the oddest thing happened—" She stopped short. "Oh, my. A tense moment, I see. Do you know what I do when I feel tense?" She stepped fully into the room. "As you know, the General isn't an easy man to be married to. But, I digress. I just pop a sugar cube into my mouth. It makes me feel so much better." She chuckled. "It's fairly evident that I've popped a lot of sugar cubes over the years."

"Nonsense, Mrs. Parris," Nebraska said kindly even though his body was as rigid as a statue.

"Mom, you mentioned something odd happened?"

No one moved.

"Yes, well, after my guest left and as I was putting my tea things away, someone else knocked on the door, which is why I unintentionally left the business card in the fridge."

"Who was it?" Justin asked.

"A pretty blonde named Detective Fenske. She said you all knew her. She didn't stay long; in fact, she never even came inside."

That threw Justin's theory about who the first visitor was out the window. Who did they know who would volunteer to remove an unconscious body? No one he could think of.

"What did she want?"

"That's the odd part. She took off just as soon as I opened the door. It seemed to me that she saw someone she recognized—there was a puzzled look on her face for the briefest moment before she looked extremely angry. She apologized, introduced herself, mentioned she knew all of you, and then suddenly sprinted down the stairs."

"You weren't alarmed or scared or worried?" Nebraska asked. Justin read the admiration in his friend's face.

"Don't be silly," she laughed a little. "This is the most fun I've had in ages. Anyway," she yawned and placed the business card on the edge of the dining table. "I'll just leave the calling card right here. Make sure you flip it over, dearies. Good night."

No one spoke until her bedroom door closed.

"Was she wearing dish gloves?" Justin asked. Her hands were definitely bright yellow.

"Your mother's delightful," Nebraska muttered and relaxed. "Jury's out on the rest of your family."

"Yes, she was—thank you—and I agree with you, actually. You were saying about the orders..."

Justin felt deflated, tired, and just beat down. Everyone wanted to know what the original orders were when... they didn't exist... not until the second or third week of taking pictures and Captain Phillips saw something—a something he didn't elaborate on—and turned into a maniac.

"No orders. No plot. No secret mission—well, not at first. I asked to use the high-def camera to take photos of those sunsets. My mom loves those. If you were ever in her house, you'd see that she has years and years of sunset photos that I've taken for her. From deployments, different assignments, even while on vacation. Cheesy, I know, but

Mom's always been amazed that the sun can look so different from different places. Anyway, one day, after I turned in the camera, Captain Phillips looked them over to ensure we hadn't revealed too much about our location, and the look on his face... my God... Nebraska will remember. The man looked stunned by one of the photos. Before you ask, I don't know which photo, precisely. The next day, he pulled us out of our normal duty and told us to take pictures of different locations at different times of the day."

"The Captain seemed deranged by that point," Nebraska added. "And got crazier by the day. If you ask me, all of this is one big misunderstanding."

"Misunderstandings don't get you kidnapped," Aaron quipped. "So, no orders?" Justin and Nebraska shook their heads. "I suppose we need to figure out who visited my mother tonight and then take another look at that camera."

Aaron looked at the forgotten business card perched on the edge of his dining table.

Then all three lunged for it.

Chapter Twelve

WHEN ALL OF this was over—Justin sincerely hoped it would be soon—he was going to sleep for days. And then he was going to think long and hard about the rest of his life.

But not right now because two hours of sleep just wasn't enough to put him a good mood.

Nebraska shook him awake. Weak rays of sun peeked through the window blinds.

"Time to get moving, buddy."

Justin groaned and opened his one good eye. He had fallen asleep on the couch. He'd rather have slept in Aaron's bed—but the mattress was still wet from their after-shower-we're-not-going-to-dry-ourselves-off-Hot-As-Hell-encounter.

"Are you wearing different clothes?" Justin asked Nebraska, then added quickly, "And cologne?"

"I went home and cleaned myself up. I do have an image to maintain, you know. I also went by your place and found some clothes for you. It's still jacked up, in case you were wondering, and I think you might have a squatter." Nebraska tossed the small pile of clothes on his stomach. "I think they're clean, but I couldn't tell since everything was on the floor."

Justin tried to sit up before he remembered that his shoulder had been re-injured after fighting over the business card. A business card that promised to lead them to another piece of the puzzle.

"You're the best." He stripped on the spot, though he

needed Nebraska's help in taking off his shirt and putting on a clean one.

"Sorry about punching you in the shoulder—" Nebraska said.

"What's going on here?" Aaron asked as he entered the living room and witnessed the disrobing. He wore different clothes, had shaved, and looked completely edible—even with the shiner Nebraska put on his cheek—and held Justin's duffle bag like it was shared property. Justin wanted to reach over and touch him.

"—I thought it was his face at the time," Nebraska continued.

"Well, you didn't miss the second time," Aaron said, feeling the bruise on his face.

"You certainly fit in now," Justin said dryly. "And it gives you a dangerous air." He looked between Aaron and Nebraska and felt some of the tension. "You two make up yet?"

"We decided to postpone our argument until after we meet up with the mysterious business card lady," Nebraska explained.

"Could be a dead end for all we know. Plus, I don't like the idea of someone else popping up out of the woodwork. What did the card say again?"

"You know what I vote for." Nebraska raised his hand. "I say we call Ashley Williams, though we'll have Justin call her since she isn't talking to me anymore, and have Good Morning Dallas to blow the lid off of this goddamn thing. Otherwise, one or all of us will be dead or locked up in some secret prison." He paused, then, "I just wanted to put that out there."

"That's comforting. Thanks for that," Aaron said. He picked up the business card, turned it over, and read, "Meet me at 6:30 am at the jogging trail entrance,

LeslieAnn Smith." On the front, it listed her name, followed by *Consultant*, and then a 1-800 number.

Nebraska raised his hand again. "Definitely a trap. I don't trust people whose first name is made up of two first names."

"If that's your only objection, then duly noted," Justin said. "You sure you know where she's talking about, Aaron?"

"Yeah. I jog it nearly everyday. Here." He handed the duffle bag over. It was lighter than Justin remembered. "Thought you might want it."

He looked through it: it had a haphazardly rolled-up uniform, boots, and his notebook. The notebook still held Aaron's letters. Justin felt Aaron watching him with interest, but he didn't say anything. He quickly put the notebook away.

They left the apartment and drove to the trail entrance using Mr. A's car. The parking lot and the trailhead were empty. The sun was already up, but it was a cloudy morning and it seemed more like dusk than the beginning of a day. The grass was wet with dew and Justin noticed, and then pointed out, a faint trail through the grass where the dew had been disturbed.

"I've got the revolver," Nebraska said to no one in particular.

Justin double-checked the clock. "Hopefully we won't need it, considering it's only as dangerous as far as we can throw it at someone. How far is the trail's entrance?"

"About a minute's walk," Aaron answered.

"Alright. Whoever LeslieAnn Smith is, she's already here. Let's hope she's a sweet little old lady that wants to chat, and nothing more. I'm somewhat tired of kidnappings and other detention-like car rides."

"And I was just getting used to that part," Aaron

quipped as they exited the car. For the briefest second, his fingers touched Justin's before he stepped away and followed Nebraska.

Justin's whole body tingled, and not because Aaron touched him—but because whatever happened in the next few minutes would change everything.

He was already sweating and, thankfully, the air was cool and damp. He caught up with his two friends and tried not to think of this meeting ending badly.

It seemed like he heard every sound: every bird chirp, every cricket cheep, their footsteps once the path turned into fine gravel, even his own heartbeat.

Then he heard the intake of his own breath and that of Nebraska's when they saw who LeslieAnn Smith was. Aaron wouldn't know her. How could he? He wasn't there the day they photographed the lovely Leia Woondiour or when they learned she had allegedly been abducted and sold into a human trafficking network.

Obviously, that wasn't true. Was anything true?

Leia Woondiour was LeslieAnn Smith, and she wasn't alone.

Chapter Thirteen

JUSTIN WAS BEGINNING to think that every woman around him was, in reality, someone other than who she said she was.

The next time he saw his own mother, he promised himself to ask her as many tricky, interrogating-type questions as he could think of to ensure she wasn't *one of them*.

Not that he knew what *one of them* actually meant as he stared at Leia/LeslieAnn and Detective Julia Fenske.

Aaron spoke first. "You were a photo subject, weren't you? Your hair is different, lighter now, but the likeness is unmistakable."

Justin blew up. "Who gives a shit about her hair?" He closed the gap and glared at her. He was yelling, and he didn't care. "I thought you were stolen. Dead. I mourned for you. And I thought it was my fault. My fault that you were hurt. Yet you stand here in perfect health, wearing designer clothing, claiming a different name, and leaving business cards in the middle of the night, all the while a part of me felt responsible. Do you know what that did to me? To Nebraska, when we found out?"

"I am sorry, Sergeant Hauten," she said in a British accent. She looked at Nebraska, and her expression was remorseful. "It was necessary."

"And you," he said to Julia. "Saying you needed a goddamn translator to take her statement. You must have thought I was so stupid. You know what? Just strap me into a highchair and feed me mashed-up peas, because that's how you've treated me this whole time: like a child. I am a Non-Commissioned Officer in the United States Army twenty-four hours a day. This isn't a make-believe world where you can pretend to fuck up the lives of everyone around you and not face the consequences. There are people mixed up in this who I think would actually kill us right here, right now. So you're going to answer every single question, starting right now."

Julia had dark circles under her eyes and her lips were pressed together so tightly they were white. She held her hands up halfway, as if surrendering, like she wasn't enjoying any of this either.

"That's not how it works, Sergeant," LeslieAnn said. "The less you know, the better."

"That's original," Nebraska said. "Then why are we all here?"

"Where are the children?" Justin yelled.

He didn't care about his own safety or that of his friends right then. He didn't care what happened next. Everything inside him hurt. He needed to know where those children were.

Aaron put a hand on his shoulder.

"I agreed to come here this morning so that you could see I was safe," LeslieAnn said. "The detective here told me how worried you were yesterday. I've already done too much. You will never see me again after this."

"What about those two kids and their families?" Nebraska asked.

"I have to go now. I've kept my bargain, detective. I need you to keep yours, too." LeslieAnn looked around her, a worried expression on her face. She looked like a hunted woman. Her hand moved out and hovered near his injured shoulder. It was a whispered touch that he barely felt. "You don't know it, but he saved your life that day."

What an odd and confusing thing to say, Justin thought. He couldn't tell if she was sad or happy about it.

The woman stepped back with a rueful smile, turned around, and quietly disappeared into the trees.

Chapter Fourteen

JUSTIN WATCHED HER go. In fact, they all did, before someone said something.

It sounded urgent, but the words didn't register. All he wanted to do was intently watch the spot Leia Woondiour walked into. The trees were full, but the small branch she passed by was still moving, like it was waving goodbye.

Maybe she would come back, and that was enough to root Justin's legs.

If Leia was alive—and thriving, by all appearances—then that could mean the two children were alive and safe and not in any danger. Did that also mean their families were alive as well? Was Mary Lovecross wrong? Did she intentionally mislead them all along?

"I don't know you and I don't think I can trust a word that comes out of your mouth," he had said as Lovecross drove him into the Badlands.

"That's the smartest thing you've said. It's simple: don't trust anyone," she had replied.

Don't trust anyone...

Justin questioned everything in those few seconds. A sudden thought barged in. He needed a phone, and not just any phone, but Mr. A's phone. It was still in his back pocket.

But then the thought vanished as a face suddenly appeared an inch away from his own, blocking his view of the spot Leia had walked into.

"Jesus Christ! Don't you listen?" It was Julia. She pushed him, and he very nearly lost his balance. "It isn't safe here. We need to go. Now!"

She turned and pulled him with her. Nebraska and Aaron were already at the grass and almost out of view.

"We need to follow Leia," Justin said instead as he tried to shrug Julia's hand off him. But her grip was firm and her nails dug into his skin.

"She won't answer any more of your questions. Besides, if you step in those woods, you'll probably be dead within five seconds."

That meant Leia had protection. But from whom? And why, before she left, did she look both scared and happy?

"Do you still have the camera in your possession?"

"No. I gave it to the first person that asked for it. Of course I still have it, you idiot."

Justin smiled at her. He liked this Julia a lot better than crazy, bimbo-acting Julia. They reached the parking lot, and Mr. A's car was still there. Justin wasn't sure why he was surprised by this fact; he supposed that in a movie, Mr. A's car would have disappeared, thus adding to the mystery. It was nice to know that in real life, cars didn't just vanish.

"Check the trunk, too," Julia instructed Nebraska. "Take everything out."

A hissing noise came from the car, and Justin noticed that Aaron was slashing the tires. He did a double take of the parking lot.

"Uh, how are we getting out of here? I don't see another car."

"I swear," Julia muttered. "I'm not going to repeat myself."

"Okay... that's not helpful."

"Jackpot!" Nebraska said happily as the trunk lid popped open. He pulled out a blue gym bag full of money.

Julia snatched it from him and did a cursory glance,

then zipped it up.

"Don't get any bright ideas. This is evidence." She checked her phone. "We've got about two minutes."

Nebraska grinned mischievously. "I can do a lot in two minutes." He immediately started ripping out the trunk's carpet.

"Two minutes until what?" Justin asked.

Julia shook her head and ignored him.

"How much money are we talking about?" Aaron asked, looking around. They were still alone in the parking lot.

Justin heard some crunching noises. Nebraska cracked opened the spare tire compartment.

"Thirty, forty grand, maybe. But the bag is half-empty, so he's gone through some bills recently. He was probably paying for information, maybe even temporary living quarters." She looked at Nebraska's handiwork. "What do we have here?" She pulled something up and whistled.

"A box?" Justin asked stupidly. He felt like a moron for simply standing there. Even Aaron was doing something now that he held the bag of money. That is, until Julia slammed the box into Justin's stomach and groin area.

He doubled over and once the nausea subsided, he saw that the box was full of folders.

Julia's phone beeped. "One minute. You checked the front and back seats? The glove box?"

"Yeah, everything," Nebraska said as he closed the trunk, then he added with a wink. "I can't do that kind of strip-down in two minutes, lady."

"Are you flirting?" Justin asked. Suddenly, he felt the urge to slap his friend.

"How would the future Mrs. Walker feel about that?" Aaron asked.

"The position might be open to additional applicants," Nebraska said. "What's it to you?"

Julia typed something into her phone, it chirped a quick response, and she said, "Time to run, boys."

Wait, what? "Run?" Justin asked. He looked stupidly at the box in his hands.

"Run!" Julia said over her shoulder. She had already started. So had Nebraska and Aaron.

"To where?"

"Don't make me shoot you."

Was Nebraska running with a tire iron?

Aaron turned around, carrying the money-filled gym bag and an exasperated expression. "I'll explain on the way."

Chapter Fifteen

SOMETIMES, ONE MILE felt like a hundred. He thought he was in pretty good shape, but Justin wasn't exactly prepared for a sprint. His face was throbbing, his vision blurred in the early morning sun glare. His shoulder felt like it was tearing apart. The box became heavy. And his breath became short and labored.

But the worst part were the horrified expressions that innocent bystanders gave them. The trail was a jogging track, after all, and it was equal parts humorous and embarrassing as the joggers running in the opposite direction spotted four individuals with a variety of wounds and facial disfigurement running by.

It didn't help that Nebraska was, in fact, carrying a tire iron.

Justin wasn't sure, but he thought he heard a woman scream as she passed them.

Thankfully, the agony ended when they reached an unassuming white Honda parked at the north entrance of the jogging path. Julia barely gave them enough time to jump in the car before she peeled out of the parking lot.

Justin needed one of Mrs. Parris' painkillers.

When he looked up, it wasn't the local TBI's office he saw, but a residential townhouse with a blue door, a sidewalk, and pottery buckets full of flowers. The townhouses on either side were similarly decorated.

"Your house?"

"It's one of our safe houses," she answered after they exited her car and filed into the house behind her. It was rather normal looking with comfortable living room furniture, bookshelves filled to the brim with books and DVDs, and homey lamps in each corner.

Nebraska flipped on a light switch, and the place flooded with bright lights. The place was clean. A little too clean for a lived-in appearance, in Justin's opinion.

Julia disappeared upstairs. Justin could hear doors opening and things beeping. It sounded like she was unlocking that safe she had mentioned earlier. He walked into the kitchen and propped his duffle bag on the tall granite countertop island in the center of the room and pulled out his notebook.

Aaron followed. "I didn't think we were staying long."

For a moment, they were alone. Justin could have turned. He felt a few jitters in his stomach, felt the lure and pull, wanted to touch Aaron's skin. Taste his lips, briefly.

Before Justin could turn, Aaron moved in closer. Justin felt his heat before he felt lips on the back of his neck. Aaron's hands brushed up against his hips, trapping him against the counter. His body followed suit and molded against Justin's backside.

Justin sucked in a breath as Aaron's hands moved around his waist, under the t-shirt, touching skin—dear God, his fingers were scorching hot. Those innocent kisses turned into small bites and sucks, his tongue rough and glorious and delicious.

He could still hear Julia upstairs, and it sounded like Nebraska was conveniently studying the books and DVDs in the next room, talking louder than what was called for.

He knew they didn't have much time and that at any moment—any second, really—they'd be discovered and interrupted. But, Jesus Christ, he wanted Aaron's hands to go down, into his pants, and touch him. To realize just how much the man turned him on. Justin's breathing became ragged.

Then Nebraska was talking louder and creaky footsteps sounded on the stairs. Aaron moved away after one last kiss. Justin cleared his throat and opened his notebook. But he could barely focus on the pages.

Julia bounced in with the camera and a laptop.

"Sorry that took so long. I couldn't find the power cord." She popped the camera's SD card into the laptop. "This way, we're not all huddled around a tiny screen."

As Julia did that, Justin moved Aaron's letters to the back of his notebook so he could flip through the pages. He remembered jotting down a few notes once when Captain Phillips had specifically asked them to take different images. If he recalled correctly, it was after he snapped the image of Leia Woondiour, er, LeslieAnn Smith. Or whoever the hell she was. At the time, she was just a lovely Afghani woman whose beauty melted their hearts. He turned the pages of his notebook rather harshly now.

"Nebraska," Justin said. Everyone was in the kitchen now. Aaron was keeping a healthy distance, observing, but Justin could feel the heat radiating from him. Julia continued working the laptop. "Do you remember when Captain Phillips flipped out after looking at our images?"

"It was like someone lit his ass on fire."

"Exactly. Now, I kept some notes, nothing elaborate or perfect or even detailed, but I think it was after Captain Phillips saw the image of the woman we knew as Leia Woondiour."

"Who we all know as LeslieAnn Smith now," Julia chimed in authoritatively, hands on hips, one resting on her firearm. Justin wondered how good of a shooter she was.

"Right. I think we figured that part out," Justin said.

He wanted to prove something first. "I have a theory, but I want Julia to fill us in." He turned to her. "I'd like for you to start from the beginning. How you got involved, why the unit is under investigation. Everything."

Chapter Sixteen

"It started fairly routine," Julia began. She gave Aaron an apologetic look. "Lieutenant Parris was reassigned here, it was within my jurisdiction, and the DC branch wanted to keep an eye on him and who he interacted with. I attached myself, literally at the hip, to your unit. Parties, mostly. I'd show up, and it didn't matter who was at the gate or who answered the damn door, someone would always let in the hot blonde wearing a short dress. Poor Justin, I have to hand it to you, you resisted me, and no, we didn't actually sleep together, even though I led you to believe it that one time. And... for the record, Aaron, I couldn't set my cap on you, now could I? I wasn't exactly your type, and I don't mean that with any disrespect. However, I saw how you looked at Staff Sergeant Justin Hauten. The All-American, muscular, good-looking guy that everyone admired. I practically forced myself on him because wherever Sergeant Hauten was, Lieutenant Parris was certain to follow."

"I'm not a puppy, detective," Aaron said before turning to Justin. "You thought you slept with her?" His face was guarded.

"She was very convincing."

"Women were always throwing themselves at Justin, though, strangely—or maybe not so strangely—he never noticed," she said. "And in the years I've been observing you, you turned them away. Why is that?"

"I don't see what this has to do with anything."

"I wouldn't mind knowing," Aaron said.

"Me, too, buddy," Nebraska chimed in with a hand on his chin, leaning against the counter, a fake, ponderous expression on his face. Always the smartass.

"My love life isn't relevant right now."

Julia looked torn, almost as if she wanted to make sure she didn't repulse him. She didn't, but Justin wasn't about to say that out loud.

"Anyway, the investigation pretty much panned out and when you deployed, I focused my efforts on combating the exploitation of children, going undercover for other operations—"

"Sleeping with my brother," Aaron interjected. "He's never been secretive about his partners."

"—and keeping a low profile." Julia's eyes turned black, but she ignored the barb, though her hand inched closer to her gun. "And then..." she hesitated and shrugged, as if they could figure out the last part on their own.

"We returned?" Justin asked.

"Exactly. A weird rumor began circulating through the law enforcement community, about a camera that had just entered the country with explosive evidence. So imagine my surprise and delight when I discovered that you had that camera."

"That's why you came over that day, shooed Aaron away, and tried to seduce me. You must have been thrilled when I asked you to protect the camera when Mary Lovecross showed up."

"It was like I had won the lottery and looked at the devil at the same time. I hope I never come across that woman again." She grimaced. "I ran the images through several federal databases. That's how I discovered Leia Woondiour was LeslieAnn Smith: her British passport."

"Did you know this before or after you detained us?"

"Before. She wouldn't talk, nor would Captain Phillips,

and when you didn't contradict me about my needing a translator to take Leia's statement, I knew then that you weren't part of some larger conspiracy. Later on, after you two left the station, I explained to LeslieAnn that you thought she was dead. She said she wanted to see you. I set everything up for this morning. But then..." she hesitated as her attention returned to the laptop. It was still downloading the photos and the progress bar was moving slowly.

"You saw her outside Aaron's apartment last night, right?" Nebraska asked.

Justin was thinking the same thing. Julia nodded, though somewhat uncomfortably, as if she had to admit that she was wrong about something. Justin noticed that she absently rubbed her belly. He wondered if she was also thinking about Aaron's asshole brother.

"Yes. I came over for two reasons; the first and main reason being that I needed to inform you that LeslieAnn wanted to see you in the morning. But when I saw her lurking outside the apartment last night, I was stunned to learn that she even knew where you would be, much less where one of you lived."

"Turns out we weren't there," Aaron said from the corner of the kitchen.

"I didn't have much of a chance to find that part out. Your mom opened the door and I hardly had the opportunity to introduce myself before I noticed LeslieAnn. Everything went through my mind, including the thought that I had been misled by you all."

"So we're liars now? Good to know," Justin said. "Curious, what was the second reason you came by?"

Julia eyed him. "You stole the station's Cherokee last night."

"Oh, yeah, right. I forgot about that."

The laptop dinged: the images had loaded. Justin opened the temporary folder and pulled the pictures up. He found the image of Leia Woondiour; she was sitting in a profile shot, watching the children play soccer. A small group of adults were a short distance behind her, near a white building. One of them was supposed to have been her future husband. It would have been one of the two men in the background. Did she dupe him? Was he somewhere, tending a broken heart, or was he in on whatever operation LeslieAnn Smith was working on?

"Consider it from my viewpoint: you claimed that you knew nothing of how she came to the United States, claimed that she was a victim of human trafficking, claimed that she was probably dead. And then I find her outside one of your apartments after I placed her in one of my safe houses? How would that look to you if the situation were reversed?"

No one said anything, so she continued, though after a small sigh. Justin listened but he continued to study the image and focus on the men in the picture.

"So, I confronted her. She was talking to someone on her cell phone, something about how a piece of something was broken and that her three-year nightmare was nearly over. Her conversation was very official sounding and cryptic, like she was talking to a superior. She jumped about ten feet when I said her name. LeslieAnn looked so scared and was shaking so much that I worried she might faint. But then I noticed the body."

"Tall man, white, jaw wired shut?" Nebraska asked proudly, to which Julia gave him an odd, how-could-you-possibly-know-that? look.

"Agent Baxter was in a serious automobile accident several weeks ago—"

"If by accident you mean my right fist, then yeah,"

Nebraska interrupted.

"Agent Baxter?" Justin asked at the same time.

"—and was the federal agent protecting LeslieAnn Smith until she reached her flight this morning. He apparently took ill, passed out, and she panicked. It was fortunate that I was there to take him to the ER and her back to the safe house."

Justin couldn't believe what he was hearing—nor, by his stunned expression—could Nebraska.

"I hate to break this to you, Julia," Justin began, "but your Agent Baxter is not who you think he is."

Her eyes narrowed, thinking. Surely the truth was obvious. "I've known Bill Baxter for a decade. We served in the Marine Corps together, joined the Bureau together."

"You have a knack for trusting the wrong men, don't you?" Aaron asked.

Any minute now, she was going to shoot one of them. Maybe all of them.

"We met him in Afghanistan. He was there when Captain Phillips shot me. Your Agent Baxter received that broken jaw courtesy of my friend here. And he didn't exactly pass out the way LeslieAnn described to you last night: Mrs. Parris drugged him, and he collapsed in Aaron's apartment, ruining a perfectly good end table by the way, while his partner, Mr. A, forced us out of the apartment at gunpoint. All in all, the beginning of a fun night."

"Impossible!"

"This might help clarify." Justin directed their attention to the image on the laptop, and zoomed in further on the men's faces. One face in particular. The man was the right size, height, and darker coloring; and even though the man had a full-beard, it was Mr. B. Julia's Agent Bill Baxter. "Leia Woondiour's fiancé."

Julia shook her head in disbelief. It was bitter pill to swallow. Justin had felt the same way when Captain Phillips shot him. "LeslieAnn Smith might not be so innocent, then," she said with a loud sigh. "And stupid me got her out of the country this morning."

Chapter Seventeen

A FEW MOMENTS went by in silence. Even the kitchen appliances knew to stay quiet.

Julia called someone. A lot of someones, even the emergency room to see if Agent Baxter was still there—he was—and Justin began to hope. Hope that LeslieAnn could be detained and questioned. Hope that Captain Phillips wasn't such a scumbag. Hope that the two other children who had allegedly been kidnapped were indeed safe, at home, and with family. He wanted to walk out of here and forget all about this. Go back to a regular life with the Army, spend time with Aaron, and take up some sort of calming, non-violent, hobby. Like knitting or racquetball. Or sex.

But three people stood in his way: Mary Lovecross, Mr. A, and Captain Phillips.

I need to know how it all ends, he thought. *I need to know why.*

Aaron stood next to him, observing, as Justin flipped through the images, hitting the laptop's keyboard a little harder than necessary.

"So which of the two do you think Captain Phillips recognized?" Aaron asked quietly as Julia shouted into her phone in the other room. Nebraska flanked Justin's other side.

"I would guess LeslieAnn; she isn't too disguised. Only her hair is darker here."

"Maybe she isn't involved in the way we think," Nebraska offered. "Maybe she's like Julia here: undercover and just got mixed up accidentally. You heard Julia earlier. The woman was scared, jittery, and if you ask me, she looked like a hunted woman this morning on the jogging trail. Like maybe the devil was on her heels."

Justin immediately thought of Lovecross. She would know. But it wasn't like he could call her up and ask a few questions. He didn't even know how to get a hold of her, or if he even really wanted to do something as stupid as see her again.

Then he instantly sobered up and remembered. He pulled out Mr. A's phone. "Do you still have LeslieAnn Smith's business card?"

Aaron found it in his wallet and placed it on the kitchen counter, next to the laptop which made several loud beeping noises. An image popped up, almost like an instant message alert, and Justin disregarded everything in his head.

It was a picture of a small, one-story ranch house with yellow shutters, a small side garden, and an old baby-blue station wagon parked in the driveway. Tall trees framed the background.

Something clattered to the floor. The cell phone.

"I never took—" Justin could barely breathe. A date-time stamp stood proudly in the bottom right corner of the image. He unexpectedly felt very sick to his stomach.

Aaron leaned over. "Who is that?" He pointed to the petite woman in the photograph.

The back and side of Nebraska's head filled Justin's vision as his friend moved in to view the screen.

"This *so* isn't good," Nebraska said. "How is this possible? I thought you secured the camera, Julia?"

"It didn't come from the camera," Aaron said. And he was right. It couldn't have. Someone must have sent the image through Julia's secure TBI network.

"What's going on?" Julia asked, her face red. Her cell phone was still plastered to her ear, and Justin could barely make out the *wok-wok-wok* voices coming through.

Nebraska turned the laptop ninety degrees to the left.

"Mary Lovecross is standing outside Justin's mother's house. It was taken five minutes ago."

+++

It was like his mind was on autopilot and laced with land mines. He didn't know how he got the car keys from Julia—did he take them from her, or did she offer them? Did they all follow him on their own accord, or did he order them?

He didn't care about the brakes or stop signs or the honking horns of other cars as he drove away from Julia's safe house.

Justin's thoughts went from bad to worse and then to whatever level was worse than worse.

Hell? Yes. His mind was torturing him, and somebody somewhere was enjoying it.

Julia said that looking at Mary Lovecross was like meeting the devil. LeslieAnn Smith had looked like she had the devil on her heels.

Mary Lovecross certainly was a mystery within a mystery. A Pandora's box. She seemed like the type of person who would lead him in circles just for fun, as if she wanted to keep him out of her way. She had an operation to control.

Operation Heart.

Was any of it true?

The photos did exist; that much was true. He took them, after all. But did they actually create what Lovecross said they did? Pictures of military bases, operations, and other agencies at work? All Justin did was take pictures of the surrounding landscapes from different angles and at various times of the day. Not to mention the precious images of those children. Captain Phillips certainly wanted something; he sent them back over and over again to snap more images within a specific five-mile radius.

Surely Justin would remember if he saw military personnel in the background. But he had to acknowledge that he wouldn't see something if it was meant to be hidden. He wasn't trained for that. He wasn't an intelligence analyst; he didn't know what to look for, and, if he wanted a bit more honesty floating around in his choking mind, Justin wasn't exactly the smartest person around. He mostly got by on common sense, Southern charm, sarcastic wit, and his ability to get along with anyone in any situation.

Including assholes.

The Army had shoved a semi-automatic machine gun in his hands, told him who the bad guy was, and said to shoot if they a) got too close, b) shot at you, and c) injured a buddy.

But this was different. Whoever the bad guy was, the rules were asymmetric. It was like a game of chess where the pieces weren't confined to their assigned squares or to their normal moves; or where the stairs were on the ceiling rather than the floor. It was the type of game where you were kidnapped and bullied and lied to, and even the lies were lies.

And then they show up at your mother's house, looking a little to innocent for Justin's comfort, and send a message to a laptop through a secured network that they had no idea you'd be in possession of. It was almost as if Lovecross knew what he'd do before he did it. Which was creepy and terrifying. And utterly brilliant, he would surmise if he wasn't so fucking pissed off right now.

He wanted to destroy everything in his path; he wanted to scream and yell and get emotional. But he did the exact opposite. A deadly calm came over him.

So the threat was clear to Justin; he just didn't want to admit it, and the way that Nebraska and Aaron were looking at him said volumes. Even Julia had a steely, determined, calm demeanor. She also had a loaded weapon.

Justin had loyalty. And love.

If they were about to face the devil, they would do it together.

Chapter Eighteen

"SO WHAT DO we know about Lovecross?" Julia asked. They were several minutes from Justin's mother's house. So far, Justin hadn't caused any accidents.

"For starters, other than being scary, she obviously had access to your safe house," Nebraska said from the backseat. Given the space and the way Justin turned each corner, Nebraska practically sat on top of Julia.

Aaron nodded. "And she must have known that we were on our way to retrieve the camera. She's watching us. So that means she probably knows we met LeslieAnn this morning."

"Or helped set it up," Justin said evenly. The steering wheel was receiving the bulk of his wrath. "Who were you texting on your phone back at the park, Julia? It kind of seemed like you were coordinating with someone."

"It was a series of alarms to keep me on track. Let's just say I had to make several promises to LeslieAnn in order for her to agree to see you. One of those conditions was that we'd be out of the park within ten minutes."

"Or what?"

"Her protection unit would have made the experience a little less fun."

"I like your interpretation of fun," Nebraska said.

"You know, I got the feeling that we were being watched the whole time," Aaron said, shuddering.

"So, back to Lovecross," Julia said. "State Department or Justice Department?"

"How about both?" Nebraska suggested with a shake of

his head. "I bet she can tap into street surveillance cameras and watch our every move."

"Sounds like a lot of work for such a small reward," Justin said.

"Depends on your definition of small reward," Julia said.

"She'd have a team at her beck and call to keep her informed," Nebraska said.

"Or a tracking device," Aaron suggested. "That'd be a lot easier and more reliable."

Nebraska grunted. "Yeah, well, I like my idea better."

"When I worked in Washington DC," Aaron said, ignoring Nebraska, "there were individuals who had access to pretty much everything. It was a special badge that granted access to multiple federal agencies, intelligence agencies, and the defense department, too. This Lovecross woman could have access like that."

"TBI is a State agency, not Federal," Julia offered, though there was doubt in her voice, hinting that she wasn't sure about anything anymore.

Join the club, Justin thought.

"But you said the Washington DC branch wanted you to keep an eye on me, right?" Aaron asked. He tried to keep his voice neutral, but Justin wasn't fooled.

"Yeah, but..."

"Is that a normal request? They probably wanted access to your files on the unit and your databases, right?"

"What are you getting at?" Justin asked. He threw Aaron a hard look. They didn't have time for this. It seemed like they were getting off topic.

Justin made the last turn, the tires screeched, and then they were there, right in front of his mom's house. The house he grew up in. He parked on the street and in plain view of anyone looking outside. A curtain moved.

"No, it isn't a normal request, at least since I've been with the TBI," Julia answered heatedly, pushing Nebraska off her. Her clipped tone made it apparent she didn't appreciate being asked procedural questions. It was also possible she didn't enjoy redheaded lumberjacks lounging on her, either. "Why?"

"I've never been one for conspiracies and the like," Aaron said. "Generally they're a waste of time and serve to keep you away from whatever nugget of information that may be true."

"Seriously, what are you getting at?" Justin repeated. His hand was on the door handle. All he wanted to do was bolt out of the car and rush into the house. But, for some reason, he held back. The look on Aaron's face was grim.

"After a while, the circumstances stop sounding like random events. My assignment to an infantry unit even though I'm not an infantry officer. Julia's told to investigate the unit. Captain Phillips gives you a special job downrange, then he shoots you, suddenly starts acting crazy. He's not even detained or charged, but is found hiding in LeslieAnn's closet, apparently waiting to, what, assassinate her? You've been kidnapped, what, twice now, by several agencies? Someone you thought was abducted and dead turns out to be an undercover State Department agent, perhaps with nefarious intentions. Julia's friend and partner, Agent Baxter is Mr. B. And now, this Lovecross character is at Justin's mother's house for some reason. Did I miss anything?"

"The Itchy Nail," Nebraska said.

"You guys have been to The Itchy Nail? I thought that place was an urban legend—" Julia said.

"The point is," Aaron cut in, "doesn't this whole thing feel orchestrated?"

Chapter Nineteen

THE DEVIL PROBABLY came in several forms, depending on who it was visiting.

Justin's devil wore her jet-black hair in a super short, asymmetrical bob, her slim figure outfitted in an expensive cream-colored designer skirt suit and red stiletto heels. Mary Lovecross looked surprisingly at ease and at home in his mother's cheerful living room, sitting on an ancient floral couch. Justin threw open the front door just as she placed her coffee cup on a coaster on the small doily-covered table in front of her. *Such manners,* Justin thought.

Mrs. Hauten's face brightened whereas Lovecross' countenance was one of boredom and amusement. She had probably timed him to see just how long it took him to get here.

"See, it's just as I suggested. I knew he'd be along shortly," Justin's mother said cheerily as she turned to him. Her expression went from being pleased to downright horrified. Her eyes rounded and she stood suddenly. "What on earth happened to your face? Cuts... Bruises? Are you limping?"

Nebraska, Aaron, and Julia filed in after him.

"I see that you have a guest, mom," Justin said evenly as he hugged her fiercely and didn't let go. She squirmed in his arms.

"Justin, I can't breathe."

He let her go just in time for Nebraska to scoop her up and kiss her forehead. "We're just so damn happy to see you, Mrs. Hauten."

"Yes," she laughed nervously, straightening her now-disheveled hair once Nebraska set her down. "I can see that." She turned to the woman on the couch. "Ms. Lovecross said she had a few more questions about the incident." Her attention moved behind Justin. "Julia, is that you? My goodness, I—I didn't recognize you in all those clothes."

Justin never took his eyes off Mary Lovecross. A smile tugged on her ageless face.

"Yes, Julia certainly has a certain chameleon effect, doesn't she, boys?" Lovecross asked. "One day, she'll start using her brain instead of her body to get the information she needs."

"That's what ugly people say," Julia said tightly.

Lovecross laughed. "You see what I want you to see."

Mrs. Hauten suddenly looked ill at ease. She started to lower herself on the couch, hesitated, and finally moved to stand near the couch, searching everyone's face for some sort of unspoken explanation.

"What's going on, Justin?" she finally asked.

"I wish I knew," he answered. "However, I don't want you anywhere near Mary Lovecross." Justin looked the woman over and didn't find any overt evidence of weapons. She had to have soldiers somewhere. The house backed up into woods. Anyone could be back there: he would know, he used to build forts and hide back there as a kid.

"How did you get into my safe house, my network?" Julia asked. She stood by the door, legs apart, arms crossed in an authoritative stance. Her fingers tickled the butt of her holstered weapon.

"I'm sure by now you will have realized that not many doors are closed to me."

"Yeah, but I doubt that you're highly welcomed,"

Aaron said.

"If my goal was to be universally liked, I'd specialize in creating cute kitten videos or running the local Girl Scouts."

Nebraska snorted. "What is your specialty?"

"Isn't it obvious?" she asked. A perfectly groomed eyebrow rose, and Justin knew he could never fathom the intelligence that was now staring him down. "To protect this country at all costs."

"You certainly have a funny way of showing it, lady," Nebraska muttered.

"Do you think that's necessary?" Justin's mother whisper-hissed at Nebraska. Even now, his mother would think about manners and proper courtesy above all else. She was a former Miss Texas, after all.

"Sometimes, I have to give a little nudge here and there before the pieces start behaving," Lovecross said. She sounded bored, like they weren't asking the right questions. So far, she didn't seem inclined to remove them from his mother's house. She was waiting on someone or something to happen.

"Are you saying we're these pieces?" Aaron asked.

"Don't flatter yourselves."

Something about the word *pieces* set his brain in motion.

"What happened three years ago?" Justin asked. He didn't know if he was on the right track, not until he saw her expression.

Justin had five sets of eyes on him. For the briefest second, a small look of surprise came over Lovecross before it disappeared.

He was the only one to see it.

Chapter Twenty

"VERY GOOD, SERGEANT Hauten," Lovecross said with something close to praise. "What do you think happened three years ago?"

"You discovered Operation Snatcher and traced it back to someone in our unit," Justin answered.

"You're getting warmer."

"Do we really have time for Twenty Questions?" Julia asked. Her fingers were definitely touching the weapon now. "I don't know about the rest of you, but I think the woman is stalling until someone else gets here."

Lovecross smiled. She took an unhurried sip from her coffee cup, adjusted the doily-coaster, and replaced the cup. "Do I look like the type of person that needs assistance, Detective? Trust me, if I wanted to disarm you of your firearm, I would have done it by now. As for the rest of you, the fact that you're even still alive is a testament to sheer stupidity on their part or luck on yours."

Justin felt a tug on his shirt. "I'm very confused, here," his mom said. "I can't tell if she's on your side or what."

"Is the devil ever on anyone's side?" Nebraska asked.

"The devil?" Lovecross asked with a smirk. "I haven't been called that in ages. It was a silly nickname, but it had its uses. It's nice to see that it's making a comeback. I really must be pissing some folks off."

"Are you referring to the Misters A and B?" Justin asked.

"Now, *those* are stupid nicknames," Lovecross said.

"Yes, those two; but more specifically, who they work for. And then who *that* person works for. I'm most interested in him."

She grinned a little crazy-like, and Justin wondered just how sane the woman was.

"Who do they work for?" Everyone asked at the same time, even Justin's mom, who was now hiding behind Justin's back. He could smell her floral perfume.

"The group behind Operation Snatcher, of course," she said evenly. "The same group whose illegal actions your company commander supposedly had you photograph, Sergeant Hauten."

"Supposedly?" Justin asked. What the fuck did that mean? Was it all for show? "Captain Phillips wasn't working with them then?"

Lovecross shook her head.

"So that's why Captain Phillips came around that day with those two idiots, demanding the camera," Nebraska said. "They must have confronted him and then he must have promised to give them the camera."

She laughed. "And why would he ever agree to do that?"

Nebraska sighed. "Well, I'm stumped."

"It was never about that, was it?" Justin asked. Everything clicked. The woman was brilliant. "The kids, their families, and Leia Woondiour. They were never harmed in the first place. You staged it so that it would appear that they were kidnapped and that their families were slaughtered, and you blamed it on this group. You were playing them before they even knew you were on to them. But how?"

Just then, the front window shattered.

Shards of glass and flying potted aloe vera plants, suddenly ejected from their normally peaceful window ledges, interrupted whatever Lovecross was about to say. Two bloody and disheveled bodies crashed through the large living room window and fell onto the floor with loud grunts and thuds and the crunching of glass.

Mr. A, looking a lot worse for the wear, stood up and yanked the other man, who turned out to be Captain Phillips, to his feet and silently put a very large knife to the Captain's throat.

Julia, almost as instantly, drew her weapon and trained it on Mr. A. "Drop your weapon!"

Justin wasn't sure how the situation could get worse, but it did when he noticed that blood was dripping from the Captain's hands and his former company commander seemed out of it. Had he been tortured? He looked resigned to his fate.

Mr. A, on the other hand, appeared extremely agitated, hyper, and on the verge of a mental breakdown. It didn't help that none of the ink had faded from Mr. A's face. DICKHEAD was still very legible on the man's forehead. In fact, it looked entirely possible that other people had written on him while he was passed out at The Itchy Nail because ARRR was also all over his face. The pirate guy?

"I said: Drop your weapon! Now!" Julia's eyes darkened when she addressed Mary Lovecross. "Is nothing in TBI's domain secure from you people?"

"Captain Phillips has a ten-inch knife digging into his neck, and that's what you're upset about?" Aaron asked.

"It's not everyday that one of my detainees leaves *my* facility without *my* permission," Julia said.

"Oliver Phillips is not and has never been a detainee," Lovecross said evenly. The woman was still sitting as calmly as before they crashed through his mother's window. "At least, not in the legal sense. And, darling," Lovecross said to Julia, "please stop your yelling and ordering and other such nonsense."

Julia sighed and lowered her weapon slightly.

"Oh, don't do that. I like the idea of your weapon trained on him. That will mean seven firearms are aimed at his head at this very moment."

"Justin," his mom whispered, "I don't like your friends."

"You mean them and not us, right?" Nebraska asked, pointing a finger in the direction of Mr. A and Captain Phillips and then at Mary Lovecross.

"Shut up!" Mr. A yelled.

"Are you okay, Oliver?" Lovecross asked.

He shrugged. "This isn't as bad as Moscow, but I've been better."

Moscow?

"I think we might remember Moscow differently," she laughed. "Yes, it has been a tiring affair. The assignment is nearly over."

"Spare us the fucking chit-chat, woman," Mr. A hissed. "I swear, I am one inch away from killing Captain Phillips unless you hand everything over."

"Oliver knows his assignment better than anyone and he agreed to it, even with the risks involved. Believe me when I say this: my agent is toying with you and has allowed himself to be put into this situation. He can free himself at any time, but, then again, that wouldn't get you here in front of me. Which is, naturally, what I asked him to do."

"My employer is not in the mood for your games," Mr. A said through gritted teeth.

"No, I don't expect that she is," Lovecross answered.

"You wanted him to come here?" Justin asked. "Do you make it habit of putting everyone you meet in danger?"

"It's a hazardous job," she replied casually. "Same as

being in the military, Sergeant."

"I completely disagree with your methods."

"What does he want you to hand over?" Aaron asked.

"It's sort of cute, actually," she said. "Mr. A's employer is under the impression that I'm willing to negotiate with those that betray our country. Sergeant Hauten, you asked what happened three years ago, and I'm proud of you for figuring that out, even though I know it was a shot in the dark. You aren't all that bright, but you possess common sense and an integrity that I admire."

"Uh, thanks," Justin said.

"Don't worry, buddy," Nebraska said over Justin's shoulder. "I think you are, you know, brighter than most."

"Who cares!" Mr. A screamed. His hand trembled, and a small bead of blood began to run down Captain Phillips' neck.

Lovecross continued on, unfazed, "Three years ago, a terrible tragedy occurred in a small village outside of Kabul. Dozens of women were abducted from this village, to include one of the United States' humanitarian teams in the region, and smuggled into an unknown, at the time, human trafficking organization."

"Mr. A's employer?" Aaron asked.

"His employer's employer," Lovecross answered solemnly. "The victims have never been recovered, and I have spent the last three years setting up this trap. I had the FBI move one of their finest detectives to this area once I selected your Army outfit as the unit to strategically place Oliver Phillips with."

"I suppose this was based on our deployment schedule?" Justin asked.

"My God, you actually believe her?" Mr. A asked. "You can't prove any of this!"

"Three years' worth of data is now in the hands of the

U.S. Attorney's Office. You'll find that if you and your employer so much as try to open a supermarket club card, your whereabouts will be sent to us and you'll be picked up within, oh, six or seven minutes. Maybe less. Oh, and guess what? Your employer was picked up forty minutes ago by a Texas State Trooper." Mr. A's face fell. "All of your financials have been frozen, which I'm sure you've recently discovered. Even the secret account." She raised an eyebrow mischievously. "Your attempt to infiltrate our secure networks through that dumb SD camera disc was rather clever, but easily thwarted. It was an honest try, though. So E for effort."

So that's why he let me have the camera after Mr. A questioned them at that old, decrepit country police station.

"Oh, my God. He saw a bigger target and thought he could exploit it," Justin said out loud.

Mr. A grunted like a wild animal. He refastened his grip on Captain Phillips and jostled him around erratically. "I will kill him."

Julia's posture stiffened as she slightly moved and re-aimed. "I'd love to shoot this asshole."

"That's not necessary," Lovecross said. "Oliver, you know what to do."

Chapter Twenty-One

APPEARANCES CAN CERTAINLY be deceiving, especially in his mother's overly knick-knack-decorated living room.

And Captain Phillips appeared to be too calm, given the circumstances.

Justin held his breath as he watched Captain Phillips' bloody fingers. They twitched slightly and then he appeared to do a countdown, each finger tick-marking against his leg one at a time until his entire body moved like that of a warrior—fluid, fast, and as one unit.

Justin noticed that just before the last finger tick-mark, Mary Lovecross picked up her coffee from the table and nodded.

The room suddenly went funeral room quiet, and a quick sucking noise came from Mr. A's mouth. The ten-inch blade clattered to the floor. Captain Phillips dislodged himself easily from Mr. A's grip, turned, grabbed the man's head and, with Herculean strength Justin had never before witnessed, threw the man over his shoulders and onto the coffee table, crushing it to the floor.

Mr. A did not get up.

"Dear Lord, is he dead?" Mrs. Hauten asked, hand over mouth.

"No," Captain Phillips said, breathing hard. Justin knew, from military hand-to-hand combat training, that it wasn't easy to hurl a two-hundred-pound man over one's shoulders. "But he'll wish he were in a few hours."

"What of his partner?" Lovecross asked as she studied the man on the floor. She crouched down and retrieved all of the items from his pockets. A small smile formed on her guarded face.

"FBI detailed him after he regained consciousness at the hospital." He turned to Justin. "Sergeant Hauten, I'm sorry about everything, man. This work can be dangerous, and I knew you were trustworthy. The shoulder... I can't even begin to apologize enough for having to do it."

Justin nodded. "I think I understand the reason why. Just don't call me for your next operation."

Oliver Phillips—if that was his real name—smiled, stuck out his non-bloody hand, and Justin shook it.

Mary Lovecross stood as several uniformed soldiers quickly entered, handcuffed, and removed the downed Mr. A.

"Stop by the downtown FBI office, collect Objective B, and take them both to bunker ninety," she told one of the soldiers.

"Roger that, Madam Undersecretary." Captain Phillips left with them.

As Lovecross walked around the bright living room, everyone gave her a wide berth. Julia looked like she wanted to ask a million questions, probably wondering if she was the finest FBI agent mentioned earlier; his mother mourned the loss of her windows, the window treatments, plants, and her coffee table. She was already wiping up the blood droplets from the floor.

"We'll fix this, Mom. I promise."

"Sergeant Hauten, a word please." Lovecross motioned for him to stand next to her. Naturally, Nebraska and Aaron followed suit. She eyed his friends, like she knew they'd follow him anyway, but she didn't order them away.

"You are an Under Secretary of State?" Justin asked.

She nodded. "Yes, the Under Secretary for Civilian Security, Democracy, and Human Rights." She studied a photograph on his mother's wall. "Did you take this?" It was one of the many sunsets he'd captured over the years.

"It was the sunset before I enlisted in the Army. I took it just as the sun hit the trees behind the house. I believe it is her favorite."

"Your skill has improved over the years, Sergeant," she said, which meant, to him, that she thought it was an unskilled-looking photograph. Which it was. "It is lovely. I can see why she displays it prominently." Then she switched topics. "When did you figure out LeslieAnn Smith was involved?"

"I guessed when I suspected the number on Mr. A's cell phone was the same number on the business card LeslieAnn Smith left at Aaron's apartment. Plus, she said something to me earlier today that didn't make much sense."

"What did she say?"

"That Captain Phillips saved my life when he shot me," Justin answered and absently rubbed his shoulder. "It didn't make sense that she'd say that. How involved is she, exactly?"

"She's the employer and Objective Heart. I've been chasing her for years."

Nebraska chimed in. "I told you I didn't trust anyone with two first names for the first name."

"That's a stupid philosophy," Lovecross said, but not too unkindly. "But she was correct. Oliver shooting you kept you from being implicated in the entire ordeal. Instead of being free to roam, being detained multiple times, and getting into several life-altering events, you would have been sitting in a real jail awaiting treason charges."

"I'm not sure which is preferable, actually," Justin said with a half-hearted laugh.

"So the images were harmless? Made to look like we were closing in on their operations?" Nebraska asked.

It appeared at first that she wouldn't answer. Doubtful she liked giving away operational secrets. But it was because of the camera they all got involved in the first place. She at least owed them an explanation, right?

"Let's just say you can keep the images," she said instead of truly answering. Justin knew they'd never know the full story. "Some of them will frame nicely."

"What happens next?" Aaron asked.

Lovecross sighed soundlessly. For a moment, she appeared small, fragile, and weary. Justin felt the urge to hug her, but he'd never dare. She would not appreciate the gesture.

"I'll make her life hell until she reveals where her father is—her employer and a ruthless criminal lord—and then I'll break her so I can I rescue or lay to rest everyone that she kidnapped, including my daughter. She was a volunteer with that humanitarian team three years ago."

"I'm so sorry," Justin said softly. A lot of things made sense now, about her behavior, her single-mindedness in solving Operation Heart—solving the pain in her own heart—even if it meant making his life hell. All things considered, she probably could have made things worse. A lot worse.

Her head tilted up, her eyes razor sharp again, Mary Lovecross had a new mission. She moved to the door and handed him a business card.

"Call me if you ever need anything, kiddo."

And then, like a ghost, she was gone.

Chapter Twenty-Two

ONCE THE DUST settled—and it was rather fast after Lovecross and her soldiers left—Justin sat down on the double rocker at the end of the porch and drank a glass of sweetened iced tea. The chair creaked. The sun was high, the weather warm, the front window was already boarded up. He would never get up again if his legs and back had any say in the matter. In fact, he might need to be carried away.

The screen door clapped and Aaron stepped out and sat beside him, their sides touching.

"Crazy day, huh?" Aaron asked playfully, squeezing his thigh. Justin studied his profile. He wanted to rub the stubble on his jaw—to memorize every feature of his face, including that newly formed bruise—and pull him in. A small smile tugged at the corners of Aaron's mouth. "Nebraska's trying to get all of us to go to The Itchy Nail for dinner tonight. He's explaining the place to your mom and confusing the hell out of her."

They'd all end up with food poisoning, for sure, Justin thought. Nebraska always confused his mother.

Justin shook his head but laughed. "He would, wouldn't he? I think I'd rather stay in. A lengthy hibernation sounds good right about now."

"So, it's all over, right?"

"Shit, I hope so," Justin said. He didn't miss the concern written all over Aaron's face. The resolution of it all certainly felt thin to him, but at least his major concerns were addressed. "All I care about is that those children were never in danger to begin with. If it was all a setup to catch Operation Heart, or whatever, then I'll let the rest of it go. Though I have a feeling that Lovecross will show up unexpectedly sometime in the future."

"I think she has a professional crush on you."

Justin's thick eyebrows narrowed. "That's stupid." He couldn't imagine that she'd be impressed with him or anyone else, for that matter. Surely they were all ants in Mary Lovecross' book. But the look in Aaron's eyes said he wasn't about to drop the topic.

"You inspire loyalty in others," Aaron answered simply. "You can't buy that. That's why Captain Phillips chose you and why one of the most powerful women in the State Department trusted you. They saw what I've always seen and why Nebraska probably wants to surgically attach himself to you. Why do think Julia felt the need to confess her pregnancy to you?" Justin shrugged. He didn't want to remember that night, or the look on Aaron's face. It would tear a hole in his heart, for sure. Hell, in reality, he just wanted to forget the last few days altogether. "She didn't want to lose your trust, that's why. I doubt she even realizes it. You might have been a job to her, following you around to work her investigation, but at the end of the day, she respected you enough to come clean, confess, and look for acceptance."

Was it true? Was any of it?

"I never set out to gain the loyalty of others. I had no idea. Not really. Is that what you want from me? My loyalty?" Justin asked. He tried to keep the insecurity out of his voice. Wasn't loyalty just another form of love? Is that what he felt for his friends, and for Aaron? His feelings for Aaron were completely different from what he felt for Nebraska. Way different.

"You already know how I feel, Justin. Nothing's

changed."

Everything inside him rejoiced. It was like a magnet pulled him into Aaron. Declare it! Say it! He swallowed hard. "I l-lov—"

But just as he was about finally tell Aaron how he felt, the screen porch clattered open loudly and Nebraska and Julia stomped out. Nebraska's beefy hands were behind his back, as if he was at parade rest, and it took a moment for Justin to realize that his friend was handcuffed.

Good Lord, now what!

Julia pushed him down the porch stairs.

"What's going on?" Justin asked. The muscles in his legs protested when he tried to stand, so he stayed put.

"Oh, don't mind us," Nebraska said cheerfully. Justin knew full well that Nebraska wouldn't be handcuffed unless he allowed it to happen.

"You don't actually think that I'm going to let you get away with stealing the station's Jeep Grand Cherokee last night, do you?" Julia asked acerbically.

"Like I said, buddy, don't mind us." Nebraska turned around to face Julia, now walking backward as she pushed him along the small stone walkway leading away from the porch. "I admire your dedication for getting the job done," he cooed. "Perhaps we can exchange strategies later on?"

Julia and Aaron both laughed as Justin groaned.

"I won't fully book him," Julia explained loudly, an eyebrow rising impishly. "But I'll make him pay for his crimes, all the same." Justin had a feeling that the day was young for those two and that perhaps a new couple was in the process of forming. He wasn't sure how he felt about that.

Julia's white Honda sped away. The only vehicle left was his mother's ancient baby blue Suburban. He wanted to laugh until he cried. He wondered how they would leave and then that thought vanished.

Aaron's thumb caressed his bottom lip and his breath caught just as he detected Aaron's warm, earthy scent. He wanted to submerge himself in that scent. He didn't care that he was on his mother's porch. Justin released the tension, released his worries, and let go of the barriers that would allow him to finally open his heart.

"So, what were you saying a moment ago?" Aaron asked, smiling.

Justin breathed in deeply. He didn't know what he did to deserve Aaron's love, but he wouldn't question it. He wouldn't question how he felt; which everyone else around him seemed to know before he did.

"I'm saying that I love you," Justin said confidently. Aaron's smile was larger than life, and surely Justin's matched.

Something glittered at Aaron's neck as they each moved in closer. Justin could barely make out that it was a silver, oblong, delicate looking object on a thin silver chain. His fingers played with it, his thumb pulsed against Aaron's neck, the heat scorching him and pulling him in deeper. It was the same design on the cigarette lighter Aaron's brother Doug had dropped at the Parris residence. A family crest? Would the Parris family accept him?

It didn't matter. He'd worry about it later. Though very briefly, in between the fluttering of his heart and the fluttering of his eyelashes, Justin did think about telling Aaron about what happened to Doug.

But not right now. Aaron's lips felt too damn good to think about anything else.

"So, about that hibernation you mentioned a few moments ago..." Aaron said in between the gentle, loving kisses that Justin couldn't get enough of.

"Hmm, yeah?"

"Want to get started on it?"

Justin didn't hesitate. There was no need. It felt right.

"Definitely."

Epilogue

Two Weeks Later

It was oh-dark-thirty, the sun was a weak orange ring, and it rained like God was pissed off at the world. Justin's uniform didn't fit because it was brand new and, for some mysterious reason, he seemed to have gained a few pounds over the last two weeks. The squatter in his apartment had nicked everything: uniforms, civilian clothes, dishes, and even the half-used bar of soap from the shower.

Justin didn't care. He was in love.

He moved into Aaron's apartment—it didn't take much coaxing from Aaron before he agreed—not that he had much to move in with. He spent his days at the brigade armory doing inventory, and steamy nights with Aaron. Exploring. Learning. Loving. He couldn't get enough of his lover and practically attacked him the second they closed the apartment door each night.

"Hauten!" someone shouted from the armory's split doorway. It was the brigade commander's executive officer. "Jesus, man. I had to call your name three times. Get with it. Colonel Winters wants to see you in his office right now."

"Roger that, sir." Justin secured the weapons room, ran up four flights of stairs—passing the executive officer in the process—and breathlessly entered the commander's office spaces. Aaron and Nebraska were standing there also, pretending to not know each other, but both of their faces lit up when he came in, though only Nebraska waved.

Aaron maintained his spot next to the commander's

ancient secretary. Fraternization between officer and enlisted was still illegal in the Army, and his relationship with Aaron had to be a secret. Only Nebraska knew, and he'd as soon as confess to the relationship than let Justin get into trouble.

If this impromptu meeting with Colonel Winters was about that, then they were all screwed. Literally.

"Lieutenant Parris," a gravelly voice barked from behind the commander's door. Aaron went in and was out again in two minutes. Justin gave him a searching look, but Aaron only winked at him as he walked out, through the reception area, and left.

Okay. Whatever it was, it wasn't too bad.

"Don't worry, Hotten. I got this one."

Nebraska hit him with a rolled-up People magazine. He'd been carrying it around ever since the magazine interviewed him about the botched Ashley Williams proposal—he didn't keep it a secret—and plastered his face on the damn cover, titling it *"A Soldier's Heartbreak"*. Nebraska was getting bags of letters a day.

"Don't be an idiot," Justin whispered so the secretary wouldn't overhear. She seemed mighty curious. It was rather early for office calls with the commander.

Nebraska was called in next. He came out two minutes later with a grin on his face, slapped Justin on the back, and left the commander's spaces.

"Sergeant Hauten!"

Justin opened the door before the commander finished calling his name, stood at attention, and saluted. Colonel Winters stood at the tall window in his office, hands behind his back, and got right to the point.

"At ease, soldier. The Chief of Staff of the Army called me this morning." He paused dramatically, and Justin remained silent. Was he supposed to be impressed?

Horrified? Happy? There was no way on earth that he was about to interrupt Colonel Winters. "It isn't often that a Four-Star General calls me at five in the morning. In fact, I'd call it highly irregular. Wouldn't you, Sergeant?"

Justin had no clue where the conversation was headed. "Yes, sir," he agreed because that's what he thought was expected of him.

The commander picked up a single white sheet of paper off his desk and scanned it briefly before indicating that Justin should take it from him. He dreaded that it was discharge paperwork or an investigation summary of misconduct. He didn't expect it to be transition orders.

"You are on orders to report to the Pentagon by the end of the month as General MacWilliams's new junior enlisted advisor," the colonel announced.

Highly irregular indeed. There was only one person who could make this happen.

Mary Lovecross. It had her scheming fingerprints all over it. Justin didn't have a doubt about it. That didn't mean he could reject the orders even if that meant moving away from Aaron. He didn't have a choice in the matter.

"This is an honor, sir. Thank you." Internally, his heart raced.

"Isn't it?" Colonel Winters asked rhetorically. "The position didn't exist twenty-four hours ago. In fact, I've never heard of a junior enlisted advisor billet before. I checked the regulations and called human resources command. Again, highly irregular." The commander paused long enough to make Justin think the office call was over.

Justin saluted again. "Roger, sir."

"You are an exceptional soldier, Justin," Colonel Winters said finally. "Obviously, you are being recognized by Army leadership. You'll be happy to know that you're not reporting alone. Lieutenant Parris and Specialist Walker are joining you, also on short-notice orders, and also at the Pentagon. I'd ask what this is all about, but given the odd situation with your previous company commander and the mysterious bruises you seemed to sport two weeks ago, I have a feeling that it's not easily explained."

"Yes, sir." Justin breathed a little easier now. He wasn't leaving Aaron or Nebraska behind. He couldn't wait to discuss all of this with them.

"So, instead, I'll offer my congratulations and my best wishes on your new assignment."

"Thank you, sir."

"Dismissed, soldier."

Justin was nearly out of the office when he heard, "Oh, and Justin. Good luck. You're going to need it where you're going."

About the Author

KELLY WRITES ROMANCE, fantasy, science fiction, and literary fiction. Past lives include Flutist, Soldier, Personal Assistant, Trainer, Intelligence Analyst, and for the last several years, a Senior Executive Assistant. She has worked for the Department of Defense for almost two decades.

Contact her anytime:
www.kellywashington.com
kellywashwrites@gmail.com
www.goodreads.com/kellywashington
For sneak peaks, and the chance to read her books for free, join her reading room at, www.kellywashington.com/newsletter or text KELLY to 22828 (*message and data rates may apply*).

*Get a sneak peek at COLLIDE INTO YOU, my
newest Contemporary, Military Romance.
Justin, Aaron, and Nebraska make a few appearances
in this story.
Publication date: October 25, 2014.*

Collide Into You

When twenty-seven-year-old Army Sergeant Keira Holtslander,
an orderly and rule-loving intelligence analyst, is reassigned to
the Pentagon for a special assignment, she agrees to room with
her brother's best friend, Dillan Pope. But there's a problem.
Several, in fact. He's sarcastic, egotistical, full of himself,
extremely attractive, and a womanizer. Within a matter of days,
her life is chaos. She didn't like him when they met nine years
ago, and her opinion isn't likely to change now.

Dillan Pope, a thirty-year-old career businessman climbing his
way up the corporate ladder, has learned to use his looks, charm,
and sexual skills to his advantage. There isn't much he cannot
accomplish. Women easily tumble into his bed and business deals
come about effortlessly. But when his best friend's little sister
moves in, he knows he's in trouble. She's rather hostile toward
him, which takes him by surprise. Not even his patented smile
works on her, but maybe that's why Keira, aka Sergeant Prim
and Proper, has always been the one girl he hasn't been able to
forget since their first meeting, nine years ago.

When a meddling barista puts a charm on the roommates,
causing them to swap bodies, they must live as the other until
they both own up to some hard truths. They quickly learn that
panic, fighting, and accusations will get them nowhere. Until
they can learn the lessons they refuse to acknowledge, they
experience life as the other. Along the way they are forced to
concede that maybe the other isn't so bad.

Maybe there's a reason they hated each other. And admitting the feelings that lay hidden may be the only way to undo the switch.

Kelly Washington's new contemporary, military romance, written with a touch of magic, will make you laugh and believe in love all over again.

CHAPTER ONE

Keira

"WOW," A MASCULINE voice says from across the living room. Not *to* me. *At* me. And he says the word "wow" in two syllables. *Wow-Wa.* It is my roommate, Dillan. Or, rather, I'm *his* new roommate. *Did he always have to talk so sarcastically?* I wait for his next comment. "Keira, whatever the opposite of amazing is, *that's* how you look today."

I look down at what I'm wearing, which is my Army Combat Uniform, or ACUs for short. My hair is pulled up in a low bun and, in the interest of time, I'm wearing pretty much zero makeup. I look exactly like what a twenty-seven-year-old sergeant in the Army is supposed to look like: like every other female sergeant in the Army.

I'm fairly close to being late for my first day at the Pentagon, and the last thing I need is for the man-slut I'm rooming with to harass me. I don't care that he's my brother's best friend, or that I've always had a secret *love-hate* crush on him, or that his abs are totally to die for and that looking at him is like looking directly at the sun. I'm rooming with him only because I need a place to crash before I find my own place.

Look away, Keira! Those abs will totally blind you.

My older brother, Jon, who's in the Navy and deployed to Bahrain, asked Dillan to let me stay here after the Army reassigned me to Washington, DC.

Dillan, shirtless and drying his hair, stands just outside his bedroom door. His wide-open bedroom door. Beyond him, I can see a naked female form sleeping on his bed. She's blond, leggy, and those are totally fake breasts.

Secret *love-hate* crush aside, in truth, after living here for only two days, I've come to the realization that I sort of don't like him. I'm glad that the living room separates our two bedrooms. Seriously, I don't want to hear sounds coming from his room at night. Not after what I heard yesterday.

I'm tired of trying to *not* look at Dillan, so I glance out the window. I still cannot believe that I'm living in a high-rise apartment with an amazing view of the Capitol, the Washington Monument, and the Lincoln Memorial. Too bad it came with a man-slut.

I try to figure out what Dillan's talking about when his lips curve in a victorious manner. I've been silent too long after the insult.

"What?" I ask, tilting my head. "Are you not used to women being clothed in front of you? Perhaps you're not exactly sure how buttons and all those crazy little fastening thingies work? Listen, can we insult each other later? I've got to catch the Metro."

He grins as he reaches for a shirt of his own, a blue, collared shirt, and purposefully buttons it up slowly, as if to illustrate that, yes, he knows how to dress himself. *What an accomplishment*, I think. *Whatever will he do next? Use his finger to pick his nose?*

I smile at the juvenile thought.

Dillan crosses the distance between us as he tucks the shirt into tailored trousers. He cleans up nicely. I know he isn't some bum. He works at a prestigious firm as some big-wig's senior executive assistant. Let me clarify: That big-wig boss is a woman. And if I've learned anything about Dillan Pope in the two days that I've been his roommate *and* all the stories Jon has told me over the last few years, it's that he can charm anyone.

Myself excluded, of course. I find something unattractive about overly attractive men. Sorta.

My roommate clears his throat as if he has some big announcement. I roll my eyes and look at my watch. *Hint, hint, buddy.*

"I was just going to say that you looked much better this morning after you came in from your run," he says in a low voice. I study his chiseled jaw, his light green eyes, and his dark hair. Not that I was smelling him or anything, but he smells like Sandalwood.

My run? That was two hours ago. "Can you please make sense, *Devon*?"

He chuckles. "It's Dillan, but you already knew that. Don't act like I don't affect you. I mean," he shrugs, "I really don't care one way or the other. You're not my type." He slips on his shoes and folds his suit jacket over his arm and turns to go. "But, for the record, *Sergeant Holtslander*," he says with a smirk. "I certainly like the little running outfit a whole hell of a lot better than whatever that—" he motions his hands up and down "shapeless uniform is called."

He winks as he leaves the apartment.

I stare at the closed door and wonder, not for the first time in the last thirty-six hours, *what have I gotten myself into?*

Dillan

I LEAVE THE apartment with a little pep in my step and walk to one of my favorite places, Ellen's Corner Bakery, and wait in the usual long line. While not technically on a *corner*, Ellen's bakery feels like your grandmother's home. Your grandmother's home on steroids.

Mix-matched, cushy chairs push up next to kitschy, antique tables. The walls are covered with famous faces, old newspaper clippings, artistic findings from all over the world, and, near the register, an older-looking wedding photo of a soldier and a young bride is on display. I love the place. So does everyone else, as evidenced by the long line.

While I wait my turn, I can't help but think about Jon's little sister.

Keira is cute, adorable, and, well, okay, she's freaking hot. I remember her little running outfit from this morning, which consisted of not much more than an orange sports bra and tiny—and I mean tiny—lime green running shorts. The outfit was bright enough to land planes. It certainly landed *my* attention.

At six a.m. this morning, Keira returned from her workout. The lights were out. She didn't notice me at the fridge, drinking milk straight from the carton. But I sure as hell noticed her. God, those tan legs, her slim waist, and her dewy, sweaty skin. I wanted to bathe her right then and there. With my tongue.

And when she bent over and began to stretch out... I nearly choked on the milk.

"You're deep in thought this morning, Dillan," the cashier-slash-baker-slash-owner, Ellen, says. She is a young fifty-year-old lady who I have seen every morning since moving to Washington, DC seven years ago.

I add up the math... I've seen Ellen at least 2,555 times. Sometimes I am here *twice* a day. That's a lot of coffee. And muffins. And innocent flirting.

"You know I can't start my day without seeing you, Ellen," I tell her, grinning, and order the usual: a large, black coffee. I can't help but flirt with her. "If I were thirty years older, sweetie, I'd romance you like it was no one's business."

"Careful what you wish for," she says in her sweet-as-pie voice. She stares at me in a manner that seems way too intense. "And I'm fairly certain that the thoughts running through that handsome head of yours would make Lucifer blush." I get the feeling that in some other life, she might have been a witch. She gives off that vibe.

"Lucifer, yeah, but not you, Ellen."

"True," she says with a laugh as she makes coffee for another customer. Ellen points to a sign above her head that announces her bakery's thirtieth anniversary party next Tuesday. "Did you get the invite?"

"I wouldn't miss it for the world."

She smiles brightly. "And how's the new roommate? Jon's sister is renting your second bedroom, right?"

I wonder if Keira drank coffee. *Did it matter?*

"If you're asking me if she's cute, the answer is yes, but I can tell she's as boring as a snail. *Sergeant Prim and Proper*. She probably does twenty push-ups at every Metro stop."

Ellen arches an eyebrow. "You've told me all I need to know, Dillan," she says in a manner that suggests she believed just the opposite of what I said. Her eyes sparkle.

"I can't wait to meet her."

"Oh, no you don't," I say. "I have no intention of bringing her here. You are mine, Ellen."

She laughs at my possessiveness. "She's a soldier?" she asks. I nod yes. "Slim, five foot eight, with brown eyes and brown hair? Carmel skin? Is her last name Holtslander?"

I wonder if she has a magic crystal ball behind the counter. "How on earth did you guess all that?"

"Because I'm standing right here, you idiot," Keira says with a biting tone. Without my realizing it, she was standing at the front of the line. "*Sergeant Prim and Proper* loves coffee, and the sign outside is big enough for a boring snail to see it."

"So you heard everything?" Even the *cute* part?

Ellen looks back and forth between us with a gleeful smile.

"Like I care," Keira says as she pours a pound of cream and sugar in her coffee and places a lid on top. She returns her attention to Ellen. "It was very nice to meet you. I'll see you again tomorrow."

I watch as Keira puts on her Army beret and leaves the store without acknowledging me at all.

"I like her already," Ellen says and smiles so large that I can count all of her teeth. "You could use a challenge, Dillan Pope."

I nearly glare at Ellen, but then realize it wouldn't be respectful to glare at her.

"What's that supposed to mean? I could use a challenge?"

Ellen only laughs. "Aren't you going to be late for work?"

I groan. "See you tomorrow."

I walk to work and take the elevator to the fourteenth floor of the Brookshire Mierkle Building in the Federal

Triangle area in Washington, DC, and think to myself, *what have I gotten myself into?*

CHAPTER TWO

Keira

I CATCH THE blue line to the Pentagon Metro Station and get jostled around in the Metro car for two stops before I eagerly exit and practically run up the escalator. I exit the Metro station and, up top, a Pentagon security guard inspects my military ID and allows me to enter through the visitor's section.

Once inside, I turn immediately to the right, enter the Pentagon badging office, take a number, and wait for it to be called.

I'm supposed to meet my military sponsor at nine. The clock on the wall reads 8:55. Good, I have five minutes to bristle about my jerk-face roommate.

How could Dillan Pope be best friends with my brother? So they went to college together. Big deal. Jon's my hero. He's an amazing officer in the Navy, he's well read, and he has the most amazing boyfriend, Tanner.

Dillan's hot. I got that. He makes good money. But he's too sarcastic. He probably has sex with anyone who nods in his direction. And he looks at me like I've got warts all over my face. There is no way on earth he could ever make it in the military. Of the nine years I've been enlisted, three have been in war zones. I've experienced things that would make his skin crawl.

I am not as boring as a snail, and I'm sure as hell not *Sergeant Prim and Proper*. I can be fun. I can be sexy. I like to hike and bike and run marathons. Those are definitely *un*boring things. I just can't do anything that will jeopardize my security clearance, like binge drinking, gambling, or stripping at parties.

Not that I would do those things even if I didn't need a security clearance.

An automated system calls my number and two minutes later, I walk out with my unsmiling face pasted on a white badge. I clip it to the pocket on the front of my uniform. Congratulations to me: The Pentagon has welcomed its newest member.

"Sergeant Holtslander?"

I turn around to face the voice. If I'm not mistaken, it had a Texas twang to it.

A male staff sergeant shakes my hand. "I'm Justin Hauten. I am the junior enlisted advisor to the Chief of Staff of the Army and I'm your sponsor."

If anyone can give Dillan a run for his money in the looks department, it would be Staff Sergeant Justin Hauten. The way he said his last name, it sounded like Hot-In.

Yes you are, I think. I inspect him. He looks great in a uniform. I wouldn't call him classically handsome; I can tell he's had a few broken noses, but he's ruggedly good-looking with a lopsided smile that could easily melt hearts and land him on the cover of a few "most handsome" magazines.

I notice the black ring on his ring finger, which declares: Not available.

"Hi, yup, that's me, Keira Holtslander, Sergeant Prim and Proper."

"I'm sorry, what? Is that a nickname?" His thick eyebrows furrow briefly.

I laugh. "No, sorry. I was thinking of something else and it slipped out. Let me start over. I'm Keira Holtslander."

Sergeant Hauten nods. He seems friendly, but not overly friendly.

"Let's walk and talk. I'll give you the quick tour since I know that this is your first time at the Pentagon. Then you'll meet the team. Your introductory office call with Colonel Benson is at thirteen hundred. He's a great guy and you'll like him a lot. He just returned from Kabul, Afghanistan. I read your file. You've been deployed a couple of times, right?"

I like that he didn't feel compelled to discuss the weather or other inane facts. Instantly, I can tell that he didn't see a *female* in front of him, he saw a *soldier*. From this point forward I know that he'll be an ally.

He leads us through a turnstile. I swipe my new badge and we go up another set of escalators. When we get to the top, he halts in a large hallway that he calls "the concourse." It reminds me of an airport, but without the planes. The hallway is huge, and it appears you can buy anything from food to greeting cards. You can even open a bank account. Also, while I'm not entirely sure, I'm fairly certain I smell roasted nuts.

I tell him about my overseas deployments. "I had a tour in Bagdad in 2006 and two twelve-month tours in Afghanistan. One in 2009 and the other in 2012. Before my reassignment here, I was stationed at Fort Bragg and worked for the JSOC intelligence chief."

The sergeant cringes. "I have a feeling you are going to be a bit out of your element here." He leads us down the hallway and we walk up an inclined ramp.

"Why do you say that?" I ask. He's not good at hiding the fact that he doesn't think I'll enjoy my new assignment. Or maybe he doesn't think I'm qualified. I try not to bristle at the thought.

"The billet Colonel Benson has placed you in isn't an

intelligence billet."

I think about this for a second. It isn't unusual to work in a different field from what you are trained in, but it generally isn't too far from the norm. For example, the Army would never put me in an infantry position. I don't have the training.

"What will I be doing, then?" I ask.

He cringes again. I can tell that Sergeant Hauten is an intelligent soldier, but he's not an intelligence specialist. He comes across as an infantry soldier, which seems a little out of place in a place like the Pentagon. I wonder how he got his position.

"Colonel Benson will brief you on your job description at thirteen hundred today." He pauses as if he expects me to question him, but I don't, so he continues. "Anyway, let me orient you."

We stop at the top of the ramp. It's a junction of sorts. In front of us, there is a massive set of stairs as well as three different hallways. Also, from this vantage point, I can see outside into the inner courtyard. My brother told me that the Pentagon often holds concerts there in the summertime.

But I can already tell that I'm going to get lost. What I need is a map.

Sergeant Hauten starts pointing and explaining. "This is the innermost ring, the A Ring, and we're at the beginning of the 9th Corridor. Each office has a unique number that identifies where it is in the building. Think of it like a spoke of a bicycle wheel."

"Uh huh," I murmur. I can imagine a bicycle easily.

"There are five rings, A through E; five floors, one through five, but if you count the basement and the mezzanine levels, then it gets a bit complicated. I've been here a year, and I still get confused if I have to go downstairs. Anyway, for each corridor, one through ten, i.e. the bicycle's spokes, generally speaking, if you're walking from the inner ring to the outer ring and the office number ends in 0-50, go left at the office number's corresponding ring identifier. If it ends is 51-99, go right. If you're walking in the opposite direction, do the opposite. I'm sure you get the idea."

Okay. The Army has not trained me for this system. "Should I be taking notes? I feel like there's a test at the end of all this."

He laughs. I didn't think it was possible, but when he smiles, it makes him even *more* attractive.

"You'll get the hang of it. Everyone gets lost. All I want you to care about right now is how to find our office and how to find the Metro entrance. Our office is 2E801."

"Two echo eight oh one," I repeat.

"It's located on the second floor, the E Ring, in Corridor 8, room 01."

I process the sentence. "Oh, now it makes sense. That doesn't sound too hard."

He laughs again, like maybe he's convinced I'm mental. "I'm glad you feel that way because I'm going to make you lead me there."

Dillan

MY BOSS, LOUANN Britton, calls me into her office as soon as I arrive, which she almost never does. LouAnn is an attractive woman in her fifties who has worked long and hard to earn a corner office and the title of senior vice president of Brookshire Mierkle Industries.

Seven years ago, she took a chance on me right out of college, and I've been her senior executive assistant ever since. Many within the company think I'm sleeping with her, or that I *have* slept with her, and that's how I earned the senior position.

While a somewhat accurate depiction of my womanizing ways—and seven years ago, I might have actually done something like that for a job—the rumors are, however, untrue. I've known the gossip for quite a while, and LouAnn only heard about it last year. I think she laughed for ten minutes straight after asking me if I knew what everyone was saying.

Another rumor surfaced last week. A rumor that I was LouAnn's biological son. Obviously, this is something my actual mother would object to hearing, but it's now out there and I assume that this is why LouAnn practically *ordered* me inside her office the second my feet landed on the fourteenth floor.

The receptionist, who hates my guts for some reason, didn't even have time to give me a curt greeting after telling me my boss wanted to see me.

"I have a job for you," LouAnn says after closing her office door. We are alone in her office, as usual, and I sit in my normal chair in front of her massive glass desk. Behind her, I can see the Old Post Office Pavilion, a building that's always nice to look at.

"Hit me with it," I say, referring to the job, not the building.

"It's a covert job. I'm loaning you out."

I smile. Sometimes LouAnn uses me to get the dirt on her rivals. Nothing illegal or even unethical. In LouAnn's world, she calls it, "integrated business partnerships" and "liaison exchanges" in order to build up the young crop of business officials, and to "cross-pollinate" the industry. So I'm not alarmed that she's decided to pimp me out again.

The last time she did this, I worked in Senator Murphy's office for four months, *assisting* in drafting the language for a small-business-friendly bill. Senator Murphy is, of course, a female, and her staff is comprised mostly of the female gender. And, yes, other than the Senator herself, I dated all of the ladies at some point or another during, or after, that liaison exchange.

In fact, Stacey, the woman probably still asleep in my bed, used to be an intern with Senator Murphy. We happened to bump into each other two nights ago at the 930 Club and didn't stop bumping into each other for forty-eight hours. We only paused when I had heard rustling out in the living room, which was when *Sergeant Prim and Proper* happened to move in.

I smile as I recall how red Keira's face had become when I opened the bedroom door to find out what was going on and she witnessed the full glory of my manliness. I'm shocked she could even look me in the eye this morning.

But, at the moment, I really didn't want to be thinking about Keira Holtslander.

"Who am I being loaned out to this time?" I pull out a

notepad, ready to take notes. Normally, I have a few weeks to prepare for such a role. LouAnn won't throw me in willy-nilly.

"I've agreed to send you to Johnson Brookshire's office."

This wasn't good. I stand up abruptly, interrupting LouAnn. "Wait a minute now. Johnson Brookshire hates my guts, LouAnn, and you know it."

"The President of Brookshire Mierkle has never verbalized his feelings for you one way or the other, Dillan. Admittedly, dating his daughter wasn't your brightest idea. If you'll remember, everyone, to include the janitor, advised you against it."

I run a hand through my hair. "Are you trying to get me fired? Are you unhappy with me for any reason?"

LouAnn chuckles. "Stop acting like a girl, Dillan. This isn't about you, it's about me. Now sit down, because what I'm about to tell you is confidential."

I sit down. "I'll never break your confidence, LouAnn. I hope you know that."

"Why do you think you're still with me all these years later, kiddo? I've heard a rumor that Johnson is retiring this summer. The board of directors will take into account my seniority as well as my thirty-five-year tenure with the company, but I know deep in my gut that Johnson will not select a female. He'll go for one of the other vice presidents. Probably that asshole Terry Richmond from the New York office. I know I should have taken up golf in order to schmooze with the bosses, but the only balls I've ever wanted to hit were the ones between their legs."

I clear my throat and cross my legs. "You want me to go in and convince him you're the right person for the job?"

"That's the end state, yes, but first I need you to convince him that you're not such a douche bag for dating and then dumping his daughter. No offense, but you are sort of a liability right now, and I'd like you clean up your own mess."

"That's harsh, LouAnn."

"You'll get nothing but the truth from me, Dillan. Johnson doesn't know I know. He thinks you're coming in to help with a new client in our federal business sector. Apparently there's hostility with, or maybe *from*, this client, I'm not sure, but Johnson was pleased with your performance in Senator Murphy's office. Johnson thinks he's 'reassigned' you, but in reality, I put a tickle in the right ear and 'offered' you. Naturally, Johnson assumes he came up with the idea. I have no intention of disagreeing with this assessment."

"When do I infiltrate his office?"

"I like how you think." She hands over an accordion-style packet. "One week. Take that time to do research on the client and the Brookshire Mierkle team handling the account. If anyone can tame the beast, it will be my *son*, Dillan Pope." LouAnn did finger quotes around the word *son*.

I couldn't hold in a bark of laughter.

CHAPTER THREE

Keira

THANK GOODNESS STAFF Sergeant Justin Hauten is a patient man, because it takes me twenty-five minutes to find the office. I think about the things I can normally complete in that time. I could run three miles. I could cook a fairly decent dinner. I could take a nice bubble bath. I could have sex, twice.

I'm a little flush, and embarrassed, when Justin introduces me to the rest of Colonel Benson's team. Benson is *one* of the Chief of the Army's military assistants. General MacWilliams has five military assistants. One is a one-star general, two are colonels, one is a command sergeant major, and the last one is Justin. I've never heard of a *junior enlisted advisor* before, and Justin didn't really explain it to me when I asked, only to say that it was a new billet and that even he was mystified about the position.

I can tell that there's more to the story and maybe in time he'll spill the beans, but for now, I let it go. There's no reason to make my first day complicated, especially with a staff sergeant who is clearly unavailable.

At one o'clock, Justin shows me into Colonel Benson's office and then leaves.

The colonel shakes my hand. "Welcome to the Pentagon, Sergeant Holtslander. The Puzzle Palace can be a little daunting at first, so the first week, we give you a bit of latitude in finding your way around. After that, however, I'll expect you to be where you need to be ten minutes before the appointed time. First and foremost, you represent the U.S. Army, and secondly, you represent General MacWilliams at all times while you are in uniform."

"Yes, sir," I say automatically. I fully expected this and am rather used to such speeches and welcomes. I've done a few of them myself when Army privates arrived at my unit while I was stationed at Fort Bragg.

"How long have you been in the Army, sergeant?"

"Nine years, sir."

"When are you up for reenlistment?"

"In three years."

The colonel doesn't answer right away. He appears to be thinking something over, and I wonder if it has anything to do with the billet I've been assigned to. I start to bite on a fingernail. After another moment, he pulls out a folder and lays it on his desk.

"I know your background, Sergeant," he begins. He's looking at my enlisted record brief, which is the report that details my entire Army career up to this point. "And I know that you are a 96B, an Intelligence Analyst, but that's not why I asked for you to fill this billet. It isn't an intel position. Well, I should clarify and say that the position isn't inherently intelligence related. You'll be reviewing documents for an internal review General MacWilliams is leading.

"Only four people know about the investigation, and you're that fourth person. I spoke with several Army commanders, looking for recommendations, and you quickly surfaced to the top of the list. You have a reputation for steady, professional work. You are not prone to jumping to conclusions and, if I've heard correctly, you somehow find reading Army manuals enjoyable. I'm happy to report that you'll be reading several more.

"I personally called every supervisor you have reported to and each have consistently praised you, your body of work, and high nature of their trust in you. General MacWilliams reviewed the findings with me and wanted you right away.

"The next few weeks will be busy ones for you as you apprise yourself of the situation. You'll have quite a bit of reading to do that can only be done inside the general's secure office. In the initial stages of the investigation, all you'll do is read the documents. In the subsequent weeks, you'll have time to write up a formal report and brief it to General MacWilliams. At this point, the position isn't permanent. Once the report is done, it is highly probable the Army will send you back to Fort Bragg. However, if you impress the general, well..." He smiles, suggesting it is possible I'll stay on board. It isn't something he can actually say out loud. He isn't allowed to promise me anything. "Do you have any questions at this point?" Colonel Benson asks.

It's like he dropped a bomb on me. Internal Review. So someone's done something wrong, and I have to read the raw material, analyze it, and present it in a coherent, unbiased manner. I do that everyday. The material and subject matter might be different, but the methodology could cross over easily. *Maybe Dillan's title of Sergeant Prim and Proper wasn't all that far off.* Uh, I really didn't want to think about Dillan at the moment.

Granted, if my job only took me a few weeks, then I'd be in and out of Washington, DC sooner than I thought, and I wouldn't have to see Dillan's sarcastic face every day.

That was a plus.

I return my thoughts to the investigation.

"Is anyone else working this with me? Who can I bounce ideas off of?"

"Obviously, General MacWilliams is not the optimal choice. You'll have your office call with him next week since he's on official travel overseas. You can come to me or Staff Sergeant Hauten. We are both cleared at the proper clearance level and understand the situation. Under no other circumstances are you to talk of this to anyone else, even if they claim to have a top secret clearance or the *need to know*."

"Roger, sir. I completely understand and know the rules of *need to know*."

"Let's get started. I'll show you to your office."

Dillan

WHEN I GET home, Keira isn't there yet and my weekend date has already left, but she wrote a naughty message with red lipstick on the bathroom mirror.

I think about removing it, but then like the idea of Keira discovering it. I want to find out what she'd do. Jon, who had become a bit more domesticated once he became serious with Tanner, would have laughed but said, "Dunno man, don't you think it's time you knocked it off and found a nice girl?"

Thinking about Jon makes me miss him more. He's been my best friend since college. I went the business route while Jon joined the Navy to fly fighter jets. The fighter jets never worked out due to his poor vision, but he was an outstanding staff officer who was recently promoted away from Washington, DC to work for the Navy in Bahrain. Tanner, a professional baseball player with the Washington Nationals, had been showing a brave face for the last month.

While I certainly love Jon like a brother, it in no way compares to how Tanner feels about him. So if I'm missing Jon this much, I wonder how Tanner is taking it? I pick up the phone, ready to call him, when I remember that Jon put the entire Nationals' schedule on the fridge. I groan. Tanner is up in Pittsburgh, playing the Pirates for the next three days.

So there goes that thought.

The front door opens and slams shut as I mentally calculate when I can invite Tanner over.

Keira walks in. I didn't think it was possible, but her uniform is more shapeless than it was this morning. Shapeless, but with wrinkles.

When she spots me, she scowls. You'd think she'd been battling an entire band of guerilla fighters all day long by the way she looks at me. It also occurs to me that I'm in the same position I was this morning when I spied on her as she stretched from her run. I wonder if she has figured that out yet.

"Rough day?" I ask. I look at the clock on the microwave. Seven p.m. Her features soften slightly. Maybe this is a good sign.

"You can say that," she says, looking at the fridge.

She moves toward me. Each step is some sort of wordless declaration of... something. Should I comfort her? Did she need a hug? I inhale when she's a foot a way. When Jon came home after a long day, I always got him a beer. God, I was totally the bitch of that relationship, wasn't I?

I swing the fridge open, lean in, and hit Keira with the door.

"What the hell?" she yells, backing up and grabbing at her shin. "You certainly know how to welcome a girl, jeez. I came over here to see if that was Tanner's schedule."

"Uh, sorry about that." I offer her the beer, but she gives me the evil eye, so I pop the top and take a large sip. "Tanner's up in Pittsburgh. I was thinking of inviting him over this weekend."

She sizes me up briefly, like maybe she thinks that's what I think *she* wants to hear after hitting her with the fridge door. I smile at her. There's no change, and normally there's a change in a girl's expression after I give The Grin.

Keira must be a robot.

"I doubt Tanner's going to be available since he's taking me to all the Nationals' games this weekend," she says, grabbing an apple from the counter. "I get to sit in the wives' box."

I must look crushed because her dry lips crack into a smile. I take another long gulp of the beer as I think of a good comeback. Damn, I've got nothing. Jon's shapeless little sister twists the knife just a little bit deeper in my back. Tanner and I were friends, right? He didn't just put up with me because I used to be Jon's roommate?

"That should be fun," I say. I look again to the fridge. I desperately want to change the subject. "Are you hungry?"

"What about sleeping beauty?" she asks, moving away from me.

I draw a blank. "What are you—*oh*, you must mean Stacey. No, she already left."

"Stacey, huh? I'm terribly impressed that you can remember their names. Thanks for the offer, but I have a lot of reading to do. I'll just have a protein bar and a glass of milk."

Right. *Sergeant Prim and Proper* probably doesn't eat anything with more than one gram of fat in it.

"Suit yourself." I finish the beer and place it in the recycle bin.

"I'm going to jump in the shower. Do you need anything in there first?"

I give her The Grin again. "Are you offering?"

Keira glares at me. "Are you always this much of a pig? Jon was so right."

"You and Jon talk about me? What about?" While I say it flippantly, something about the fact that she said, *Jon was so right* pierces doubt right through me. Like maybe Jon had serious concerns about me. I know he'd been joking for me to find the right girl, but when there are so many *right girls* out there, it certainly makes it difficult to choose just one.

Besides, what business does she have prying into my life? Just because she's Jon's little sister doesn't mean she has the right to judge me.

"You'll have to ask Jon," Keira says over her shoulder. She walks into the bathroom and locks the door. Seconds later, I hear her cuss rather loudly. She opens the door harshly. "I am not amused by sleeping beauty's message, Casanova."

I laugh as she slams the bathroom door shut again.

CHAPTER FOUR

Keira

PEELING OFF MY uniform, I give the mirror—and its lipstick-written message—the darkest look I can muster. Who writes that kind of stuff? I mean, how cliche. *"Dillan - I can't wait to taste you again. I loved it when you put it there. xoxo Stacey."* The word *there* is underlined. The rest of the mirror is filled with red hearts, X's and O's. The *entire* mirror.

I can't even see my own reflection as I start the shower, just an entire tube of lipstick smeared across the glass. Which is fine. I don't need to see myself to disrobe. I also don't need to see how flush my face is. I can feel the heat emanating as I remember what happened two nights ago, when I walked in the front door and accidentally found Dillan standing there. In the nude.

I had had a suitcase in each hand and a green Army duffle bag strapped on my back, and I shuffled into the apartment with about as much noise as an ogre would make stomping through the woods. It was no wonder he flung his bedroom door open, turned on the lights, and spied me without shame. "Oh, it's you," he had said without a sense of urgency or embarrassment. It was almost like he was glad he was showing me his goods. Like he got that part out of the way right away.

I didn't know he had a woman with him until the next day, not until I heard the *sounds*. Sounds that made me wonder just what exactly he could be doing to garner those particular moans. Admittedly, he had an amazing body and, uh, perfectly proportioned *equipment*, but I would never, ever say so out loud. Even if I had a gun to my head. Even if I had *two* guns to my head.

God, what a way to move into your brother's best friend's apartment. It wasn't like I had never met Dillan before. I had, several times, but he was always wearing clothes and he wasn't having day-long sex one wall away from me.

I had to hand it to him: Dillan was consistent. He wasn't presenting a false front with me. He was being himself, and I could at least appreciate that, even if that meant he was a pig and a womanizer. I couldn't wait to summarize the last few days to Jon and Tanner in an e-mail.

Drying off and dressing in comfy clothes, I leave the bathroom. I'll let Dillan clean the mirror. I refuse to touch it.

As soon as I open the door, though, a delicious aroma and the sounds of sizzling ground me to the spot.

Dillan is cooking something. Something that smells appetizing.

Keep going, Keira. Nothing to see over there in the kitchen as your roommate cooks what smells like barbecue chicken. You have a mouthwatering protein bar waiting for you in your bedroom. Plus, you have a 108-page Army manual to read before tomorrow morning.

"I was going to tell you that I had thawed out chicken," Dillan says. His back is presented to me as he works a skillet. I can tell he's wearing an apron. Its strings are tied low on his back.

If I don't acknowledge him and keep moving, by the time he turns around, I'll already be in my bedroom. He won't know that I stopped dead in my tracks.

I only make it a few feet across the living room.

He turns around. "I made enough for you, Keira." He looks at me, my bedroom, and takes note of whatever weird expression I have plastered on my face, and says, "You can eat it in your bedroom, if you want."

Damn.

Why'd he have to be so accommodating right now? Why couldn't he have been a jerk? Now I feel bad about lying to him about Tanner's invitation. Yes, Tanner invited me to attend the games this weekend, but he also asked me to extend the invitation to Dillan. Both of our names will be at the will-call window.

"I, uh," I start, not knowing where to begin. Confess the lie or accept the food?

Dillan turns around and prepares one plate and then moves the skillet over the trash can.

"It's okay," he says neutrally. "I'm not good at remembering to eat leftovers, so I'll just throw out the extra."

"Wait," I say. I don't believe for one second that he'll actually throw it out, and I know what he's doing in order to get me to agree to eat his food. Guilt. He's guilting me into eating it. "Don't waste it," I say through clenched teeth. It kills me to compliment him. "It smells good. Let me put this stuff away," I indicate my uniform, "and I'll be right out."

I hang up my ACUs in the closet and grab an old, thin, long-sleeve shirt to wear over my tank top. I retrieve the unclassified army manual from my backpack. I'll eat his chicken, but it doesn't mean I have to talk to him.

"Ah, I see that you're not the only one who has brought work home tonight," Dillan comments as I sit down beside him at the small kitchen table. I notice he has a stack of folders on the chair next to his. He peeks at my manual. "Army Regulation Twenty dash One. *Inspector General*

Activities and Procedures. Sounds fascinating, Sergeant." He bites into the chicken.

"There's no need to be rude just because you've never met a female that relies on her brain, rather than her looks, to get ahead."

He smiles. "You are right, and I apologize. I'm sure that all the women I've dated with MBAs and PhDs would completely agree with you. Not to mention those that have interned with Senator Murphy or worked at the White House. Such bimbos, each and every one." Dillan takes a victorious bite.

So he dates beautiful, smart, educated women. Big deal. He moved through them fast. *That* is the issue. *But what's it to me?* I think. Oh, right, they write on bathroom mirrors.

"Perhaps you can clean Stacey's PhD lipstick diploma off the mirror tonight?" I take a bite of his chicken and very nearly moan. Wow, it's really good. Much better than a protein bar. *Don't let on how good his cooking is, Keira.*

He watches me as I eat. He's waiting for an indication if I like the food or not. His eyes narrow when I don't satisfy his inquisitive stare. I finish the chicken and pull out the Army manual.

"Yeah, I can do that," he says, standing. He takes my plate, stacks it on top of his, and puts both in the sink. I see him take something out from a lower cabinet. Dillan walks to the bathroom. Half a minute later, he returns. He shows me a red-stained paper towel. "All gone."

I nod and say "Thanks" before diving back into the manual on Inspections, Assistance, and Investigations. Earlier, during my office call with Colonel Benson, he tossed the regulation manual at me and said, "Memorize this before you arrive tomorrow morning." I spent the rest of the day, alone, in the general's secure office. When it was time to leave, it took thirty minutes to find my way to the Metro entrance.

Dillan sits down next to me and opens a folder. The room is silent for a while.

"Thanks for dinner," I say after reading and taking notes on the first three chapters. "The chicken wasn't completely terrible."

I feel him looking at me, so I glance up. A small smile forms on his lips. I'm blown away at its simplicity. I doubt he even knows he's doing it. That big, fake grin he likes to give everyone is just too over the top. But this—this boyish smile—*almost* makes me smile back at him. Almost.

"You're welcome." He goes back to his reading and I think that that's the end of the conversation until he says, nonchalantly, "Some of it is stuck in your teeth."

I give him a black look, but he refuses to look away from his folder, so I grab my stuff, head to my bedroom, tune the TV to Tanner's ball game, and finish reading the manual there.

Dillan

I watch Keira semi-storm away from the kitchen table. She isn't really mad. She's just not used to my personality. Which is fine. I'm not trying to impress her or flirt with her.

Not at all.

Not one bit. She's Jon's little sister. She's way too stuffy and boring and unlike anyone else I've ever met. *She is completely off-limits.*

I agreed to that weeks ago, after Jon called me up and asked for a favor. Asked if Keira could rent my second bedroom after her all-of-a-sudden reassignment to the Pentagon. After she settled in at her new job, if she didn't like the arrangement, she could find a new apartment.

"Dillan," Jon said over the long distance phone call, "Keira is off limits. You know what I mean." I knew what he meant, but if I remembered correctly, Keira was twenty-seven years old. A grown woman who could decide for herself if I was worth her time or not.

"Is your sister easy, Jon?" I had asked him. In hindsight, I realize it was the wrong question to ask.

"Let me be clear," Jon said without any hesitation in his Navy Commander voice. "If I find out you've tried to, or successfully, seduce my sister, our friendship is over. She's not your type. Do you understand?"

It irritated me to no end that Jon would mistrust me like that. Was the sentiment earned? Yeah, probably, but I thought Jon had known me long enough to know that I would never jeopardize our friendship over a quick hook-up.

"Wow, ease up, buddy," I said to my best friend. "I was only kidding. Sorry. I've met Keira before, remember? She's totally not my type. If I recall correctly, she's a by-the-book type, right? Besides, she's a sergeant in the Army. She'll totally kick my ass if I try anything with her."

After that, the conversation took on a friendlier tone.

But now, as I think back on that phone call and how I've been acting toward Keira, I realize that if she tells Jon everything, then I might be in the market for a new friend. However, Keira didn't seem like the type to complain to anyone. In fact, she was as sarcastic toward me as I was to her. I wasn't used to that. *You could use a challenge.* That's what Ellen said.

I sigh. The first challenge I want at the moment is the one with Johnson Brookshire and this new federal client. The second challenge I want is for LouAnn to succeed Johnson and for me to move up in rank with her.

Ignoring Keira is not a challenge. And ignoring her from here on out is what I plan to do. There. A plan. I'm good with those. Before I return to LouAnn's documents on the federal client, I send a quick email to Jon and Tanner.

I type: "Keira moved in this weekend, and she seems to have survived her first day at the Pentagon. All good here. I'd like to tell you that she sends her love, but she's not one for conversation, and she'd probably accuse me of putting words in her mouth. So I'm sending my love, instead. Stay safe. Dillan."

I check for missed calls or emails. I see one from Stacey and another one from a girl I met several weeks ago. I don't click on either of them.

Returning to LouAnn's documents, I immerse myself in her quirky sidebar notes. My boss comments on everyone and everything in such a non-politically correct manner that I can't help but laugh out loud.

Everyone once in a while, I look at Keira's closed door, as if by my looking at it, it will open up. But it stays closed. I can hear a slight murmur from the TV in her bedroom. Once the light goes out from under the door, I stop looking altogether.